THE RECYCLED CITIZEN

Harry Burr couldn't have been far away. When he
came, Max was still standing in the same spot,
looking down at the grotesque unreality of a
pickaxe with a heavy oak handle, one tine pointing
up at the roof, the other buried in a well-cut, neatly
buttoned, expensive light brown suede sports
jacket. There wasn't any blood showing, just that
deadly sweep of tempered steel.

Max couldn't see whether the pickaxe was
pinning the body to the floor, but it was standing so
stiff and firm that he thought it must be. Ashe was
lying quite peacefully on his back. His legs weren't
contorted, his arms were not raised to ward off the
blow. His dead face showed no look of horror, but
dead faces seldom look anything but dead . . .

Also available in Mysterious Press by
Charlotte MacLeod

THE FAMILY VAULT
THE WITHDRAWING ROOM

THE RECYCLED CITIZEN

Charlotte MacLeod

A Sarah Kelling Mystery

Mysterious Press books (UK) are published
in association with Arrow Books Limited
62—65 Chandos Place, London WC2N 4NW

An imprint of Century Hutchinson Limited

London Melbourne Sydney Auckland
Johannesburg and agencies throughout
the world

First published in Great Britain 1987 by
William Collins Sons & Co. Ltd
Mysterious Press edition 1989

Printed and bound in Great Britain by
Anchor Press Limited, Tiptree, Essex

ISBN 0 09 958820 X

THE
RECYCLED CITIZEN

CHAPTER 1

'Coffee, Theonia?'

Mrs Adolphus Kelling was a strong woman for her age and size. She managed to lift Dolph's great-aunt Matilda's baroque silver pot without a quiver, and pour without a splash.

'Thank you, Mary dear.' Mrs Brooks Kelling stretched a graceful hand from the chaise-longue on which she was reclining like Madame Récamier to accept the ornate gold and green demitasse.

'Sarah, what about you?'

'I'd love some.' Bulgy young Mrs Max Bittersohn, née Kelling, caught her husband's stern eye and sighed. 'You'd better make it mostly cream.'

'Good girl.' Max collected two coffees, one black for himself, and brought them back to the chunky Biedermeier sofa on which he and his wife had been sitting. 'Cheer up, süssele. It won't be long now.'

'Thirty-seven days,' said Brooks Kelling, who had done a good deal of work on breeding statistics, though mostly among the confusing spring warblers. 'Right, Sarah?'·

Sarah's Uncle Jeremy's wrathful pink face poked around from behind the wing of a Queen Anne chair. 'Can't we let our dinner settle without dragging in the disgusting subject of obstetrics?'

'What's so disgusting about babies?' snapped his cousin Dolph. 'Unless they go from puling infancy straight into doddering dotage the way you did.'

'Now don't you boys start picking on each other,' Mary intervened. 'Come on, let's have some ideas. How are we going to raise that money?'

Max, who was feeling rather overstuffed himself, looked from the overstuffed furniture to the overstuffed mantelpiece to the overstuffed whatnots in the corners. 'What you need is an auction.'

'What you need is a lighted match,' grunted Jem.

There was merit in both suggestions, Sarah thought. Back in their sedate Beacon Hill brownstones, the Kellings of yore had lived austerely enough. Once they'd emigrated to the surrounding suburbs, though, they'd been all too prone to hunt up architects with delusions of grandeur and tell them in essence, 'Let 'er rip!'

Sarah didn't know who'd perpetrated the monster Dolph had inherited from Great-uncle Frederick, but he hadn't been one to stint on space. Naturally, finding themselves stuck with so many excess rooms, the Kellings had felt it their duty to fill them up. By now the whole house was crammed with much that was good and more that was ghastly.

She herself wouldn't mind owning that Empire chaise Cousin Theonia was occupying so decoratively at the moment. Theonia herself might well be coveting the coffee cups. However, nobody in his right mind would ever give houseroom to those inspirational mottoes done in pokerwork on birch bark and framed in dried seaweed.

Great-aunt Matilda's æsthetic leanings had found their ultimate outlet in seaweed. Her chef d'œuvre had been a wreath of bladderwort and kelp formed around a bent coat-hanger and preserved for posterity inside a heavy gilded frame whose glass bumped out in the middle much as Sarah would be doing for another thirty-seven days. She couldn't see the wreath from where she was sitting, and she was glad.

Dolph didn't seem too keen on the idea of an auction. 'We can't go peddling Uncle Fred's personal belongings to God knows who,' he started to object.

'Dear, nobody's said anything about personal belongings,' said Mary. 'But what about all this other stuff? I don't see why we shouldn't clear out enough so a person could walk into a room without cracking her shins every third step.'

She'd never met the aunt and uncle who'd taken custody of little Adolphus after his parents were killed in a crash between the Norumbega trolley-car and a runaway brewer's wagon. She'd attended one or two spiritualist meetings with Theonia, hoping Fred and Matilda would manifest

6

themselves so she could give them a piece of her mind about how they'd browbeaten and brainwashed a helpless orphan child; but so far they'd been contrary in death as they had been in life. Theonia was all for having another go, but Mary's Irish Catholic upbringing made her reluctant to try again.

Anyway, Mary had more urgent business on her mind. 'Let's face it, Dolph, somebody's got to deal with the overflow sooner or later. Why shouldn't we get the good of it? We can use the money as well as the next one.'

'And a damn sight better than some,' Dolph conceded, glaring at Jem from force of habit.

'That's a matter of opinion,' his cousin retorted cheekily. 'Were you planning to pass the decanter, old bane of my boyhood, or are you planning to auction it off with the rest of the impedimenta?'

'What the hell, why not?' Dolph picked up the handsome piece of cut glass, shook his head sadly at the inch or two of red wine left in the bottom, and handed it over to Jem. 'Won't have anything to put in it once you've swilled the dregs down your ungrateful craw. We've opened the last of Uncle Fred's port. Haven't we, Mary?'

'Two bottles left, and you needn't start looking pitiful, Jem. I'm saving those for Dolph's birthday party in November.'

'Don't know what anybody wants to celebrate that for,' Dolph growled, looking pleased nevertheless. 'Go ahead, Jem, hog the last of it and rot your gut. I'm surprised you haven't died of a pickled liver long ago.'

'My liver is a happy liver,' Jem replied without rancour. 'Here's to your seventieth, old crock, in case I'm too soused to make an appropriate toast when the day rolls around. Egad, that's a real milestone. Next stop the boneyard for you, my boy.'

'Nonsense,' said Sarah. 'Dolph will live to be ninety-eight like Great-uncle Frederick. Don't you agree, Brooks?'

The neat little man who'd been occupying himself in jotting down some of the birch-bark mottoes for the family archives gave a qualified assent. 'Ninety, I should say. Not much older. Dolph is pugnacious but not cantankerous like Uncle Fred. It seems to me one might need that extra streak of general cussedness to hang on as long as Fred did.'

'Good point, Brooks,' said Jeremy. 'You've mellowed lately, Dolph. You'd better quit immersing yourself in good works to the exclusion of a little healthy debauchery now and then, or you'll go soft at the centre as well as in the head.'

'That's a hell of a thing to say to a man when you've snaffled the last of his port,' Max chided. 'Okay, so Dolph and Mary have decided to hold an auction, to weed out the dead wood and make some dough. What's next on the agenda?'

'Wait a minute,' Jem insisted. 'They don't need money. They've got too much already. Almost too much, I mean,' he amended hastily. Jem was, after all, a Kelling.

'That shows all you know,' said Mary. 'I guess Dolph hasn't told you we're planning to expand our facilities.'

'Facilities? You're not by chance referring to that high-class junk-yard you've been running? What's the matter? Are the empty beer cans piling up too fast for you?'

'The Senior Citizens' Recycling Center is doing just fine, thank you.' Mary had once sold hats to Boston ladies, so it took more than a bit of ribbing from Jeremy Kelling to shake her equilibrium. 'But there's so much more to be done. Boston has better facilities for helping its needy elders than a lot of other cities, but there are still far too many who aren't getting a square deal. There are subsidized apartments for those who have the resources, and shelters where the down-and-outers can find a bed if they're lucky. What we have in mind is a facility that fills the gap in the middle.'

'Would you care to tell us your plans?' said Brooks.

'Well, you know Dolph inherited various properties from his uncle. One's a smallish factory building that a paint company just moved out of. He's had a couple of offers already. There's one real estate trust that's been pestering the life out of us, but we've turned them down. You see, 'what we hope to do is convert the building into something like a great big boarding-house.'

'You mean make it into bedrooms?' said Sarah.

'Essentially, yes. Cut it up into dozens of nice little rooms that people could rent for very small fees by the week or month. They'd have a reasonable degree of comfort and privacy and a safe place to keep their possessions. That way they wouldn't have to tote everything they own around in shopping-bags and never know where they're going to sleep at night.'

'We're charging the rent to keep them from feeling like objects of charity,' said Dolph. 'If they don't have the money, we'll find ways for them to earn their way by doing chores. Give 'em a sense of pride, keep 'em self-supporting to the best of their ability.'

'How big is this warehouse?' Brooks looked as if he might already be drawing blueprints in his head.

'Big enough,' said Dolph. 'It's four storeys high, two hundred feet deep and six hundred feet long. We'll have room for several different kitchens, dining-rooms, and recreation areas so the tenants won't have to trek all over hell and gone to reach the facilities.'

'And plenty of bathrooms on every floor,' said Mary.

'But that will cost you millions!' Theonia exclaimed.

'Dolph has millions,' drawled Jeremy, holding the decanter upside down over his glass to catch the last drop of Uncle Fred's port.

'Not so many millions as you think I have,' Dolph retorted. 'Why don't you lick the stopper, you old soak? We'll have to run a major fund drive. Sarah can handle it.'

'Me? Why don't you simply turn this mausoleum into a boarding-house instead, the way I did with mine?'

'Because our people wouldn't come out here, that's why,' said Mary. 'Don't think Dolph and I haven't thought of that. We've brought a few SCRC members out here thinking they'd enjoy the change, but they hightail it back to the city the minute we give them a chance. They all claim they can't stand the quiet.'

'What quiet?' Jem demanded. 'Birds squawking, leaves

rustling, blasted squirrels chomping on acorns. All you have to do, Mary, is make a lot of asphalt paths through the grounds with wooden benches like the ones on Boston Common, import a flock of ill-behaved pigeons, strew a few truckloads of rubbish around to make the place look homey and provide wholesome occupation for your scavengers, and set up a public address system with horns honking and sirens yowling. You might have a cop stroll through the grounds and pinch someone for loitering every now and then,' Jem added as an afterthought, 'and pump whiffs of exhaust fumes through the house during rush hours. It would cost you a damn sight less than rebuilding that warehouse.'

'Yes, but the noise of Great-uncle Frederick's ghost thumping around the hallways in a tantrum would scare them out in no time,' Sarah objected. 'Besides, your neighbours would be sending their gardeners over here with jack hammers to tear up the asphalt. I'm sorry, Mary, I made a silly suggestion. Even if the SCRC people would come, can you imagine what would happen in this neighbourhood if you tried to upset the status quo?'

'The status hasn't been all that God damn quo since the second Roosevelt administration,' snarled Dolph.

'Now, dear, you know what the doctor warned you about Roosevelt the last time he checked your blood pressure,' Mary interrupted. 'Anyway, you're a social reformer yourself now.'

'Like hell I am.'

'Like hell you're not. Yes, Henrietta, what is it?'

'Mr Loveday's on the phone,' said the maid. 'He needs to speak to Mr Kelling right away.'

'Mr Loveday?' said Sarah. 'I thought you'd pensioned him off when Great-uncle Frederick died. Don't tell me you've got him working for you now, Dolph?'

'Why should I pay Osmond Loveday money for doing nothing? He's a damn sight younger than I am. Uncle Fred hired him straight out of college, don't ask me why. I was already full-time whipping-boy. Anyway, Osmond used to handle the books for those ridiculous foundations Uncle

Fred kept setting up, so I've been keeping him on to help me dissolve them, which we've pretty well succeeded in doing, thank God. Now Osmond's working almost full time for the SCRC. He's liaison man with the recycling plants, pays the bills, keeps track of the membership lists, all that sort of thing. He's a blasted fussbudget, but he's capable enough in his way.'

'You'd better go see what he wants, dear,' Mary suggested mildly.

'Huh. Probably mislaid a decimal point somewhere and wants me to help him hunt for it. Back in a minute, everybody.'

Adolphus Kelling was a big man, tall as well as broad. He hefted himself out of the oversized wing chair he'd been sitting in and marched from his great-aunt's drawing-room like a man well trained to do his duty in that sphere of life to which he had been summoned. Mary watched him go, the wrinkles deepening around her still lovely blue eyes.

'What's happening now, I wonder? It's not like Osmond Loveday to bother us at this hour on a Sunday night. The Center's not open. I'm surprised he's even awake. Osmond's one of those early to bed fellows. He gets up at the crack of dawn and takes walks in the Public Gardens.'

'Ought to be exterminated, all of 'em,' grunted Jem, who never walked any farther than the nearest martini if he could help it. 'Setting a bad example to the youth of America.'

Cousin Theonia adjusted the lace flounces over her comely wrists and moved the conversation to a less controversial plane, as was her wont. 'Dolph looks wonderful, Mary. You must be taking splendid care of him.'

'I try to.' Mary's pleasant face became, for the moment, almost as beautiful as Theonia's. 'The Lord knows Dolph's been a good husband to me.'

'Why, Mary,' teased Sarah, 'a person might think you were absolutely batty about him.'

'And did you think I'd married him for his money?' Mary's Irish was up. 'If you want the honest truth, I'd had a crush on Dolph since I heard him speak that time at the West End Senior Citizens'. I couldn't believe my good luck when I met him at your house not long after that, and he asked me to have dinner with him at the Ritz. I felt like Cinderella meeting the prince.'

Jem made a spluttering noise he didn't quite manage to cover up. Mary turned on him.

'Oh, I know Dolph's no Rudolph Valentino. He acts kind of pompous sometimes and I'm not saying he's any great intellect compared to his smart relatives, meaning no offence to yourself, Jem, since you've been so nice about coming to the Center and singing dirty songs to the old ladies, God bless 'em. But Dolph honestly does believe it's his bounden duty to do some good in the world. It shines right out of him. If you were a person with nothing in this world to hang on to, and here came this big, important, rich man willing to treat you like one of his own and help you put food in your mouth and money in your pocket—'

She had to pause. Then she went on, almost fiercely, 'Well, I'm not the only one who loves him. Down at the Center they think he's God, or darn close to it. And you can laugh all you want to, Jem Kelling.'

'I shouldn't dream of laughing at you, Mary me darlin',' Jem assured her, quite soberly for him. 'Any man who managed to live with Aunt Matilda and Uncle Fred all those years without bopping either one of them over the head in a house strewn with articles admirably designed for bopping should *ipso facto* become a candidate for sainthood, in my considered opinion.'

Jem raised his glass and finished off his drink in a solemn and reverent manner. 'And now he tells us he's still putting up with that perambulating pipsqueak, Osmond Loveday. Remind me to step around to the Cowley Fathers and take up the question of beatification first thing tomorrow morning, will you, Sarah? On second thought, you'd better make it sometime during the afternoon. Ah, here comes his potential holiness now. What's up, Adolphus?'

CHAPTER 2

What was up was nothing good. They all knew that before Dolph opened his mouth. Mary reached up and took her husband's hand.

'What's the matter, dear?'

'Chet Arthur got mugged.'

'Oh, Dolph! Chet's been one of our regulars ever since we opened the Center,' Mary explained to the others. 'Is he hurt, dear?'

'He's dead.'

'Who—'

'I don't know, Mary. Somebody noticed him lying in the alley between Beacon and Marlborough Streets, down near the Massachusetts Avenue end. They thought he must be drunk and called the police. The only identification he had on him was his SCRC membership card, so the police tried to call the Center and got the emergency number, which is Osmond's because he's nearest.'

'And Osmond flew into a tizzy and started pestering you. What does he expect us to do about it?'

'Well, damn it, Mary, somebody has to go over to the morgue and identify the body.'

'Why can't Osmond go himself? He's right there in town, for goodness' sake.

'He says he's not feeling well. Neither am I, but what the hell? Sorry, everybody, don't let me break up the party.'

Max Bittersohn was already on his feet. 'Come on, Dolph, I know you hate driving in the dark. I'll drive your car, and the rest can go in mine when they're ready to leave.'

'I'm going with you,' said Sarah.

The upshot, of course, was that everybody went except Mary.

'You won't mind going with Max, will you, Dolph? I really ought to stay and help Genevieve clean up the kitchen. She must be tired.'

Sarah doubted that. Genevieve had put in a good many years under Great-aunt Matilda's iron heel; working for Mary must be her idea of heaven. The truth of the matter was that Dolph was all geared up to spare the little woman and do his duty like a soldier, and Mary was too good a wife to crab his act.

As they sorted themselves out for the ride, Sarah couldn't help thinking they were an unusual group to be so closely allied. Theonia, the raven-haired, sloe-eyed, almost alarmingly well-mannered offspring of a gipsy mother and an Ivy League anthropology student who'd got more closely involved with his subject than he'd meant to, was perhaps the most exotic.

Certainly she was the most striking to look at, and showed every intention of remaining so. Theonia still carried her height proudly although she'd given up wearing high heels when she married Brooks. She walked every day to maintain a reasonable balance between her excellent appetite and her Rubens-esque figure. During the daytime she dressed in simple black or dark red with a modest string of pearls. At night she burgeoned forth in wondrous creations of her own.

This being a brisk September evening, Theonia had put on a sumptuous wine-coloured velvet dinner gown she'd first espied as a marked-down negligée in Filene's Basement. She'd remodelled the velvet to follow the lines of her expensive foundation garment and trimmed it with creamy lace taken from what would have been called a teddie by Sarah's late mother-in-law, to whom the teddie had once belonged. With a sombre black stole draped carefully over her high-piled hair and flung around all that lace and velvet, she rather suggested a middle-aged Tosca on her way to stab Baron Scarpia.

Brooks Kelling, standing five feet six inches tall and weighing perhaps a hundred and thirty pounds, might have been considered a laughable consort to so queenly a spouse, but nobody laughed at Brooks. Something about him put one in mind of those unassuming chaps John Buchan used to write about: the ones who could speak fluently whatever foreign dialect their perilous situation demanded, could baffle the foe by contriving an impenetrable disguise with a handful of dust and a trick of the mind, could destroy the enemy stronghold by some ingenious device constructed from whatever bits and pieces might lie to hand, then go back to scratching the backs of their pedigreed pigs and taking twenty-mile strolls across the moors with Carlyle's Essay on Burns for company.

Brooks was a photographer of ospreys' nests and a former entertainer at children's birthday parties. He could build almost anything but was inclined to be fussy about his materials. He spoke only Andover-Harvard and had no trouble making himself perfectly understood in it anywhere, under any circumstances. He altered his appearance by wearing a straw boater with a feather of the crested grebe tucked into the hatband during the summer, and a greenish-grey felt hat with a feather of the ruddy turnstone in the winter. The only perils he'd ever quailed at were bossy widows who wanted to marry him, but Theonia had relieved him of those.

Jeremy Kelling was about Brook's height and roughly twice his girth. There was a cousinly resemblance between them, but Sarah could never have pictured Uncle Jem photographing an osprey's nest or thwarting a foe by agility or guile. He might, she supposed, succeed in paralysing a foe with a jug of his special formula martinis. More likely, he'd yell for his man Egbert to handle the matter. Lately, to Sarah's annoyance, he'd taken to yelling for Max.

In Sarah's personal opinion, Max Bittersohn was far and away the most distinguished member of the group. She could well believe his ancestors had been priests in the temple of Solomon while the Kellings were still painting themselves blue and being nasty to the Picts. Max was just about six feet tall and looked less than the forty years he'd soon have attained. His dark brown hair had a marvellous wave to it, his grey-blue eyes saw a great deal more than most people realized they did.

Lately the expression on Max's handsome though by no means pretty face had been anxious. That was due to impending fatherhood; normally Max was a cheerful man, though never boisterous like Jem. By profession Max was a private detective specializing in the recovery of precious art objects. Recently he'd developed a sideline: fishing members of the enormous Kelling tribe out of hot water.

Sarah herself had been Max's first Kelling catch, and the only one he'd never felt any urge to throw back. She was small and slight like Brooks, had a modified version of the square Kelling jaw, but had mercifully escaped the Kelling nose. Her hair was brown, much lighter than Max's, and was showing a tendency to curl now that she'd had it cut short. Her skin was delicate and inclined to be pale except when she blushed. She was still under thirty and as happy as an expectant mother could be, considering how many relatives' good advice she had to endure.

The luxurious car Max drove was his only step in the direction of ostentation and not much of one at that since he used it often on business, needed plenty of trunk space to bring back the rescued Rembrandts, and dealt mostly with rich clients who expected him to look successful. Dolph plunked himself down in the front passenger seat without waiting to be asked. Sarah shrugged, slid under the steering-wheel and put her feet up on the hump in the middle. Max checked to make sure his impending offspring was in no danger of being squashed, then took his place behind the wheel. Theonia sat in back with Brooks on her right and Jem on her left, like a hybrid tea-rose between two Boston baked beans.

All but Dolph lived on Beacon Hill. Jem shared a memento-filled flat on Pinckney Street with his long-suffering henchman, Egbert. Brooks and Theonia were at present managing the historic brownstone on Tulip Street that Sarah had inherited from her first husband, Alexander Kelling, and turned into a remarkably high-toned boarding-house. Sarah herself had retreated with Max to a small apartment next door while waiting for their new house at Ireson's Landing to be finished.

At this time of night, it was about a twenty-minute run from Chestnut Hill. Max made it in fifteen. 'I'll drop the rest of you at the boarding-house and get Sarah up to bed before Dolph and I go on to the morgue, if that's okay.'

'I don't want to go to bed,' Sarah protested.

'Then stay with us till Max gets back. Mothers-to-be must be humoured,' said Theonia.

Theonia herself had never been a mother, but she had a way of investing her pronouncements with an authority it would have seemed folly to question. She might have acquired the knack during her earlier career as a tea-leaf reader, but anyway, Max yielded. Sarah went into the house with the rest and accepted a glass of hot milk in deference to her delicate condition. Jem asked for black coffee. Brooks and Theonia drank something called Snoozybye Tea, and thus it was that Max found them when he got back from his direful errand.

'It was Arthur, all right,' he told them. 'Dolph's pretty cut up. This is the first violent death they've had among the SCRC members, and he's blaming himself. He thinks it wouldn't have happened if he'd got that warehouse remodelled sooner.'

'Poor Dolph,' said Sarah. 'Mary's right about him, you know. Where is he now?'

'I ran him back to Chestnut Hill. We weren't long at the morgue. There was nothing to stay for. Dolph promised to send an undertaker around in the morning, and they presented us with Arthur's personal effects.'

He held up a worn and ripped brown paper shopping-bag with SCRC stamped in big green letters on one side. 'This is it, except for the membership card in his pocket and the clothes on his back. He'd been hit over the head from behind with a tyre iron, which was left at the scene. Dolph thinks he might have had a little money on him. Arthur was a conscientious collector and came in with a bunch of bottles and cans to be redeemed every day. The cops who picked him up said there were maybe a dozen empty soft drink cans scattered around the body, presumably from the torn bag.'

'Died with his boots on, eh?' said Brooks. 'I suppose there might be worse ways for a person in his situation to go. Will there be a funeral?'

'Oh yes, it's a perquisite of membership. The members are all elderly, you know, so they lose one to Father Time every so often, and they always make a point of giving them a decent send-off. Dolph says it was Mary's idea. Maybe it doesn't help the dead person much, but it makes the rest feel better. They go to a community church nearby, one of their members who used to be janitor in a church or something conducts a non-sectarian service, then they troop back to the Center for coffee and cake.'

'How perceptive of dear Mary,' said Theonia softly, 'letting those dear people know they'll be decently cared for even after they're gone. Brooks darling, do you think I ought to bake something?'

'Why don't you check with Mary in the morning, my dear? She'll know better than I. Max, what can I offer you? Tea? Brandy?'

'Brandy, if you don't mind. I could use it.' Max was fiddling with the tattered shopping-bag. 'Poor bugger. Hadn't a damn thing but this, and some son of a bitch wouldn't even let him keep it. I suppose these printed bags were Mary's idea, too?'

'No, I think they were Dolph's,' said Sarah. 'Look out, Max, there's sugar or something dribbling out on to the rug.'

'Sugar?'

'One takes it, you know,' said Theonia, 'those little packets they put out at lunch counters. The extra carbohydrates help get one through the night if one has to sleep in a cold doorway.'

Max nodded, but he didn't seem to be listening. He'd spread a newspaper over the library table and laid the bag on top. Now he was ripping the folds apart, finding a few grains still caught inside.

'That doesn't look like sugar to me, unless it's brown sugar. Got something we can examine it with, Brooks?'

'Just a second.' Brooks ran lightly up the elegantly proportioned but rather steep and narrow staircase. In a moment he was back with an old-fashioned brass microscope in his hand.

'Picked it up years ago at the Morgan memorial,' he explained, fiddling with the adjustments. 'Now let's have a speck or two of that stuff on a slide.'

He produced a pair of needlepointed tweezers and a slim oblong of glass, selected a few grains, and arranged the slide under the lens.

'Ah yes, very interesting. Not salt, surely. Rather like sugar in its crystalline structure and you know, Max, that doesn't surprise me.

'So what do you think it is?'

'I think it mightn't be a bad idea to get this over to the police laboratory.'

Max shook his head. 'I'd rather get my own chemist to run the analysis if you don't want to take the responsibility, for which I wouldn't blame you. I'd prefer not to go to the police unless I'm sure there's something to go for. And then I'll want to even less,' headed soberly. 'You know, Brooks, we could put Dolph and Mary out of business if we let it be even suspected somebody's running drugs through the SCRC.'

'Then what would happen to all those waifs and strays who are looking to them for a nice, cosy funeral?' grunted Jem. 'Far be it from me to indulge in an excess of sweetness and light, but I have to admit it would disturb me to see some poor bum lying around unplanted because my cousin Adolphus was in the jug for peddling dope. Gad, can't you see the old blowhard sitting in a concrete cell with a honey bucket beside him, bellowing for the warden to bring him a martini and the *Wall Street Journal*?'

'Uncle Jem, that's not a bit funny,' Sarah protested. 'Don't you realize Dolph actually could wind up getting arrested?'

'But surely not convicted?'

'No, of course not. Merely detained long enough to ruin his fund drive and break Mary's heart.'

She hadn't realized how close she was to crying until Max did something he normally wouldn't have dreamed of, to distract her. He picked up one of the cups that had held the Sleepytime Tea, a piece of blue and white export china that

19

had come back in one of the Kelling clippers from Hangkow sometime during the late 1800s, and handed it to Theonia.

'Okay, you're the expert. What's your prognostication?'

Theonia inclined her head, took the cup in her fingers, tilted it upside down and let a few dregs run out into the saucer. For some little time, she gazed at the flecks adhering to the inside. Then, without saying anything, she hurled the precious bit of porcelain straight at the back of the fireplace, smashing it to slivers against the soot-blackened bricks. She stood up, smoothed down her velvet skirt, said in her usual dovelike coo, 'If you people will excuse me, there are some things I have to attend to upstairs,' and went.

'We now assume,' said Jem, 'that the party is over. Call a cab, will you, Brooks?'

CHAPTER 3

Max was on the phone to Marseilles when Sarah got up, giving somebody named Pepe urgent instructions about two Paul Klees and a Winslow Homer.

'What an unusual combination,' she remarked when he at last hung up. 'That would have been Pepe le Moko at the other end, I suppose. I thought you'd intended to go to Marseilles yourself.'

'I had, until this business of Dolph's came up. Pepe can handle the French end without me, I hope. It's high time I began delegating more responsibility. Actually his last name's Ginsberg, pronounced GeensBAIR. You met him when we were in Paris, remember? The guy who looks like a mink wearing a purple T-shirt. How's the kid this morning?'

'I haven't asked. I don't think he's awake yet. Would you like a glass of milk?'

'God, no.'

'Neither would I.' Nevertheless, Sarah went to the refrigerator. 'It's always the woman who pays,' she sighed, licking a narrow white moustache off her upper lip. 'Do you actually mean to say you're staying home because of what happened last night?'

'Why not? I'm practising to be a family man. Dolph and Mary are family, aren't they? Frankly, *kätzele*, I've been holding my breath for fear something like this would come up. Those printed scavenging bags were a serious mistake, in my opinion.'

'But they're meant to give the SCRC members a feeling they're doing a real job instead of just pawing around in trash bins,' Sarah protested. 'It's part of the self-esteem thing. Besides, Dolph got them for nothing from that old crony of his who owns a printing company.'

'I know.' Max poured juice for himself and Sarah. 'The only trouble with building up an identity is that it makes you too damned easy to identify.'

He drank some of his juice. 'Suppose I'm out on the corner dealing and I see somebody who looks as if he might be a narc bearing down on me. Naturally I don't care to get caught with a pocketful of drugs. I see this nice old guy shuffling through the garbage and I see he's carrying a nice, convenient shopping-bag that says SCRC on it in nice, conspicuous letters. I figure he's not going to be too far away after the narcotics agent frisks me and finds me clean, and that bag will be easy to spot. I drop my merchandise in among his junk, let him wander off on his appointed rounds, follow him as soon as the coast is clear, and engage him in light conversation while I rip his bag open and get my goods back.'

He drank the rest of his juice. 'Or else I join a respectable organization, get myself an official SCRC membership card and a bag that will make it easy for my customers to spot me. I run my business right out of that shopping-bag until some dissatisfied customer hits me over the head and robs my store.'

'Which do you think happened to Chet Arthur?'

'I'm trying not to think anything about Chet Arthur until we've got a chemist's report. That powder might have been something he used to cure his athlete's foot, for all I know.'

'Yes, dear. I'm sure you'd cancel your trip to Marseilles

for a case of athlete's foot. How about scrambled eggs and toasted bagel?'

'How about a toasted bagel and a little kootchy-koo?'

'That's what you said to me eight months ago, and look what happened.' Sarah gave her husband a chaste kiss on the brow and went to toast the bagels, which she still tended to regard as glamorous and exotic gourmet fare. 'When do you plan to see the chemist?'

'As soon as I can get away. I'm expecting a call from Ghent.'

'Good news, I hope.'

'So do I. Ah, that must be it now.'

But it wasn't Ghent, it was Mary Kelling. 'Max, I've been thinking.'

'Would you care to share your thoughts?' he prompted when she seemed reluctant to go on.

'Well, I don't want to make a bad matter worse, but after you folks left last night, I got to wondering what Chet Arthur had been doing over in the Back Bay. The thing of it is, Chet had his little quirks, as most of us old fogies do, and one of them was that he was scared stiff of going anywhere beyond Arlington Street. Chet wouldn't have gone down Marlborough Street if you paid him a hundred dollars a step, so how did he get 'way over near Mass Ave?' She used the abbreviation as a born Bostonian naturally would. 'I haven't brought this up with Dolph and I'd just as soon not, until after the funeral's out of the way, but I didn't think it would be right not to tell you.'

'I'm glad you did,' Max lied gallantly. 'So you have no idea how he could have got there? He wasn't desperate for a place to sleep, for instance?'

'Why should he have been? It wasn't that cold last night, and anyway Chet was no common vagrant. He collected Social Security every month and earned more from the Center than any other member we've got. Which still wasn't much, goodness knows, but it kept him off the streets. He rented a room from the janitor of an apartment building up off Cambridge Street somewhere. Osmond Loveday could tell you. The address is in his file.'

'What time does Loveday get in?'

'He ought to be at the Center by now, I should think. He walks over every morning at half past seven to unlock the door so whoever's on breakfast duty can get in to make the coffee and set out the cereal or whatever we're serving. Then he walks back uptown and eats his own breakfast at a cafeteria across from the Common, and comes back to the Center at half-past eight on the nose. He walks home at eleven, does his exercises, has an apple and a glass of skim milk for lunch, takes a nap, shows up again at two o'clock and works till half past five. That only comes to a six hour day, but he works Saturdays from nine till twelve, so it evens out more or less.'

'If you say so. Getting back to Arthur, couldn't he have taken the subway or got a lift in a car?'

'Chet hated cars, and he wouldn't ride the Green Line because it goes through the Back Bay.'

'Can you think of anything Chet liked?'

'Money,' said Mary. 'Chet always knew how much he had coming to him when he brought in his salvage, and he made darn sure he got it, right down to the last penny.'

'Now we're getting somewhere, maybe. What if somebody owed him money and wouldn't pay? Would Chet chase after the welsher and try to make him cough up, even if it meant going into the Back Bay?'

'I suppose we never know what somebody might do under pressure,' Mary conceded. 'All I can say is, it doesn't seem likely.'

'You're probably right. I'll drop in at the Center later on. Are you going to be there?'

'If I'm not, I expect Dolph will be. But Osmond can tell you anything you want to know. How's Sarah feeling this morning?'

They exchanged a few courtesies, then Max hung up and told Sarah what Mary had said. Then the call from Ghent came through. Then Max said he was ready to roll and was Sarah coming with him?

'I certainly am. Give me one minute.'

'Take two if necessary. I'll get your coat. Which one do you want?'

'That white loden jacket you brought me from Austria, please. I can still fasten the top button, I think.'

Sarah had bought herself a full-cut jumper dress in a darkish green that matched the jacket's braid. The chemist was favourably impressed. 'Let me get you a chair, Mrs Bittersohn. This won't take long.'

It didn't. He came back looking a little frightened.

'Foot powder?' Max asked him.

'No, as a matter of fact it's heroin. You're not supposed to have that sort of thing in your possession, you know, Mr Bittersohn. By rights I ought to turn it in to the police.'

'I'll turn it in myself,' Max promised him.

'Er—soon?'

'As soon as I possibly can.'

'That's good enough for me. Anything interesting in the art line these days?'

The chemist, an elderly man with a face like an eagle's, wanted to chat about art forgery techniques. Max didn't. 'We'll see what we can dig up for you, Mr Smithers. Thanks for the quick service.'

'My pleasure. Glad to have met you, Mrs Bittersohn.'

Sarah, who was feeling rather sick from the laboratory odours and especially from what she'd just heard, said she was glad, too, and they left.

'Heroin?' she said when she'd got enough fresh air to quiet her stomach. 'Max, that's terrible.'

'It's not good, baby. How do you feel?'

'How do you expect? Come on, we'd better get over to the Center and see what Mr Loveday has to say.'

'Are you sure you're up to it?'

'The doctor says I have to exercise.'

'He didn't say you had to get mixed up in a drug-related murder.'

'He didn't say not to. Darling, I can't sit home and crochet booties all day. I can't crochet anything, it just comes out one big tangle. Anyway, your sister Miriam's handling that end of the business. She's up to three sweater sets and a fancy afghan for the baby carriage already.'

'Do we have a baby carriage?'

'We have that adorable wicker stroller your mother used to wheel you in when you were a year old, and the pram Aunt Emma's parents ordered from London before Young Bed was born. Of course the pram's carried her own sons, their children, and a few grandbabies by now, but she assures me there's still plenty of mileage in it. Aunt Appie wanted to give us Lionel's, but those four hyenas of his had reduced it to shreds long ago. His wife threw the remains out with the trash that time she cast off the shackles of motherhood and went to live with Tigger. Whatever happened to Tigger, I wonder? She used to be one of Aunt Appie's standard nuisances, but she hasn't been around for ages.'

Max shrugged. 'Maybe she washed her face and died of the shock. Last time I saw her was in Rotterdam.'

'Max, you beast! You never told me.'

'Did you really want to know? As a matter of fact, I'd forgotten all about it till you mentioned her just now.'

'What was Tigger doing in Rotterdam?'

'I didn't stop to ask.'

'Did she see you?'

'I made damn sure she didn't.'

Sarah supposed one couldn't blame him. She herself had never been sure whether Tigger was one of her cousin Lionel's old girlfriends or just a leftover from one of her aunt's neighbourhood Hallowe'en parties. Tigger had merely shown up at various gatherings, glaring out from under a mat of uncombed black hair, snarling like a cornered coyote if anybody tried to engage her in conversation. They'd last seen Tigger at a funeral up on the North Shore. Tigger had been wearing a hairy brown poncho and filthy corduroy pants tucked into muddy hiking boots. Sarah decided not to think about Tigger any more, for the baby's sake.

'Darling, what did you think of that performance Theonia put on for you last night?'

'I thought it damned peculiar, since you ask,' Max replied. 'Theonia's not in the habit of hurling good china around, is she?'

'Heavens, no. Theonia takes far better care of things than I ever did.'

'You don't suppose I offended her by asking her to read the tea-leaves? I only meant it as a joke.'

'She knew that. Theonia isn't stupid. But she was brought up as a gipsy, after all. If you really want to know, I think she was doing what she'd been taught was the right thing to do in the circumstances.'

'What circumstances?'

'She saw something in the teacup, of course.'

'Sarah!'

'Darling, there's no earthly point in your asking me questions if you don't want to hear my answers. Surely you can't think Theonia was a mere charlatan throughout her professional life?'

Max's lips twitched.

'All right, I suppose there were times when she had to stretch a bit. With some customers it's like trying to see through mud, she told me. But you have to tell them something because they've paid their three dollars, so you do the best you can. With others, you begin picking things up as soon as they sit down. When that happens, you're infallibly right.'

'Infallibly, eh?'

'That's what she said, and Theonia doesn't lie. Not to me, at any rate.'

'She did once.'

'Only because she thought she had to. She never has since.'

'You're sure of that?'

'Believe me, I'd know. Wait thirty-seven days and I'll prove it.'

'Oh yeah? What's her prognosis?'

'A boy.'

'And what if our son turns out to be a daughter?'

'Then I'll never trust another tea-leaf and your mother won't be cross with me. You know how Mother Bittersohn's been saying she already has a grandson and now she wants a girl. She'll think I had a granddaughter just to spite her.'

Actually, Sarah was on pretty good terms with her mother-in-law these days. Last Christmas, she'd accidentally filled Mrs Bittersohn's long-felt but never expressed yearning for a genuine handmade tea-cosy like Agatha Christie's. Even so, Max's mother felt the strain of having a swarm of WASPS in the *mishpoche*, and couldn't help showing how much she'd have preferred having her only son married to a nice Jewish girl.

They'd work it out. Sarah wasn't going to worry. She was excited about her baby, she felt marvellous, and she was enjoying the walk. The Senior Citizens' Recycling Center being situated over towards North Station, she and Max had decided to walk along the Esplanade as far as it would take them. With the wind whipping off the Charles River, she was glad she'd put on the white beret that went with her outfit.

'It will be nice when I can button this jacket again,' she remarked. 'I do love it so.'

'Maybe I'd have been smarter to buy you a cape,' Max answered. 'That woman up ahead of us has one.'

'The brown thing that looks like a horse blanket? Ugh, I wouldn't – good heavens, I know that poncho! Speak of the devil and she appears. Max, it's got to be Tigger. Slow down, for goodness' sake. We don't want to catch up with her.'

They had no trouble avoiding Tigger, she was making good time. When they got up to where the shops were, they saw her cross the road, flap into a coffee shop, and sit down with her back to the window.

This was only one of several eating places in the area. Sarah wondered why Osmond Loveday still bothered to walk all the way back to Beacon Hill for his breakfast. Because he always had, she supposed, or because this neighbourhood was too grubby to suit him. She'd never known Mr Loveday well, but he'd always impressed her as being a fussbudget.

It was strange a man who balked at rubbing elbows with

27

hoi polloi had worked all his life for charitable organizations. But then he hadn't been working for charity, he'd been working for the Kellings. Perhaps that had made the difference.

CHAPTER 4

Anyway here they were and there he was, off in a cubicle by himself. They could see him through the big front window. This must have been some kind of store once. Now Mary's taste and Dolph's cheque-book had turned a drab, bare space into an inviting place for their elderly members to meet, eat, and rest from their labours.

Coloured tiles brightened the floor. A good many armchairs, covered in hues of blue, green, and orange were grouped around yellow plastic-topped tables. A long counter at the back, also plastic-topped, held a couple of big urns and enough cups and saucers to stock a tea-shop. They were real cups and saucers, Sarah noticed, not thick institutional mugs. Mary had used far more plastic than she'd wanted to in the decorating because it was the only way to keep the place clean, but she'd drawn the line at utility china.

Attractive green draperies were looped back from freshly washed windows. Between them a big vase of chrysanthemums from the Kelling estate sat next to a discreet green and gold sign announcing that this was in truth the Senior Citizens' Recycling Center. A tipped-over SCRC collecting bag with some debris spilling out of it in a tasteful and decorative manner completed the window display and served as a visual aid to those who couldn't read the sign. Mary thought of everything.

A number of the members were sitting around the tables drinking coffee or tea and chatting. Others were playing checkers or dominoes and getting more advice than they wanted from onlookers. One man sat alone with his eyeglasses down near the tip of his nose, reading a church magazine. Perhaps this was the man who preached, getting some ideas for Chet Arthur's funeral sermon.

Though the day was still young, members were already coming in with full bags and being ushered into the back room, not by Osmond Loveday, but by an affable hostess wearing a dress that Sarah recognized with some sense of shock as having once belonged to her own mother. When they opened the Center, Mary had gone around the family scrounging respectable hand-me-downs and Sarah had been delighted to unload. It was interesting to see the old duds still going strong.

The woman wouldn't be a paid employee, but one of the SCRC members putting in some volunteer time. She'd be recompensed with a discreet gift of hosiery, underwear, another hand-me-down, a hot bath and a haircut, or whatever she happened to be most urgently in need of at the moment. Dolph was too wily to start paying for services at the low rate the Center's budget would allow and risk falling afoul of the regulations that beset employers. Those who chose to work at the Center were content with this arrangement; those who preferred cash could earn it by selling their salvage.

Part of Mr Loveday's job, Sarah assumed, would be to keep track of the volunteers' schedules. He'd have rubber stamps, no doubt, to mark their time cards. Mr Loveday had always had a passion for rubber stamps. Sarah remembered how intrigued she'd been as a child by the neat little rack of them he'd kept on his desk.

Her parents had taken her to Great-uncle Frederick's office up behind the State House every so often. They'd always insisted she save half her weekly ten-cent allowance, to teach her the New England virtue of thrift. When she'd saved up enough to make the excursion worthwhile, she was given the privilege of bringing it to Mr Loveday and forking it over to whatever cause Uncle Frederick was espousing at the moment. This was to teach her the particularly Brahmin virtue of public charity.

Sarah hadn't thought much of her parents' teaching methods, and she'd especially resented the fact that Mr Loveday would never let her play with his stamps. She'd never protested because children weren't supposed to, but the grievance had rankled.

Sure enough, Mr Loveday was stamping something, with a finicky dab and his little finger sticking out straight, just as he always had. He might as well have been a goldfish, in his glassed-off corner. No doubt it made sense for him to have a place where he could work undisturbed and still keep an eye on what was happening in the room; but Sarah knew perfectly well the old prune had insisted on being separated because he really didn't like being so close to the people who provided a reason for him to keep working for the Kellings.

The members must know it, too. Sarah wondered how Mary managed to keep the peace, but she had every confidence that Mary did manage.

Naturally Sarah and Max got some curious looks when they went in. The hostess bustled over to meet them. Mr Loveday bustled out and tried to outflank her, but Sarah eluded him and offered her hand to the woman.

'I'm sure you don't remember me. I'm Dolph Kelling's cousin, Sarah Bittersohn, and this is my husband. We stopped by to tell you how sorry we are about your friend, Mr Arthur. We happened to be with Dolph and Mary last night when they got the news. What a dreadful thing to have happened.'

The hostess said it sure was and they were nice to call, and would they like some coffee?

'Yes, get them some coffee.'

There was no way Osmond Loveday could have been prevented from taking charge. 'If you please,' he added with a professional smile, remembering just in time that he was supposed to be a model and a beacon to the disadvantaged.

'Well, well, little Sarah Kelling. It seems like only yesterday.' He didn't specify what seemed like only yesterday. 'Did you get my letter at the time of your terrible bereavement?'

'You were so kind to write,' Sarah replied automatically. 'Mr Loveday, this is my husband, Max Bittersohn.'

Loveday cocked an interested eye. 'Ah yes. How do you do, Mr Bittersohn? Come to see how the other half lives, have you? What can we tell you about the Center?'

'Not much,' said Max. 'We helped set it up. How long have you been working here, Mr Loveday?'

'Only since last June, when all Mr Frederick Kelling's good works were finally dissolved and Dolph decided to phase out the office on Bowdoin Street which had been my little domain for thirty-seven years. This is quite a change for me, doing what might be called field work after having been so long in a purely administrative position, but no doubt a new stimulus was what I needed. Not that working with Frederick Kelling was ever dull, I must say.'

'I should say not,' Sarah agreed, 'with Great-uncle Frederick setting up some new foundation about once a month and dissolving them just as fast. Or forgetting to, and landing in another idiotic legal tangle over the mess he'd created. I'm sure you find working for the SCRC a good deal more restful.'

'I must say I haven't had a chance so far to think of this position as restful,' Osmond Loveday replied with a wry smile. 'Ah, here's your coffee. Set the tray on the table—er —Annie. May I offer you a chair, Sarah? Or must I call you Mrs Bittersohn now that you're all grown up?'

'Whichever you prefer,' Sarah told him sweetly. 'As a matter of fact, we're here on a little errand for Dolph. Max, what was it he asked you to get from Mr Loveday?'

'The address of that man Arthur who was killed last night, and any other information about him you may have in your files. I'm assuming the Chet is short for Chester Allan?'

Loveday shrugged. 'It could be short for Chester Anything. We try to keep accurate records, but it's uphill work considering the sort of people we have to deal with here. Dolph needs the information for the undertaker, I suppose?'

'I believe he wants it for the police.'

'The police?' Loveday so far forgot himself as to stare at Max. Then he shrugged. 'Oh, of course. They have to go through the motions, no doubt, for whatever good it may do. Excuse me just a moment.'

He walked into his office, flipped through a file, copied

down a few words on a slip of paper, and brought it back out.

'Here you are, Mr Bittersohn, such as it is. Arthur listed no next of kin, but one would hardly have expected him to. He's written down "foreman" as his last employment, but failed to specify in what capacity or with what firm. I'm afraid that's rather typical among our membership.'

The man sounded both annoyed and a trifle self-satisfied over the late Chester A. Arthur's unsatisfactory records. He was presenting an excellent example of what the late Henry Adams had called 'a certain irritability—a sort of Bostonitis —which, in its primitive forms, seemed due to knowing too much of his neighbours and thinking too much of himself.'

What a pity Dolph was still caught up in the feudal system, Sarah thought. If he'd felt all that responsible for Uncle Fred's old retainer, he'd have done better to pension Osmond Loveday off even if the man was still fit to work, rather than putting him here where he so patently didn't belong.

She was sure Osmond Loveday wouldn't be acting so supercilious if Mary or Dolph were here. Still, his manner annoyed her. He'd got under Max's skin, too. She could tell that from the way her husband took the slip of paper, glanced at it, and put it in his pocket with a too polite 'Thank you.'

Even the hostess was burning. As she was seeing them out, she made a point of letting them know, 'My name's Joan, not Annie. Annie didn't come in yet.'

Sarah shook hands again. 'Goodbye, Joan. Thank you for your hospitality.'

After they got outside, she asked Max, 'Don't you think we should have asked Joan and some of the other members what they knew about Chet Arthur?'

'With Loveday around? Forget it, he'd never have let anybody else get a word in edgewise. Mary says he goes home for a nap at lunch-time, so we can stop back later if we feel the need. In the meantime, what do you say we go take a look at the place where Arthur lived?'

'Will the janitor let us in?'

'There's only one way to find out. What the hell, it's on our way. Unless you'd rather take a cab straight home?'

'Darling, I'm fine. Truly, I've never felt better. Don't I look well?'

Max had to admit she did, and switched his fretting to whether the house at Ireson's Landing would be finished in time for the coming-out party. The baby would be born here at Phillips House, of course, where Sarah herself had been born. Aunt Appie was terribly upset about their plan to go directly to Ireson's Landing afterwards.

'She was all set to pop over every day and babysit for us.'

'Did you tell her that's why we're getting out of town?' Max asked her.

'No, dear. I told her we simply couldn't afford to have all that land sitting out there without our getting any good from it. She could accept that, though she still can't imagine what possessed us to tear down the dear old house.'

The dear old house had been hideous, dilapidated, uninsulated, unheatable, totally unlivable in during nine months of the year and endurable in the summertime only among those who believed in rising above physical discomforts and keeping their thoughts fixed firmly on the higher planes. It was the sort of house Bronson Alcott would have parked his family in.

Max Bittersohn was less transcendental in his ideas. He believed in plumbing that worked, heaters that heated, windows that let in the light and kept out the draughts, rooms that were planned to serve their functions efficiently, and architecture that didn't lacerate the eyeballs. Sarah, having learned to her astonished delight that such amenities might yet be hers, had cheered on the wreckers and couldn't wait for the new house to be done.

Since they'd gone to the expense of renovating the apartment over the old carriage house, they'd decided to keep that building standing as a separate guest house. Aunt Appie could stay there, in the unhappy event that she couldn't be dissuaded from coming at all. Appie herself was tolerable for brief periods at well-spaced intervals, but couldn't be trusted not to turn herself into a Trojan horse and let in her son Lionel, along with his awful wife Vare and their fearsome foursome: Jesse, Woodson, James, and Frank. Sarah would sooner have thrown her forthcoming babe into a den of wolves than let the rat pack near him.

They were discussing the possible advantages of a moat and portcullis as they struggled up the steep, narrow streets on the back side of Beacon Hill, but had to set the question of fortifications aside when they got to the address Loveday had copied out for them. No. 47B took a good deal of finding. At last they located the minuscule door that led to the basement, not only below street level but also tucked into a niche down an alley so narrow as to be almost invisible to the naked eye.

'It's a good thing we came when we did,' Sarah remarked as she edged her way into the alley, trying not to let her white coat rub against the sooty bricks. 'By tomorrow, I doubt if I'd be able to squeeze through.'

Max started to say, 'Maybe you should wait up on the sidewalk,' but remembered he wasn't supposed to be over-protective and confined his admonition to, 'Take my hand going down. These steps must have been built by a midget with the hiccups.'

At least they hadn't sought in vain. The janitor was just inside the door, banging trash cans around and not at all loath to be interrupted. Max opened negotiations.

'My name's Bittersohn. This is my wife.'

'Yeah? My name's Montmorency and what the hell is it to you?'

'We're from the Senior Citizens' Recycling Center, Mr Montmorency. It's about Chester Arthur. We understand he was a tenant of yours. I expect you know what happened to him last night?'

'Oh, sure. The police woke me up. That's right. Chet was with me—Let's see, I moved in here right about the time Kennedy was assassinated.'

'1963,' said Max. 'And Arthur moved in then, too?'

'Nah, he didn't come till after George Wallace was shot. 1972. See, how I happened to get this place was, the guy

34

that was here before me got shot in a robbery. So I applied for the vacancy.'

'Naturally,' said Max. 'And how did you acquire Chet Arthur as a tenant?'

'I was coming to that.' The janitor sounded a trifle hurt. 'What happened was, I was in a bar down on Charles Street. They had this programme on the TV about Abe Lincoln getting shot, so I'm sitting there watching and Chet's sitting next to me. So we got to talking. You know how you do. So he tells me the rooming-house he's been living in ever since that guy took a pot shot at Harry Truman and got the other guy instead is going to be torn down on account of urban renewal. He wants to know if I know of a place he could stay. Cheap.'

Mr Montmorency rattled another trash can. 'So I figure what the heck, I can use a few extra bucks a month. So I said sure, I could rent him one of my rooms. I got two, see, and I don't need them both because I'm kind of what you might call a man about town. I don't stay in much if I can help it. And I didn't have to charge him much because I get the place for free as part of the deal. I didn't tell Chet that, but that's how it is. Anyway, Chet said that was fine with him, so he moved in and it worked okay, so he never moved out.'

'I suppose you and he got to be great friends,' said Sarah.

'Nah. We got along okay, don't get me wrong, but Chet was never much for company. Maybe he'd go down to the corner with me on a Saturday night for a beer, but mostly he'd sit in his room and watch the fights on television or read the old magazines the tenants threw out. It didn't make no never mind to me what he did. Chet paid his rent on the button and never bugged me about nothing, that's all I cared about. I got trouble enough with them kooks upstairs.'

'Nevertheless, I expect you've been wanting to know about the funeral plans.'

'Not specially. It isn't like he was shot instead of just mugged. This is my week to wash the hallways, and I got to clean out Chet's room. There's a guy I know from down at the bar who's still got a bullet in him from when he used to drive for the mob. He wouldn't mind moving in.'

'Sounds as if you were made for each other,' said Max. 'We might be able to help you a little by taking Chet's things away. Some of his friends at the Center might like something to remember him by.'

'You can if you want, but Chet didn't have much. And what there was ain't worth taking. The television's mine, remember, and the lamp. I rented Chet the place furnished, and I'll need all the stuff for the next guy. He don't have much, neither.'

'At least he's bringing his own bullet,' Max reminded him. 'Then we'll just go take a look.'

'Be my guest. The door's unlocked. Turn left at the boiler and look out for the busted drain in the floor. I got to get on with my work.'

Max drew Sarah aside while the janitor went upstairs, thumping his mop and bucket against the railings. Then they navigated the basement by the light of one dust-coated forty-watt bulb and found the place that had been Chester A. Arthur's home ever since George Wallace was shot.

They had no problem deciding which of the two rooms was Arthur's. His had to be the one that didn't have newspaper clippings about assassinations stuck up all over the walls. In fact, it didn't have much of anything: an iron cot with a once gaudy Indian print bedspread some tenant must have discarded years ago, a small chest of drawers with a gap where the bottom drawers should have been, a dingy padded armchair with a rickety metal table drawn up beside it. On the table was a lamp some misguided person had made from a large purple plaster pig, the kind they give as prizes at carnivals. Pink toenails and a pink snout had been daubed on with nail polish and a pink shade with purple ball fringe added as a final insult to the eyes.

An old portable black and white television set was propped up on an orange plastic milk crate facing the chair. The rug underneath was so filthy there was no telling what its colour might have been. On the whole, though, the room was reasonably clean and almost painfully neat. There was no closet, but hooks had been screwed into a board fastened to the concrete wall and a few garments hung from them.

'I suppose we ought to take those,' said Sarah. 'Somebody might be able to get some use out of them.'

'Who, for instance?' Max demanded. 'Why don't you just stand there and try not to inhale while I go through the pockets?'

'I could search around a little.'

'Go ahead, but be careful what you touch. Leave the bed to me.'

There weren't really many places to look. Those of the dresser drawers capable of holding anything didn't hold much: a change of underwear, a few holey socks, some ragged T-shirts, a thick sweater with the elbows worn through. There was a helmet of imitation leather with earlaps and a thick fleece lining that might have saved Chet Arthur's life if yesterday had been cold enough for him to put it on.

Sarah got excited over some packets marked sugar and instant coffee, but when she called them to Max's attention and he'd slit them open with his pocket knife, they proved to contain only sugar and instant coffee. They found no sinister packet taped to the back of a drawer, nothing stuck between the pages of the dogeared magazines that had beguiled Chet's leisure hours. They found, as Max said in disgust fifteen minutes later, not a damned thing.

'Except this.'

Sarah held up a heavy brown paper envelope she'd just discovered tucked in between the speckled glass and the buckled cardboard backing of a cheap mirror that hung over the ruined dresser. In it were a tidy bundle of bills and four savings bank certificates from a Boston bank. The sum to which they added up was by no means meagre.

CHAPTER 5

'Forty-one thousand, three hundred and twenty-six dollars.' Max whistled. 'Not bad for a guy who lived in a cellar.'

'Do you suppose it's possible Chet bought the certificates

with his retirement money?' Sarah asked.

'I might, if I knew where he worked and how much he earned. And when he started investing. These certificates were issued within the past two years, but it's conceivable he'd been renewing them over a long period of time. He could have been taking the interest for living expenses, though I can't see what the hell he spent it on.'

'Maybe he gambled.'

'Or squandered it on loose women. Or gave it away to the deserving poor, like that uncle of yours who inherited a fortune and lived like a bum.'

'But Chet Arthur *was* the deserving poor. At least he made Dolph and Mary think so.'

'You're right, he did. Let's have another look at that mirror.'

With the blade of his helpful pocket knife, Max probed carefully down into the backing and eased out another envelope. 'Well, well. Look at this, *kätzele*.'

It was a will form, the kind that can be bought in stationery shops, meticulously filled out in ungraceful but perfectly clear printing, signed by Chester Allan Arthur, and leaving everything of which he died possessed to Mrs Mary Kelling of Chestnut Hill and the Senior Citizens' Recycling Center.

'Damned good thing Mary has an alibi for last night,' Max grunted. 'This is exactly what we don't need. If the police see it, they might get the idea Dolph and Mary had Arthur rubbed out to start their fund drive.'

'And if we report the heroin you found in his collecting bag, they'll say Dolph put him up to peddling drugs to raise the money. Max, what are we going to do?'

Sarah looked stricken, then faintly hopeful. 'Maybe the will isn't legal.'

'That wouldn't cut any ice, the intention would still be there. Anyway, the will looks okay to me. Arthur had it properly witnessed. Joan Sitty and Anne somebody or other.'

'Joan Sitty? What a delightful name. Darling, do you suppose she's the woman who brought us coffee at the

Center? Mr Loveday called her Annie, remember, and she said her name was Joan. This Anne whose name we can't read might be the Annie who hadn't come in yet.'

'It certainly wouldn't hurt to ask,' Max agreed. 'The odds are that Arthur would have asked people from the Center because it looks as if he didn't have anybody else. Except his landlord, and he'd surely have more sense than even to hint to El Moppo that he had anything to leave. Let's get out of here before that guy comes back and starts asking questions.'

He quickly scooped up the contents of the drawers and the clothes from the hooks, and dumped them in a heap in the cot. 'Got a pen in your handbag? We can leave a note saying we didn't see anything here worth taking, but maybe he can find a use for it. If you're set on making a donation to the Center, I'll give you something of mine. Like that necktie your Aunt Appie knitted for me.'

'Or perhaps those pink silk shirts you got from that luscious widow in New York?'

'Will you lay off those shirts? Mrs Vanderschlep was only showing her gratitude because I got her Jan Steen fornicating scene back for her.'

'And she has so much to be grateful with,' Sarah murmured. 'How did she happen to know your size?'

'She didn't. They're too long in the sleeves and too small in the neck. Look, next time the Mafia runs a rummage sale, you contribute the shirts and I'll take them off my income tax as a charitable deduction. Now where do you want to go?'

'To a bathroom, since you ask. Uncle Jem's is probably the closest to here.'

Men with pregnant wives either adjust to the facts of female physiology or spend nine months with red faces. Max wasn't the sort to embarrass easily. He merely took Sarah's arm and helped her over the worn brick sidewalks to Pinckney Street, indulging in rude jocosities along the way. Luckily the elevator was in the foyer, so they made it up to Jem's apartment in the nick of time.

Learning from his man Egbert that he had company,

Jeremy Kelling decided to get up. He emerged from his bedroom wrapped in a dashing tobacco-coloured velveteen bathrobe with black turnover collar and cuffs, and a big sash knot riding jauntily atop his little round tummy.

'Good morning, good morning. To what do I owe the honour?'

'To your niece's delicate condition,' Max told him. 'She'll be out in a minute. We've been over collecting Chester A. Arthur's personal effects. We didn't wake you up, by any chance?'

'Not at all, my boy. I was just lying there musing. I think I was musing. I may have been merely ruminating. Collecting Chet Arthur's effects, you say? Find any more cocaine, for instance? You're not going to tell me it turned out to be bug powder, after all?'

'No, as a matter of fact it was heroin.'

'Heroin? How *déclassé*. Max, this is appalling. Is the chemist going to tell the police?'

'No, I told him I would.'

'And will you?'

'I'll have to, sooner or later. Only we've run into a further complication.'

Max showed the papers Sarah and he had found hidden behind the mirror. Jeremy Kelling didn't have to have their implications explained to him.

'Great Cæsar's ghost! He was in love with Mary, I expect, and imagined that if he were rich enough, he could entice her away from Dolph. So he took the only way a man in his position might reasonably hope to make a great deal of money in a hurry.'

Max stared at his uncle-in-law. 'I'll be damned. That's one angle I hadn't thought of.'

'That's because you're insufficiently versed in the art of *l'amour*, my boy.'

'Who says he is?' demanded Sarah, emerging refreshed from her brief retirement.

'Sarah,' said her uncle, 'marrying a personable member of the opposite sex and begetting a child upon her does not constitute a grand passion.'

'In a word, Uncle Jem, balderdash. How did you get started on grand passions, anyway?'

'Jem says Chet Arthur had one for Mary, which drove him to dealing in drugs so he could lure her away from Dolph with his ill-gotten gains,' Max explained. 'Sounds reasonable to me.'

'It's positively brilliant,' Sarah agreed. 'Of course Chet Arthur would have had to be stark raving to think it might work.'

'Oh, I don't know,' Jem argued. 'Dolph's no Rudolph Valentino, as Mary herself pointed out only last evening. I still cannot for the life of me understand what a woman like her ever saw in that oaf.'

'Uncle Jem, Mary Smith was no Theda Bara, either. I do mean Theda Bara, don't I? I'll grant you Mary is a marvellous person, but can you honestly picture her in the role of a *femme fatale*?'

'What has my picturing her got to do with it? The question is how this deluded goop Arthur pictured her. Look at Don Quixote and his Dulcinea.'

'Not fair. That's only a book.'

'Then look at Samuel Johnson and his Titty. Look at Dolph himself, confound it. He took one bugeyed gander at Mary and fell for her like a ton of bricks. I was there, you know. I saw it happen. Strangers one minute, sweethearts the next.'

Sarah read through the will again and shook her head. 'I suppose Chet Arthur might have loved Mary as a mother.'

Her uncle hooted. 'What do you mean—a mother? He must have been older than she is.'

'Not necessarily. Anyway, a surrogate mother. A mother figure, as Cousin Lionel would say. A kind woman who gives you wholesome things to eat and talks to you kindly. A stabilizing influence.'

Jeremy Kelling continued to be amused. 'If Mary was a surrogate mother, Dolph would be a surrogate daddy.'

'Oh, Uncle Jem! All right, then perhaps she was only a sister to him. What difference does it make?'

'Quite a lot, I should think. You wouldn't go out peddling

heroin so you could woo your sister. Even Lord Byron didn't go that far.'

'He didn't have to,' Sarah snapped back. 'He was rich.'

'So he was. Who knows, Chet Arthur might have been another Byron if he'd shown a bit more forethought in picking his ancestors. It's a sobering thought, quite wasted on me at the moment since I haven't had my first drink of the day. Speaking of which, would you care to join me for breakfast? Egbert could make us a pitcherful of nutritious, vitamin-rich Bloody Marys.'

'Ugh,' said Sarah. 'Not for me, thank you. My child and I are abstaining for the duration.'

'Hell of a way to bring up a kid, in my considered opinion. How about you, Max?'

'Sorry, I'm working.'

'Gad, what a depressing pair you turned out to be. What are you going to do now?'

Max glanced at his watch. 'Quarter past eleven. Loveday must be off to his skim milk by now, I think we might stroll back to the Center. Unless you'd rather have me walk you home, or stay here and watch Jem guzzle, Sarah?'

'No, I'd rather go with you. Perhaps we could drop in at the Union Oyster House for a bowl of chowder afterward. I'm so sick of plain milk.'

'Must you go using words like milk in my presence?' Jem groaned. 'Take her away, Max. I'm in a delicate condition myself.'

When they returned to the Center, they found Dolph and Mary both there. Mary was helping Joan and another woman set out a lunch of soup and crackers. Dolph, much to Sarah's surprise, was doing something to the coffee urn in a brisk and competent manner. The room was filling up, already a line had formed at the buffet table.

As Sarah and Max hesitated, not wanting to break into the line, Mary caught sight of them and waved. 'Hi. Come to have a bite with us?'

'Not today, thanks,' said Max. 'The little mother's clamouring for pickles and ice-cream. We just wanted to talk to you and Dolph for a few minutes, but it looks as if we've come at a bad time.'

'Oh no, we're all set up. Annie and Joan can serve. Would you mind, girls? Harry, could you take over for Dolph at the coffee urn?'

'Glad to.'

A shortish man in a wrinkled but clean plaid shirt stepped out of the line. He was the one who'd been reading the church magazine earlier, Sarah noticed, and he made an almost laughable contrast to the man directly behind him. Whereas Harry was spruce and shaven, the other had carried dirtiness almost to the point of becoming an art form. His hair looked as if he'd washed it in used crankcase oil, powdered it with grit, then combed it backwards to achieve the maximum effect of spiky dishevelment. His face and hands were so thoroughly begrimed that his bright blue eyes came almost as a shock. His clothes—but Sarah didn't want to think about his clothes. She turned her eyes to Mary and kept them there.

Mary gave the clean man a smile and a nod of thanks, then came around from behind the serving table, rolling down the sleeves of her cheery green smock. Dolph was right after her.

'Now then,' said Mary, 'why don't we go into the kitchen? Nobody's there at the moment. Is it about Chet?'

They were still too close to the waiting members. 'About the funeral,' Sarah said quickly. 'Theonia wants to know what to bake.'

Mary hustled them into the back room and over to the area that had been partitioned off from the salvage depot to hold a stove and a sink. 'What did I do?' she asked when she'd got the door shut. 'Open my mouth and put my foot in it as usual? What's the matter?'

'Now, dear,' said Dolph, 'don't you start worrying. Whatever it is, Max and I can take care of it. Why don't you go out to the desk and call Theonia?'

'I've already spoken to Theonia, she's making brownies, and you needn't go thumping your manly chest at me, Tarzan of the Apes. Come on, Max, spill it.'

'Okay, Mary. Chet Arthur left you some money.'

'You're joking!'

Dolph gave his wife a puzzled look. It was inconceivable to him that anybody would joke about money. 'How much?' he said simply.

'Over forty thousand dollars.'

Max showed them the will, the savings certificates, and the wad of cash. Dolph gaped.

'My God! Where did he get all that?'

'Good question.'

Mary, quicker on the uptake, saw at once what Max was driving at. 'Did you find out what that powder was you got from his bag?'

Max gave them the chemist's report. Mary answered him first.

'So you think Chet was using the SCRC as a front for peddling drugs.'

'Max didn't say that, dear,' Dolph objected.

'I know he didn't say it. I say that's what he's thinking. Isn't it, Max?'

He shook his head. 'At this stage, all I'm thinking is that we ought to get these papers into Redfern's hands as soon as we can.

'Can we?'

'Why not? He's named Dolph as executor. I'd also like to talk to the two women who signed the will. Joan Sitty and Anne—looks like Bzkmz or something. Do you know them?'

'Yes, of course. It's Annie Bickens. Osmond Loveday could have told you that when you were here earlier.'

'We didn't have the will then,' said Sarah. 'Anyway, Mr Loveday doesn't even know who she is. He got her mixed up with Joan.'

'I suppose that's understandable. They're usually together. Anyway, Osmond's not good at names.'

'Depends on whose names they are,' Dolph grunted. 'If they're names he can drop, he remembers them well enough.'

'In any event, I'd rather leave Loveday out of this,' said Max. 'The fewer people who knew anything about this matter, the better off you'll be. I hate to say this, but you've got to realize not only the SCRC but also you personally are in a highly dangerous position. The heroin found with the body was trouble enough, but this will is a disaster.'

'What's so disastrous about forty thousand dollars?' Dolph demanded.

'Don't you see, dear?' said Mary. 'If the police get hold of this, they'll think we put him up to running heroin to make money for our building fund. Max, can't we just tear up this will and forget we ever saw it? Then the state will get his money, and who cares?'

'I'm afraid we'd be taking a still worse risk if we did that, Mary. Two of your people know Chester Arthur made a will. Annie and Joan may have read it before they signed it. We don't know whom they might have told, or whether Chet Arthur himself mentioned what he was doing to somebody else. If the will doesn't show up, there's bound to be a hue and cry. Those two women may not realize that being asked to sign as witnesses means there's nothing in it for them, and think they're entitled to an inheritance. Or they may know he was leaving it all to you and don't want you cheated out of your rights.'

'But nobody knows the will's been found, except us.'

'Okay, I'll grant you that. The guy Chet rented his room from doesn't know anything about the will and the money, or that roll of bills would have disappeared before we got there. He does know, however, that a man and woman representing themselves to be from the SCRC went and searched the room this morning. He can identify us and you can bet he will if anybody puts up a squawk, because otherwise he'd be the prime suspect himself.'

'Now look here, Mary.' Dolph had been checking the totals and finding them good. 'Chet meant for you to have his money. It's our duty to carry out his wishes whether we like it or not.'

'Well, I don't like it,' Mary insisted, 'and I'm not going to say I do. We don't need the money that badly.'

'Who says we don't? Tell me a better way to spearhead our fund drive. Hot damn, if Uncle Fred were alive, he'd be on the phone already. Loyal SCRC Member leaves savings of a lifetime to establish fund for seniors' boarding-house. That's no good, it needs more zing. Sarah, you'll have to write a publicity release.'

'Me? Dolph, I've never written a publicity release in my life.'

'Then draw a picture. We've got to start this drive rolling while the iron's hot. Come on, Max, let's get over to Redfern's and make sure we shan't have any trouble getting this will through probate.'

'While you're at it,' Mary sniffed, 'you might ask him if he can see any way to save our necks. You're right, Max, I was foolish to think of destroying the will, and you'd be even sillier not to let the police know about the heroin. You mustn't lose your detective licence on account of us, not with a baby coming along. Only I know darn well they'll be at us to close the Center as soon as they find out what Chet was up to, then what will happen to our members? Never mind what's going to happen to us. I wouldn't mind going to jail if I had to, but Dolph would absolutely hate it.'

'I could stand it if you could,' Dolph insisted.

'I'm not so sure of that, dear. I've had first-hand reports from a few of our members. They say the beds are hard and the food's just awful. And they don't even let husbands and wives stay in the same prison.'

'You're dreaming, Mary. Surely no judge would separate a man from his lawfully wedded wife. It's—it's indecent!'

'Happens all the time,' said Max. 'Okay, Dolph, we'll go see Redfern. Only I'd like a word with those two witnesses first.'

'Why don't you leave Annie and Joan to me?' Mary suggested. 'They'll be busy for a while yet, and they wouldn't open up for a stranger, anyway. As soon as they're finished serving, I'll sit down with them for a cup of tea, and lead the conversation around to Chet. That won't be hard. He's the big excitement around here today. You two take Dolph along to lunch with you and buy him a martini before you see Mr Redfern. Make sure he eats something that's not fried. Dolph, you'll come back here as soon as you're through at the lawyer's, won't you?'

'We all will,' Sarah promised.

'Not to be rude, but I'd as soon you didn't, if you want the honest truth. It's not that I don't like having you, but the members are going to smell something fishy if you keep popping in and out. Why don't I give you a call at the apartment later and we'll get together and compare notes. Darn it all, why did this have to happen, just when everything was going so well?'

CHAPTER 6

'This is real nice of you, Mrs Bittersohn,' said Annie Bickens.

They were in a restaurant on Canal Street. Rather than endure a boring visit to the lawyer's office with the two men, Sarah had suggested a compromise arrangement. Mary had agreed. With a little conniving, she and her two assistants had bumped into Sarah coming from the Oyster House, and Sarah had invited the three of them to join her for the dessert Max allegedly hadn't let her eat.

'Not at all,' Sarah told Annie. 'Frankly, I'm hoping to pick your brains a little. Mary's been asking me for advice on decorating the new housing facility and I'm wondering what colours the tenants would like best. We want the rooms to be cheerful and homey, but it would hardly be practical to paint each one to suit the particular tenant of the moment. Should I be thinking about neutral shades or bright colours?'

'Just don't make them pea green,' said Joan. 'When I was in the hospital for two months that time, everything was yucky pea green, even the orderlies' uniforms. It got me so down, I used to just lie there and cry.'

'What gets to me is that awful tobacco spit brown,' said Annie. 'My old man used to chew tobacco and spit in the sink, then he'd make me clean it out. I ran away when I was thirteen, but I still feel sick to my stomach thinking about it.'

She was making Sarah sick, too. 'Let's talk about what

47

you do like,' she begged. 'How about a cheerful sunshine yellow, for instance?'

Joan said yellow was okay, but she liked peach better. Annie said peach was too blah and what about a nice purple? Purple was her favourite colour. Joan made a crisp comment on the kind of women who preferred purple walls, and said, 'Why not shoot the works? Paint them in rainbows.'

'That's not a bad idea, you know.' Sarah was beginning to feel she'd bitten off a good deal more than she'd anticipated having to chew. 'We might think about using the rainbow as a decorative theme for the entire building. We could do the rooms in order, each in a different rainbow shade, have rainbow stripes painted along the corridors, hang rainbow-striped curtains in the dining-rooms and lounges. There are various ways it might be done.'

'They got cute rainbow stickers at Woolworth's,' Annie suggested, 'and rainbow decals you stick on the windows and they look like stained glass.'

Sarah tried not to wince. At any rate, she'd given them a reason for her sudden involvement with the Center, and got them talking. From here it was only a step to choosing rainbow-hued chairs for the Chester A. Arthur memorial lounge, and thence to Chet himself.

'How many do you expect at the funeral tomorrow?'

'We'll get a good turnout,' Joan replied. 'Nothing like a funeral to bring out the old folks, you know. He got in the papers, too, that'll count. Annie cut out the piece and stuck it up on the bulletin board. It's not much of a write-up, considering, but something's better than nothing, I always say.'

Annie said that was what she'd always said, too. 'I wouldn't miss it for anything, not that I was ever any great pal of Chet's.'

'Who were his pals?' Sarah asked her.

Annie shook her head. 'Far as I know, he didn't have any. Chet wasn't mean or ugly or anything, he just wasn't much of a mixer. Like when Harry Burr was getting up the checker tournament, for instance. Chet just grunted and said he had better things to do with his time. Which didn't stop him from hanging around down by the Broken Zipper, I noticed.'

'When did you see Chet at the Broken Zipper?' Joan sounded quite put out. 'You never told me.'

'Because I knew what you'd say if I did, honey. Okay, so I drop over there myself once in a blue moon, to see if there's any of the old gang around. What the hey, I worked there twenty-three years, didn't I? That was before they went topless,' Annie explained to Sarah. 'I'd still be shovin' the drinks if them bra burners hadn't come along.'

'Sure you would,' said Joan. 'What was Chet doing at the Zipper? Not picking up girls, for God's sake?'

'Picking up muscatel bottles out of the gutter, any time I saw him.'

'Yeah? How often did you see him?'

'Once or twice. It was no big deal. I don't see what you're getting all steamed up about, Joanie.'

Mary Kelling shook her head. 'I don't know, Annie. That's an awfully rough section these days. I'm surprised Chet Arthur would trust his precious hide in it. He was always so careful. Do you remember how he'd never set foot in the Back Bay?'

'I sure do,' said Annie. 'I was saying to Joan a while ago, how come his body turned up 'way over near Mass. Ave.? He used to rant and rave about them big buildings like the Hancock and the Pru getting washed away underneath and falling down on top of everybody. That's about the only thing he ever did talk about.'

'He talked about his will,' Joan reminded her friend.

'Not what I'd call talked about it. All he said was would we witness it for him, and we did.'

'That was nice of you,' said Mary. 'When did Chet make a will?'

'Maybe a month ago. He was all hush-hush about it, like as if he was the spy that came in from the cold or somebody. He got me and Joanie in the kitchen one morning, about a quarter to ten. You know that little quiet spell after breakfast and before we start getting ready for lunch. Anyway, nobody was around but us, and he took out this will he'd written up.'

'It was on a form he said he got at a stationery store,' said Joan. 'Only he hadn't signed it, see. He told us he was supposed to sign first with us two watching him. Then we had to sign underneath, to prove it was really him that signed it. He said that was what made the will legal.' She shrugged. 'So we did. Why not? It wasn't going to hurt anybody.'

'Mr Arthur followed the correct procedure,' said Sarah. 'Did he show you what he'd put down in the will?'

'No, just the printed part about him being of sound mind,' said Joan.

'What the hey, Chet was no nuttier than the rest of us, as far as we know,' Annie added. 'Like about them buildings falling down in the Back Bay. I almost got clobbered myself once, back when the windows were falling out of the Hancock Tower. They had to keep the sidewalk roped off for I don't know how long. You can see where Chet got the idea the whole place might go. He used to be in some kind of construction himself, wasn't he, Joanie? Maybe he knew something we didn't.'

'I thought he'd been a foreman at the Navy Yard.'

'Did he tell you that himself, Joan?' Sarah asked.

'Gosh, Mrs Bittersohn, I don't know if it was Chet or somebody else that told me. Or maybe one of the guys said they used to see him over in Southie and just assumed he worked at the yard. There's always a lot of talk around the Center, people shooting their mouths off and half the time they're talking through their hats just to have something to say. Me included, I suppose.'

'I just wish I knew if Chet was talking through his hat about that will.' Annie was casually tucking sugar packets into her bag as she spoke. 'I asked him how come he bothered, and he said everybody ought to make a will. So I kind of kidded around a little about who was he leaving his millions to, but he just clammed up. All he said was he couldn't talk about it or it wouldn't be legal. I don't know if he was giving us the business or what. Do you, Joanie?'

50

'I sure don't, kiddo. I never knew anybody before who made a will. I never knew anybody who had anything to leave. Did they find it, Mrs Kelling?'

Mary glanced at Sarah, got a nod, and replied cautiously, 'I believe my husband has some papers Chet left, but I can't give you the particulars. I expect we'll all hear sooner or later, if there's anything to tell. Well, girls, I'm afraid I'd better get back to the Center before Osmond Loveday puts a black mark on my card for loafing on the job.'

Annie and Joan took the hint and made their goodbyes.

'What are you going to do, Sarah?'

'I'm going straight home and give my child a nap. Why don't you and Dolph stop over later? We have lots to talk about, don't you think?'

'Looks that way, doesn't it? Perhaps we will, but not to eat. Genevieve's making Dolph a boiled dinner.'

Sarah shuddered and turned away. She really did want to lie down. Nobody had told her how badly a pregnant woman's feet could swell. Of course not all pregnant women spent the day traipsing from one side of Boston to the other. She was tempted to take a taxi back to Tulip Street, but the Puritan ethic proved too much for her and she walked. A couple of hours later, Max found her on the sofa with her shoes off and her eyes closed.

He knelt and scooped her into his arms. 'Feeling all right, sweetheart?'

'Just resting.' She grabbed a fistful of his hair and pulled his face down for a kiss. 'Mm, that was lovely. Oh, I meant to call Brooks and Theonia. I've asked Mary and Dolph to come for a drink. What time is it?'

'Quarter to five.'

'Then I'd better stir my stumps, if I have any left. Give Theonia a ring, will you, and see if they'd like to pop over for a little while. I'll get the ice out.'

'Shall I call Jem, too?'

'If he's free.'

Sarah wormed her way into the undersized apartment kitchen to begin cutting cheese and setting out glasses. It was going to be heavenly having a kitchen she could move around in and she'd enjoy having Max's people closer, but she was going to miss the daily contacts with her own relatives. And what should she do about the house next door?

She'd given Brooks and Theonia the job of managing the boarding-house when they got married a while back, not because she'd cared about keeping it going but because they'd needed a place to live. Theonia hadn't a cent and Brooks's little trust fund couldn't have supported them in any kind of comfort. But Brooks wasn't hard up any more. He'd inherited Uncle Lucifer's coin collection and Christie's were making him pots of money auctioning it off.

Suppose she converted the house back to a private dwelling, would Brooks and Theonia like to stay on and share the expenses? Mariposa the maid and Charles the butler, who'd been such props and mainstays during these hectic years, could have the basement rooms for as long as they wanted them. The top floor rooms would be reserved for however many Bittersohns and Kellings might need an intown *pied-à-terre* in the years to come.

As she was arranging the drinks tray, Max came back to report. 'Jem and Theonia will be along. Brooks is going to hold the fort next door. Shall I set this tray in the living-room?'

'Please. I suppose I ought to put the gin in the freezer till Uncle Jem gets here. You know how he is about getting his martinis cold enough.'

'I know he'd drink 'em red hot in a pinch.' Nevertheless, Max paused to set a cocktail glass in beside the chilling gin. 'Did you get anywhere with Annie and Joan?'

'I think so. They did sign the will and they did witness Chet Arthur's signing, but he wouldn't let them see the provisions. They confirm what Mary said, that Chet Arthur had a phobia about the Back Bay, and they thought it odd that his body was found where it was. Annie supplied a new bit of information, for what it's worth, that Chet used to hang around the Broken Zipper sometimes. That's over in the Combat Zone, isn't it? Mary said it was an awful section. Annie used to work there. She says they have topless waitresses.'

'Was she one?'

'No, she claims to have been a victim of mammarian emancipation, but I rather doubt it. Annie must be well over seventy, from the look of her. She's rather fun, I thought. So is Joan, and they're both longing desperately for a decent place to live. You know, Max, I do think this warehouse project of Dolph's and Mary's is a marvellous idea. I want to help all I can on their fund drive. You won't mind, will you?'

'Of course not, so long as you don't wear yourself out. Oops, there's the bell. That must be Theonia.'

For once, Max was in error. It was Dolph and Mary. 'We skun out a little bit early,' Mary explained. 'Osmond Loveday offered to stay on through the supper-hour, much to our surprise. He's all excited about the benefit auction, and he's going to update his mailing list of the *haut monde* for us,' she added with a wicked grin.

'Count on Loveday to know whose pockets to pick,' Dolph grunted. 'You talked to Sarah about the will yet, Max?'

'I haven't had time, I just got home myself. What are you drinking?'

Mary wanted a little bourbon and water and lots of ice. Dolph said scotch and ice and damn the water. As Max was fixing their drinks, Theonia rustled in wearing her new black taffeta with the Merry Widow flounce and said she'd like sherry because theirs was so much nicer than the boarding-house's, which came out of gallon jugs at about ten cents a drink. At last Jem chugged down the hill and up the stairs, and the party was on.

CHAPTER 7

Sarah sipped at the glass of fizzy grape juice she was trying to pretend was champagne so that she wouldn't have to listen to another of Uncle Jem's lectures on the perils of teetotalism, and let them all chat until Max finished fixing the drinks. Then she called the meeting to order.

'Max, why don't you fill everybody in on what's been happening?'

'God, you sound like your Aunt Caroline at the Beacon Hill Uplift Society,' Jem cackled.

Dolph said, 'Shut up, you old boozehound,' and Max began his report.

'Most of you know about Chet Arthur's will already, so I'll be quick about that.' He was. 'So Dolph and I took the papers over to Redfern this afternoon. He says the circumstances are somewhat unusual—'

'Old poop,' Jem growled.

'But that the will itself appears to be perfectly legal and should be filed for probate according to the usual procedure. He believes that unless some relative comes out of the woodwork and tries to contest it, Mary should get her forty thousand without a hitch.'

'Less expenses,' Dolph modified.

'But what if it does get contested?' asked Jem. 'Would those two witnesses hold up in court?'

'I don't see why they shouldn't,' said Sarah. 'They struck me as responsible women. Don't you think so, Mary?'

'Absolutely. Their work records at the Center are excellent and we've got Osmond Loveday's cute little file cards to prove it. Don't you fret yourselves about Joan and Annie.'

'What's their story on the signing of the will?' Jem insisted.

Sarah repeated the women's words pretty much verbatim, with a few assists from Mary.

'So you see, there can't be any question of Chet Arthur's intent. He knew what he was doing and he was concerned to do it right. He was wrong about its being illegal for the witnesses to read the will, of course, but I expect he only said that to discourage Joan and Annie without hurting their feelings. Don't you, Mary?'

'Oh yes. He wouldn't want them to know he had money for fear they'd spread the word and somebody would try to rob him. Gosh, do you think it did get around and some skunk took the notion he carried his savings with him?

Anyway, I don't see that it matters if Joan and Annie didn't see the whole will.'

'Not a bit,' Dolph assured her. 'They only had to testify that Chet signed the will in their presence, which he did. Redfern's going to file right away. He did natter a bit about telling the police but I told him we would when we were damn good and ready.'

'You're taking an awful risk, though, you and Max.'

'And we're all accessories,' said Jem cheerfully. 'Not that I personally give a hoot.'

Theonia said she didn't give one, either. Dolph snorted.

'What risk? Be sensible, Mary. We can't even guarantee that bag belonged to Chet. I got a thousand of them, all alike, and at least half are gone already, God knows where. The police had the bag before they turned it over to us. They didn't find any heroin in it, so why should they think we did? If it was in fact Chet's bag, did he know the dope was in it? And what if he did? Suppose he bought a dose from some street peddler just to see what it was like? What are the police supposed to do about that, haul his body out of the coffin and ship it off to a Methadone clinic? You didn't tell that chemist where you found the heroin, Max?'

'No, I only said I'd run across it in a case I'm working on, and wanted to find out what it was.'

'There you are, dear, nothing to worry about. Hell, I've run risks a darn sight more hazardous than this one.'

Jem sneered. 'Like what, for instance?'

'Like the time Uncle Fred took a notion to reform the girls at Madame Jolene's Palais de Joie. Osmond Loveday damn near had a heart attack over that one. Jolene took umbrage in a big way, and Jolene had connections. Before she was through, she'd come within a hair of getting both Uncle Fred and me jailed on a charge of moral turpitude. I beat that rap, and I'll beat this one if I have to. My head is bloody but unbowed, in case you hadn't noticed.'

'Really?' said Jem. 'I'm always so put off by the disgusting general effect that I never notice the details. Bloody but unbowed, you say?'

While Dolph was trying to think of a sufficiently crushing

comeback, Theonia defused the situation. 'I have always felt strongly that dear Dolph is the master of his fate and the captain of his soul. Jem, wouldn't you like Max to fix your drink?'

Jem said that would be a splendid idea. The captain of his soul cleared his throat and took charge of the quarterdeck.

'So as far as I'm concerned, it's a case of damn the torpedoes, full speed ahead. Redfern says we're better off not publicizing the will, except for the mandatory announcement of probate, but that won't hinder us from starting our fund drive, and the sooner the better. Mary wants one section open by Christmas, if it's humanly possible.'

'If we don't, we may find we've lost some of our members by Easter,' Mary sighed. 'The shelters get filled up so fast, and there are so few rentals available at prices our members can afford. Half of them wind up sleeping in the bus terminals. How soon do you think we can hold our auction, Sarah?'

'How soon do you want it?'

'I'd say tomorrow if I could, but I know it's impossible. I don't know anything about arranging those swell affairs. What'll it be, next month sometime?'

'How about Saturday night?'

Mary gasped. 'This coming Saturday? Are you serious?

'I don't see why not. We'll call it a secret surprise auction. Goodness knows the patrons will be surprised enough when they see some of that stuff we're going to sell. I'll hand-letter an invitation tonight, take it to one of those instant copying places first thing in the morning, and we can have them in the mail tomorrow night if Mr Loveday has his list together and Theonia will help with the addressing. Uncle Jem, you'll be auctioneer. I can't think who could do a better job.'

'Neither can I,' said Jeremy Kelling, 'but I'm supposed to be dining with the Whets Saturday night.'

'Tell them it's an emergency situation and that they're to bring their guests and come along. We'll serve wine and things. Dolph, you still have all those crates of champagne Great-uncle Frederick ordered for that victory celebration he never got to hold back in 1977 because his candidate lost. It ought to be drunk up anyway, champagne doesn't keep long. Theonia, has Mariposa any relatives we can hire to be waiters and runners?'

'My dear, we shan't have to hire anyone. Charles knows scads of out-of-work young actors and actresses who'll be thrilled to do it for a free meal and a chance to mingle with the right people. It would be divine if they could all come in costume.'

'There are lots of old clothes in the attic,' said Mary. 'Gay Nineties, Roaring Twenties, all that stuff the hand-me-down boutiques are peddling nowadays. We could have the actors put on a fashion show and auction off the clothes.'

'That's a marvellous idea.' Sarah got up to fetch paper and pencil. 'I'll make a list, like Aunt Emma. And I'll phone her this evening and tell her to come and bring her orchestra.'

Emma Kelling did in fact have her own band of musicians. Among the Kellings, this was not considered unusual.

'If I know Aunt Emma, she'll charter a bus and bring all her friends. That would be lovely.'

'Provided she leaves Mabel home and doesn't expect us to pay for the bus,' Dolph grunted.

'Of course Aunt Emma wouldn't ask you to pay,' Sarah retorted. 'When has she ever? And I'm sure she'll have presence of mind to tell Cousin Mabel everybody's expected to spend wads of money and give a large donation besides. You know Mabel, that will keep her away if anything would. Isn't it lucky Great-uncle Frederick never went ahead with that notion of his to turn your ballroom into an indoor skating rink? That will be the perfect place to hold the auction. The room is in usable condition, I hope?'

'It's clean and empty, if that's what you mean,' said Mary. 'Nobody ever goes in there except to brush down the cobwebs. I don't think it's ever been used much since Dolph's Aunt Matilda gave up fencing.'

'That was after she speared Uncle Samuel straight through the brisket,' Dolph reminisced fondly. 'Remember, Jem? You and I were hiding behind the draperies and made the mistake of yelling *touché*! Uncle Fred thrashed us both with that rattan fly-swatter he brought back from Tierra del Fuego.'

'Who cared?' said Jem. 'It was worth every welt. Ah, the golden memories of a misspent childhood.'

'You did a damn sight more misspending than I ever got a chance to. All right, Sarah, have it your own way. I dare say if we spread the word around and sent out plenty of invitations, we'll get enough customers to make the evening worthwhile, even if it is awfully short notice. Do we have to ask Appie?'

'Why not? She's wallowing in money, and I can't think who else would be likely to buy those seaweed mottoes.'

'Darling Sarah,' cooed Theonia, 'always so ready to see the best in everyone. I shall be delighted to help with the addressing. Shall I also make myself responsible for the decorations and the buffet? Perhaps I might also choose the costumes for the models and plan the fashion show. Brooks would love to pitch in, too, I'm sure. He can arrange the merchandise for the auction and set up the chairs.'

'I'll send Egbert to help,' said Jem, nobly making his ultimate sacrifice for the cause.

'You will not,' said Mary. 'We've got Genevieve and Henrietta to clean the house and fix the food. Once we get some kind of idea how many chairs we're going to need, we'll call the rental place and get their men to set them up. Theonia, you can do some flower arrangements and help me hostess on the night, and pick out the clothes for the fashion show if you want. We can get plenty of people from the Center to lend a hand. Harry Burr would, I know.'

'Is he that nice-looking man who was reading the church magazine?' Sarah asked her. 'I noticed him at the Center.'

'Must have been. I can't think who else would. And that sidekick of his.'

'Billy Joe McAllister?' Dolph shook his head. 'I wouldn't trust that bird within two hundred feet of a bottle.'

'Who said anything about bottles? Billie Joe can lug the knick-knacks downstairs, can't he?'

'I don't know that I'd trust him with a knick-knack either,

58

not if he thought he could pawn it for the price of a drink. What about that new feller, Ted Ashe? He looks husky enough.'

'What you can see of him for dirt,' Mary sniffed. 'Ted would be fine if you could get him to take a bath first. We do have a shower at the Center,' Mary explained to the others, 'but some of the members don't seem to have any clear idea what it's for.'

'Bad as those whelps of Lionel's,' Dolph grunted.

'Worse, because our folks have had a heck of a lot longer to get dirty in,' Mary agreed cheerfully. 'I'll leave it to you, dear. If Ted shows up too ripe, we can always keep him outdoors to park the cars. I'll grant you Ted would be better than Billy Joe. He's a lot younger, for one thing, or looks to be. I've been wondering why he comes to the Center at all. If Ted would clean himself up, I should think he could get a steady job as a night watchman or something. Oh well, no use trying to arrange other people's lives for them. We gave that up the week after we opened the Center. Now, dear, don't you think we'd better head for home and let Sarah start her dinner?'

CHAPTER 8

Max sat down on the edge of the bed and began admiring Sarah's nightgown. ''Morning, *angela mia*. How's it going?'

'Mother and child are doing nicely, thank you.' Sarah sat up and took the glass of orange juice he'd brought her. 'What got you up so early? Did you have to call Pepe Ginsberg again?'

'Oh yes. He's deeply touched to know I still care. Pepe sends you his compliments the most respectful, by the way.'

'How kind of him. Is he getting anywhere, do you think?'

'He sounds as if he's hot on the trail. I only hope it's the right trail. As for getting up early, I didn't. Nor did you, which doesn't surprise me. You sat up half the night lettering that invitation to the auction, remember?'

'So I did, and I'd meant to have it all printed up by now. I must get going. There are also the stamps and envelopes to buy, and I have to pick up that list of names and addresses from Mr Loveday before we can start the addressing. I do hope I wasn't over-optimistic, rushing Mary into this. It is awfully short notice.'

'Ah, you'll get a decent crowd. Did Emma say she'd come?'

'She called back shortly after you went to bed to say she'd rounded up fourteen patrons, a flute, a bassoon, and a viola da gamba so far. She's going to keep trying, bless her. Marcia Whet's bringing the Tolbathys and a few more, and no doubt Aunt Appie will drag along a bunch of her cronies. They won't know what it's all about because she'll have got the information mixed up, but no matter. If we don't raise enough at this auction, we'll hold another. At least it's a start, and it will give Dolph and Mary something besides that awful Chet Arthur affair to think about. Are you planning to attend the funeral, by the way? It wouldn't hurt for one of us to put in an appearance, don't you think?'

'I do and I am. I'm also going to see whether I can get any sort of line on that forty thousand dollars. The police could trace it better than I, but I'm not ready to tempt fate by alerting them yet.'

'No, dear.' Sarah picked up his wandering hands, kissed them both—Max had wonderful hands—and put them firmly away from her. 'Don't, dear, I really must get up. Do you think you could manage to start the teakettle boiling? Only put some water in it first, this time.'

'How much?'

'Never mind.' She ought to know better by now than to turn Max loose in a kitchen. 'I'll be right there.'

Over at the boarding-house, Theonia would have already presided over a gargantuan breakfast buffet of eggs, fruit, creamed salt fish, ham, bacon, toast, hot rolls, muffins, and perhaps even baked hominy grits. In the apartment, Sarah rejoiced that she no longer had to cook those breakfasts, and poured cereal from a box.

They were neither of them dawdlers. Max ate his cereal

standing up while he made some more expensive phone calls to agents in faraway places with strange-sounding names like Taormina and Meddy Bemps. Then he kissed his wife and was gone with the wind. Sarah made her simple toilette, whisked the cups and bowls into the dish-washer, and made sure her artwork was still in the big envelope she meant to take with her, because life had taught her to take nothing for granted. Since what she could see of the sky looked a bit iffy, she put on a raincoat and felt hat, and set off across the Public Garden. There was a copy shop near Arlington Street that she'd often patronized back when Aunt Caroline was alive and forever pestering her to do bulletins for one civic organization or another.

The shop was in a basement, half way down a narrow alley which in Boston passed for a full-grown street even though unloading trucks and piled-up trash waiting for the collectors made it all but impassable. The stairs down from the pavement seemed steeper than Sarah had remembered them, but of course she hadn't been carrying a passenger then. She waited until a messenger had been dispatched on his rounds with a pile of letter-sized grey cardboard boxes and a secretary wearing a businesslike tweed suit and high-heeled red sandals with fluffy pink ankle socks had got a handful of graphs duplicated, then handed her invitation over the counter.

'Cute.' The operator smiled at Sarah's lively artwork, picked up a ream of the India buff paper she'd specified, and started the machine.

The swish-swish-swish of the emerging copies was pleasant and the crisp reproduction of her neat calligraphy and her saucy cartoon of Uncle Jem as auctioneer was satisfying. Sarah paid the modest bill and picked up her own grey cardboard box. Now to get the envelopes and collect the list. Brooks would buy the stamps, he loved being asked to do errands in a worthy cause. She was half way up the stairs when the yelling began.

Nobody down in the shop was paying any attention, probably they heard plenty of yelling from the alley. Why should she let it bother her? Nevertheless, Sarah hesitated before opening the glass-fronted door to the street. In front of her she saw nothing but trash and trucks. The racket was coming from farther down, near the Berkeley end. She had a clear path to Arlington.

But Sarah didn't go. She'd caught sight of the two people who were shouting at each other. One was the vigorous-looking middle-aged man whom she'd noticed yesterday at the Center because he was so much dirtier than anybody else. This must be the Ted Ashe Dolph and Mary had been talking about last night. The other was a youngish woman with matted black hair and blue jeans tucked messily into clumpy laced boots, wearing a hairy brown poncho Sarah had seen only yesterday. What in heaven's name was Tigger doing, staging a public brawl with a member of the Senior Citizens' Recycling Center?

It was probably a stupid thing to do, but instead of heading for the safe exit, Sarah picked her way around the trucks and the trash towards the scene of battle. This was the first time she'd ever heard Tigger utter more than a surly yes or no, and at first she thought Aunt Appie's unlovely protégée must be speaking some foreign language. Then she realized Tigger was merely using words Sarah herself had never run across except in Restoration comedies.

Before she could make any sense of the fight, the man who must be Ted Ashe caught sight of her, broke off in mid-epithet, and hurried away. Tigger glanced back over her shoulder, saw Sarah approaching, and stayed where she was.

Sarah had no earthly use for Tigger. To turn around now and go back the other way, however, would be to give her a direct snub. Sarah hadn't the heart to do that. Moreover, she thought the stationery shop where she meant to buy her envelopes was in this direction. She kept walking and Tigger kept on standing. At last it became impossible not to speak.

'Hello, Tigger. What was the fuss all about?'

Instead of the stony glare Sarah would normally have expected, Tigger actually answered her question. 'Bastard tried to rape me.'

'No! He couldn't possibly.'

That was hardly tactful of Sarah. Rapists didn't pick victims for their sex appeal. On the other hand, if Ted Ashe's appearance reflected his personal tastes, Tigger might have looked to him like the girl of his dreams. 'At least you managed to fend him off,' she temporized.

Tigger merely gave her a look and changed the subject. 'Where you going?'

'To buy envelopes. I've just had some invitations printed back there—' Sarah waggled her box—'and now I have to send them out.'

'What for?'

'An organization my cousin Dolph and his wife are interested in.'

'The SCRC.'

'How did you know that?' Sarah asked in some surprise.

But Tigger had run out of conversation. When she didn't answer, Sarah moved on. Tigger stayed with her. That was another surprise, and not a welcome one. The only explanation seemed to be that she felt genuinely threatened by whatever Ted Ashe had said to her, and was afraid to go on alone. That meant Sarah could not in decency do anything except tolerate Tigger's company and get on with her own errands.

The stationery shop either was no longer where Sarah remembered it or never had been, but she did find one of those cut-rate places that carry all sorts of odds and ends. They had the long white envelopes she wanted, but only in boxes of fifty apiece. Ten of these made a fairly awkward bagful. To Sarah's further surprise, Tigger insisted on taking the bag from her.

'Really, you needn't,' she expostulated. 'I can manage. Besides, now I have to go all the way over to North Station to pick up the list of addresses.'

It didn't work. When Sarah went down into the subway, Tigger was at her heels, still clutching the bag of envelopes. When she bought her token for the turnstile, she could hardly avoid buying a second one for her unwanted companion. When at last she entered the Senior Citizens' Recycling Center, Tigger was still one step behind.

The front room was empty except for Osmond Loveday, seated in his glassed-off cubicle, playing with one of his rubber stamps. Everyone else must still be at Chet Arthur's funeral. The coffee urns were plugged in, though, Sarah could see their little red 'on' lights gleaming at the back of the room. A faint aroma of pastry suggested full trays already arranged in the kitchen, ready to be set out when the hungry mourners got back.

Somehow or other, Tigger was now ahead of Sarah. When Osmond Loveday looked up and saw her with her poncho and plastic bag, he came scurrying out of his cubicle.

'I'm sorry, young lady, but this recycling facility is open to senior citizens only.'

'I'm with her,' Tigger growled.

'What?' Loveday stopped, stared, stammered. 'S-Sarah, do you know—er—'

'We've met at my Aunt Apollonia's,' Sarah hedged. 'I'm sorry, Tigger, but I don't believe I've ever heard your proper name.'

Tigger probably wouldn't have noticed a hint unless it came wrapped around a thrown brick. She only jerked her head at the sixtyish man in the neat brown suit. 'Who's he?'

'This is Mr Osmond Loveday, who was assistant to Great-uncle Frederick for many years and is now coordinator here at the Center,' Sarah explained. She wasn't at all sure what Mr Loveday's title actually was these days, but he'd called himself a coordinator at various times in the past and didn't appear to mind being one now.

'Yes, indeed.' Mr Loveday was warming up to coordinate Tigger, Sarah could see. Any connection of the scatty but filthy rich Mrs Apollonia Kelling might well be another eccentric philanthropist. If there was one thing Osmond Loveday adored, it was an eccentric philanthropist. 'Perhaps—er—Tigger, you had some thought of doing a little volunteer work?' he ventured.

'What happens?'

This was more conversation in one hour than Sarah had heard from her in all the years of their acquaintance, if such it might be called. However, she wasn't about to listen to any more.

'Right now,' she said firmly, 'Mr Loveday's going to hand me that list of names I came for, so that I can address those envelopes you've been kind enough to carry for me. Then I'm going home to get to work. I know you'd rather stay and learn about the work of the SCRC, so I'll leave you in Mr Loveday's capable hands. Thank you. Goodbye.'

It was a rotten thing to do, but Osmond Loveday was getting paid for working here and Sarah Bittersohn wasn't. Throwing the Puritan ethic to the winds, she hailed a passing Boston Cab and made her getaway before Tigger could decide to follow her again.

Poor Max! If he went back to the Center after the funeral, maybe Tigger would try to attach herself to him, now that she'd lost his wife. Tigger would know who Max was, she'd seen them together more than once. Sarah wasn't much worried about her husband's ability to dump an unwanted shadow; he'd had to do it often enough; but it would be a shame if he found himself having to bother. Whatever had possessed Tigger to get so chummy all of a sudden?

There was absolutely no way Sarah was going to believe Tigger's rape story. It was possible, she supposed, that Ted Ashe had made some insulting remark to which Tigger had taken violent exception. She hadn't sounded frightened back there in the alley, only furious.

And what had Ashe been doing over in that part of town, anyway? Why wasn't he at the funeral with the other SCRC members? Attendance wasn't obligatory, of course, and since Ashe was a newcomer, perhaps he'd felt he hadn't known Chet Arthur well enough to bother. Still, the occasion offered a chance to socialize and get some free food of a sort the Center didn't often serve. People who spent their days picking up discarded trash usually welcomed any civilized diversion, according to Dolph and Mary.

Maybe he was an atheist and didn't believe in funerals. Maybe he had more urgent business elsewhere. Maybe somebody had told him he'd have to get cleaned up for the occasion. Sarah paid the exorbitant cab fare, went upstairs, and phoned Theonia.

Mr Loveday's list was a long one. The two women spent the better part of the afternoon addressing and stuffing the envelopes, writing 'Mrs Adolphus Kelling' and the Chestnut Hill address in the upper left-hand corner of each envelope. Loveday had clued them in that the Kelling name and address would stand them a better chance of catching the recipient's attention. They'd dispatched Brooks to the post office with the bundles of envelopes, all stamped and sorted by zip code, and were easing their writers' cramp with cups of hot tea when Max came home.

'How's the mailing coming along?' he asked.

'All done and gone,' Sarah told him. 'Did the funeral go off all right?'

'Great. Everybody enjoyed it but the corpse. Maybe he did, too, for all I know. You'd never believe what happened afterwards, though.'

'You went back to the Center and found Tigger passing the cookies.'

Max stared at his wife. 'How the hell did you know?

'Theonia saw it in the teacups. Want some?'

'Sure. See if you can fish me out a leaf that has Chet Arthur's old boss's name on it.'

'Haven't you had any luck on that?' Theonia asked him. 'I'd rather thought you would, somehow.'

'Actually I did make some progress,' Max admitted. 'I decided to follow up on that rumour that he'd worked at the South Boston Navy Yard, which he apparently didn't. But anyway, I was over in the area and feeling hungry. I hadn't stayed for refreshments at the Center when I saw who was dishing them out. So I stopped in at a corner deli that looked pretty good. It was one of those neighbourhood landmark type places that must have been around for quite a while, so I showed the counterman a photograph of Chet Arthur.'

'Wherever did you get one?' Sarah asked him.

'I'd borrowed Dolph's Polaroid camera and got the undertaker to let me take a couple of shots before they closed

66

the casket. Your friend Annie said Chet didn't look much different dead than alive. Anyway, the counterman took one quick glance and said hell, yes, that was the guy who hit the lottery. It turns out the shop has sold only one ticket that paid anything like real money, and Chet Arthur was the man who bought it.'

'Did the man know him personally?'

'Only as Chet, but he'd been one of their regulars for years. The counterman thinks he must have worked close by, because he'd stop in there every noontime, five days a week, for a fried egg sandwich and a cup of coffee. The guy said as soon as he saw Chet coming through the door, he'd slap another egg on the grill so Chet wouldn't have to order. He says Chet didn't like to talk much because he was deaf.'

'Was he really? Dolph and Mary haven't said anything about that.'

'Maybe they never realized. He might have been able to lipread enough to get by with. The counterman thought Chet's deafness might have been work-connected. There used to be a boiler factory not far away and it wasn't unusual for the workmen to suffer a gradual loss of hearing from the noise, just as the kids today are ruining their ears with that God-awful hard rock.'

'Did you check with the boiler factory?'

'I couldn't. It went out of business about ten years ago. After that, the counterman says they didn't see much of Chet. For a while he'd still drop in occasionally to eat his egg sandwich for auld lang syne, I guess, but he never showed up again since the day he walked in with his winning ticket. They assumed he must be off somewhere, living it up on his lucky money.'

'How much was his prize?' asked Theonia.

'Twenty-five thousand, less tax. Assuming he did work at the boiler factory or somewhere, as the regular lunch-hours suggest, it's not unreasonable to assume he might have saved up the rest of Mary's inheritance, or got it as a pension lump payment when the factory shut down. I said something about his having been a foreman, and the counterman was surprised. He said Chet didn't act like a foreman, whatever that's supposed to mean.'

'Mr Loveday says they all lie,' Sarah observed.

'That guy's a real sweetheart,' Max snapped. 'I wonder how he ever got into the charity business.'

'Attraction of opposites,' Sarah suggested.

'Snobbery,' said Cousin Theonia. 'My own uncharitable opinion would be that Mr Loveday is one of those "little people fed on great men's crumbs" who seize any chance to rub elbows with the rich and prestigious even though they themselves have little prospect of rising to such heights. Charitable organizations involve themselves with the up and coming as well as the down and out, as I don't have to tell you considering what we've been doing all day. And certainly not everyone had the opportunity to associate on a day-to-day basis as he did with the famous Mr Frederick Kelling.'

'Not everyone would have wanted to,' said Sarah. 'Most people shunned him like a case of measles. Tea, Theonia?'

'No more, thank you. I must be getting back. I mustn't stick Mariposa with the cooking two nights in a row, after she's been cleaning all day. No, Max, don't bother to come down with me.'

CHAPTER 9

She kissed them both and was gone in a waft of Arpège. Sarah took away the tea-tray, came back to the sofa, put her feet up, and leaned against Max's shoulder.

'You say Tigger actually stayed and helped with the refreshments? I'm boggled. Did she comb her hair first?'

'Don't ask me. Anyway, she wasn't glaring out from under it like the last time we saw her. In fact she wasn't glaring at all. I'd never have recognized her if she hadn't been wearing her combat boots.'

'Did she speak to you?'

'She most likely didn't notice me. I only saw her through

the window. All I did was walk back from the church with Dolph and Mary, and leave them at the door. I hadn't meant to go in anyway. How did you know Tigger would be there?'

'Because I took her, in a manner of speaking.'

Sarah told him about the episode in the alley and Tigger's subsequent tenacity. 'It was strange, Max. I can't imagine what got into her, unless she was really frightened, which I find hard to believe, or unless she's trying to worm her way back into the family's good graces any way she can. Aunt Appie used to give her a lot of attention, you know, until she made herself *persona non grata* over that insane business with Vare.'

A while back, Apollonia Kelling's daughter-in-law, Vare, had abandoned Cousin Lionel and their four bloody-minded offspring for a brief exploration of alternative lifestyles. Why she'd chosen to do her experimenting with Tigger was something nobody could fathom, but why Tigger had latched on to Vare was obvious enough. She'd goaded Vare on to milking Lionel for money enough to support them both in grand style until Vare decided it was better to be a rich man's wife than a hyena's mate. Now that Appie had come into a great deal more than money than she already had, Tigger could be hoping for another free ride on the gravy train.

'Then why doesn't she simply go to your aunt and ask her?' said Max. 'She must know what a soft touch Appie is.'

'Darling, there's no earthly use in your asking me how Tigger's mind operates. She's always struck me as being pretty crazy. I haven't the foggiest notion whether she was actually working some dark and devious scheme today or merely going on blind instinct, the way a stray dog will trail after the first person who happens along. Mr Loveday asked her if she was interested in volunteering, and I suppose she thought she might as well, since she was there.'

'What possessed Loveday to ask her that?'

'Well, you see, I had the box of invitations, and then I bought this big plastic bag full of boxes of envelopes to mail them in. The bag wasn't at all heavy, just a bit of a nuisance, but Tigger insisted on carrying it for me and I wasn't about to risk physical violence by trying to take it away. When she walked into the Center wearing those awful clothes, Mr Loveday naturally assumed the bag was full of trash she wanted to redeem. He came flapping out and told her the Center was only for senior citizens. She said, "I'm with her," and he started wagging his tail and licking her hand. He wanted to explain what the Center was about and began burbling about volunteer work, at which point I saw my chance to grab the list and ditch Tigger, so I took it. Do you think I should have stayed?'

'God, no! The farther you stay away from that woman, the better I'm going to like it.'

'Me, too. But don't you think it's odd, the way she's been popping up in unexpected places all of a sudden?'

'A screwball like her?' Max shrugged. 'I'd say the unlikely's always more likely than the likely. What's for dinner?'

'Not a great deal, I'm afraid. I meant to stop for something on my way home, but between trying to duck Tigger and getting that mailing out, I forgot. Are you terribly hungry? I could manage an omelette and a salad.'

'Unless you'd like to go out. How about the Ritz Carlton?'

'I don't think I'm quite up to the Ritz Carlton. Let me fix you something to drink and we'll think about it.'

Sarah's guileful plan was to ply Max with cheese and crackers until he was ready to settle for something simple, so that she wouldn't have to put her shoes back on. As it turned out, she didn't have to work her gastronomic wile. Theonia phoned, sounding somewhat less dovelike than usual, to say that after she'd gone to the not inconsiderable bother of preparing Chicken Kiev, two of her boarders had called at the last minute to say they'd be dining out. Could Sarah and Max possibly come and fill out the table?

Max, who'd taken the call thinking it might be Pepe Ginsberg calling back, said they'd be glad to help out in an emergency. He wouldn't go so far as to wear his dinner jacket, of course. Theonia wouldn't expect that. He never had when he was a boarder, although most of the others dressed up to the nines and sometimes a good way beyond. One of his London-made suits with a white shirt and a discreet silk tie would do nicely.

Sarah, on the other hand, was delighted to put on her gold mesh necklace with the little diamonds and a floor-length chiffon caftan in shades of mauve and pink. That would please Theonia and enable her to ease her sore feet into soft bedroom slippers which nobody would see. An hour later, she had the pleasure of finding herself a welcome guest in her own dining-room.

The room itself hadn't changed much since Sarah had presided there as landlady during her brief widowhood, but Theonia and Eugene Porter-Smith were the only two left of the original boarders. Soon even Eugene would be gone. He'd recently been promoted to a post of grandeur and affluence at Cousin Percy Kelling's accountancy firm. He'd toned down his wardrobe and gone in for good works such as befit a man of serious purpose. Instead of hanging around the Charles Street coffee-houses during his spare time, he'd been putting in a good many hours over at the SCRC, setting up an improved accounting system for Dolph.

Now he was ready to set up his household. Not long hence, he intimated, Mr and Mrs Bittersohn as well as Mr and Mrs Brooks Kelling would be receiving invitations to what would no doubt be a pretty splashy wedding. The bride to be was not the Miss Jennifer LaValliere who'd once captured his fancy in this very room—she'd been Mrs somebody else for quite a while now—but a Jennifer whose father was so big in real estate that Eugene didn't have to say how big he was. Miss Wilton-Rugge held her degree from Babson Institute and shared her prospective bridegroom's passion for a real knock-down, drag-out, rough-and-tumble audit.

'Then you won't be doing volunteer work at the SCRC any more?' Sarah asked him.

'I doubt if I would have in any case,' he told her. 'What I've been doing, basically, is to set up a simple, workable bookkeeping system for the Center. They have rather an interesting problem over there, you know, with so many different members bringing in all those different kinds of junk, and all the different salvage places they work with. Once I've got things running smoothly, though, they should be able to function without a hitch.' Porter-Smith went on to explain in totally incomprehensible detail just how simple and foolproof his system would be.

'But I take it you haven't been working in direct contact with the members,' Max put in when it became possible to do so.

'Not really. I pass the time of day with them, you know, and try to answer their questions about social security and old age benefits. It's appalling how ignorant some of those people are about handling their finances.'

'I dare say most of them have never had any finances to handle,' said Brooks Kelling.

'I wouldn't say that,' Porter-Smith contradicted, as he was always ready to do. 'One fellow tells me he used to be the bookkeeper for a big meat-packing plant, until he became a vegetarian and his principles cost him his job. According to Loveday, they all lie about what important jobs they used to have, but this man does at least appear to understand the basic principles of accounting. A good deal better than Loveday does, I must say. I've never seen a worse mess than those books were in before I took them over. Loveday himself admits figures aren't his forte. I can't help wondering how much his ineptitude's cost the Kellings, though I suppose I shouldn't say so in front of their relatives.'

Brooks and Sarah burst out laughing. 'Don't worry about Dolph's losing money,' Sarah assured the accountant. 'I can't say about the books, but I can guarantee you that Dolph has a running record in his head of how much the Center has taken in and put out ever since the day they opened. If you asked him this minute what the balance of their checking account is, he'd tell you right down to the penny. It's a family joke that most of the Kelling men have adding machines in their heads. So do some of the women, for that matter. Right, Brooks?'

'Oh yes, I do it myself, though money has never been among my primary interests. Sorry, I wasn't meaning to pun. Even my Cousin Jeremy, whom I believe you all know, isn't quite the devil-may-care spendthrift he likes to pretend he is. I've sometimes suspected his penchant for martinis stems from the plain economic fact that good gin costs less than good whiskey.'

'I never thought of that, but you could be right, Brooks,' said Sarah. 'Getting back to that bookkeeper who swore off meat and ruined his career, Eugene, do you think he could by any wild stretch be telling the truth?'

'Probably not about the vegetarianism,' said Porter-Smith, 'since I've noticed he eats whatever they give him at the Center, but he must have worked with figures somewhere. I can't understand why that man doesn't pull himself together and get a decent job, instead of foraging in trash cans for a nickel here and a nickel there. Even if he is getting on in years, there's plenty of part-time work for bookkeepers and tax consultants. Of course his appearance is against him.'

Eugene Porter-Smith shot the cuffs of his brand-new dinner jacket to show off the engraved golden cufflinks in his starched white cuffs. Time was when he'd gone in for ruffled pink shirts and maroon velvet tuxedo jackets with satin lapels. Now that he was a coming man, he'd put such youthful follies behind him in favour of sober black of conservative cut, though there was still a devilish *je ne sais quoi* about the way he tied his tie.

'His appearance?' said Sarah. 'Are you talking about Ted Ashe?'

'Why yes, I believe that's his name. Tallish, on the heavy side, rather young-looking for a senior citizen, it seems to me, though his face is always so dirty it's hard to tell. That's another funny thing about him, because he's always fairly clean-shaven. I suppose I shouldn't be mentioning such things at the dinner table, but I've often wondered how he manages to shave himself every day without disturbing the dirt.'

'Indian or oriental blood,' said Brooks promptly. 'Other

races tend to be less hirsute than the Caucasian. But then we have more to cover up.'

Porter-Smith shook his head. 'He doesn't look it. Besides, I usually see him late in the day when he's grown a little stubble. But the next time I see him, the whiskers are no longer and yet he's just as filthy as he was before.'

'Electric razor, then.' Brooks wasn't to be daunted by a faceful of stubble. 'That's the only kind you can use without lather, unless you don't mind raking your skin off.'

'Good thinking, Brooks,' said Max, 'only where does he plug it in? Back alleys and public rest-rooms don't have outlets, so he can't be sleeping rough even if he looks as if he is. If he goes to a shelter, they'd have facilities for him to shave, but they'd also make him clean himself up. Ergo —I knew I'd find a place to use that word some day—he's got a pad of his own somewhere. Would Loveday have the address?'

'I suppose so,' said Porter-Smith. 'I never touch the personnel files, myself. That's Loveday's territory and he doesn't like me, after what I said about his ledgers. How come you people know Ted Ashe, if you don't mind my asking?'

'We don't,' said Sarah. 'It's just that his name keeps cropping up lately. For instance, Cousin Dolph was wondering whether Ashe would be a suitable person to help at the auction Saturday night. You're going, aren't you?'

'Wouldn't miss it for anything. Mrs Dolph's asked me to clerk. My fiancée's all excited about it. Jennifer hopes to pick up some real conversation pieces for our new home.'

'She'll find plenty of those,' Sarah assured him, thinking of the seaweed mottoes.

A couple of the other boarders were looking interested and another one decidedly put out, so Sarah thought she'd better issue a blanket invitation. 'It was a spur-of-the-moment inspiration and it's not open to the general public, but of course you and your friends would be welcome.'

Max's lips were twitching a little, and Sarah could see why they might. She and Theonia had sent out well over four hundred invitations that afternoon. Aunt Emma must have rounded up her busload by now. Marcia Whet would be bringing a party, so would Aunt Appie and no doubt a few more. What if everybody they'd asked came and brought a friend? She'd better curb her hospitable impulses and start praying for a fine night and a full moon so the auction could be held out on the lawn if the crowd overflowed the house.

Boarding-house custom decreed that the proprietors spend half an hour in the library after dinner, dispensing coffee and chitchat to those boarders who chose to linger and enjoy their company. Eugene Porter-Smith was the first to leave tonight. This would probably be his last session with the SCRC debits and credits, he told them, before he and his Jennifer buckled down to more serious business like picking out the wedding rings. The moment the half-hour was up, Brooks rose.

'I'll take out the tray. Charles is treading the boards tonight.'

Having a butler who was also an actor, though not a terribly successful one, fortunately for the Kellings' domestic economy, added glamour to the ambience but sometimes led to a certain amount of confusion with the operational mechanics. 'Oh, too bad,' said Sarah. 'Can I help clear up?'

'There's no need. Charles will be back soon, I'm sure. He gets stabbed halfway through the first act. You people go upstairs with Theonia. I'll join you in a few minutes.'

Back when Sarah was running the boarding-house, she'd turned her late mother-in-law's boudoir into a sitting-room for herself. Except for Brooks's Audubon prints in place of Sarah's Philip Hale tea-party and Charlotte Lamson portrait drawing, and Theonia's sewing materials in place of Sarah's art supplies, the room hadn't been changed much. The loveseat on which Max had managed to undermine a young widow's inhibitions was still where she'd put it, and the two of them quite naturally settled themselves there.

'This is nice,' Sarah observed with a satisfied little sigh. 'I'm so glad your boarders conked out, Theonia. Poor Max would have had rather slim pickings if they hadn't.'

'I don't see that he looks particularly abused.'

Theonia settled her taffeta flounces in one of the bergères

that would perhaps have been put up for auction this coming Saturday night if Mary and Dolph hadn't donated them to Sarah instead. 'Do tell Brooks about the funeral, Max. I haven't had time to talk with him, myself.'

'As soon as he comes up.' Meanwhile, Max obliged with a description of the simple service, because Theonia liked to know about these things. He regretted that he was unable to report on how the mourners had liked her chocolate brownies because he hadn't stayed for the refreshments.

'Why not?' said Brooks, who'd by now joined the party, smelling faintly of dishwashing liquid. 'I'd have stayed.'

'No you wouldn't,' said Max. 'Lionel's wife's former girlfriend was passing the platters.'

'You don't mean that strange person they call Tigger, who glares at one from behind her hair like a wolverine out of a thicket? What in the world was she doing there?'

'Sarah got her a job. Tell him, *kätzele*.'

Sarah explained once more how she'd inadvertently acquired Tigger and led her to the SCRC, and how Osmond Loveday, hearing the magic password Kelling, had trapped the woman into volunteering.

'Leave it to Osmond,' said Brooks. 'He may be and usually is totally ignorant about the motivations behind whatever cause he's working for, but he knows all the tricks when it comes to raising the funds. His philosophy may be summed up as, 'Never give a sucker an even break.' Not that Osmond's dishonest, you understand. It's just that he's developed the technique of arm-twisting to its ultimate stage of refinement.'

'He'd better not try twisting Tigger's too far,' said Sarah. 'I think she's a mental case, or the next thing to one. You should have heard her this morning, berating that Ashe man.'

'What was she saying?'

'I wouldn't repeat that kind of language even if I knew what it meant. All I can say is, she must have had a thorough grounding in the gamier Elizabethan dramatists.'

'Or spent a good deal more time hanging around on street

corners than one might expect from a young woman of her background,' Theonia suggested. 'Though in fact I have no right to make such a remark, since I have no idea what her background actually is.'

'Does anybody?' said Max. 'Sarah doesn't even know her proper name.'

'Well, don't ask me to enlighten you,' said Brooks. 'I've made it a lifelong policy to steer clear of Appie and her good works. She's the one to ask, if you really want to know.'

'Appie wouldn't be available at the moment,' Theonia informed him. 'She's taking her transcendental meditation class.'

'What for, I wonder? Appie has both feet planted firmly in the clouds already.'

Brooks straightened the creases in his somewhat threadbare evening trousers. He could have afforded to buy new ones, of course, but why should he? At his time of life, he could look forward to no more than another twenty or thirty years of formal dining. That would hardly give him time to get a new suit properly broken in.

'I'll make it my business to call Aunt Appie first thing tomorrow morning and get Tigger's name and address,' Sarah promised. 'I should have done it today, only I was so wrapped up in the auction. Theonia, do you realize we may have unleashed a monster?'

The older woman laughed. 'Better a monster than a midget, my dear. Let's not worry about drawing too big a crowd. There's plenty of room for an army in that great ark of a house, and they do have an astonishing amount of stuff to get rid of. I think Mary would be happy to see every room stripped to the boards and the house itself auctioned off to wind up the sale, if it weren't for putting the servants out of work.'

'All right, if you say so,' Sarah replied. 'We'll simply make sure Dolph has enough champagne on hand to float a battleship and alert Genevieve to prepare for anywhere from a hundred to a thousand.'

'Surely not a thousand,' Theonia protested. 'Three to four hundred would be the most we could expect on such short notice, but even half that number would be a respectable crowd.'

'Whatever happens, Genevieve and Henrietta will know what to do,' Brooks reassured them. 'Uncle Fred was always sticking the staff with last-minute receptions for visiting dignitaries and whatnot. If there's too much food, Dolph and Mary can serve it next week at the Center. If we run short, we can remind the guests that this is a charity auction and we didn't want to spend so much on the entertainment that we had no money left to donate to the charity, as has been known to happen. Let's get on to more important matters. Max, do we interest ourselves seriously in this fellow Ted Ashe?'

'Why not?' said Max. 'I'd interest myself in everybody who's in any way connected to the SCRC, if I could think of a way to manage it.'

'I know how,' said Cousin Theonia.

CHAPTER 10

Anybody curious enough to observe it could have noticed a small and rather curiously assorted procession strolling across Boston Common the next morning.

First came a stately, handsome matron wearing a plain but good black coat and a plum-coloured turban. In her plum-gloved left hand she carried not only a large black handbag but also a small white paper bag. She sat down on a park bench not far from the convenience station, took peanuts from the little white bag, and began to shell them in an efficient but unhurried manner. Her object was clearly to provide more wholesome nutriment for a ratty-looking grey squirrel than the plastic potato chip bag it was chewing on nearby.

The lady had succeeded in luring the squirrel away from its unrewarding researches when a much younger woman, noticeably pregnant and carrying a cloth tote bag with an appliqué of a barn owl on its side, strolled up the path and entered the ladies' side of the convenience station. Shortly thereafter, the large woman appeared to weary of playing Lady Bountiful to so rudely clamorous a group of petitioners, for the squirrel had by now been joined by several loudly cooing pigeons and a rackety mallard duck.

She scattered the rest of her peanuts, which they all began fighting over, for Boston Common fauna are not genteel in their habits, and also went into the rest-room. The pregnant woman came out, still carrying her tote bag, and hurried away without paying any attention to the squirrel, the pigeons, or even the ill-tempered duck. She also ignored two well-dressed men who came strolling towards her engaged in earnest philosophical discourse, albeit the taller of them was good-looking enough to attract other women's glances and the smaller bore an interesting resemblance to the squirrel.

Whereas the mother-to-be had been in a rush, the two men were not. One might almost say they dawdled. If perchance they were hoping to encounter the gracious lady in the plum-coloured turban, however, they were doomed to disappointment. She must have slipped away by a different route; for during the whole time they lingered, deep in some Socratic nicety, the only person who emerged from the haven was a much older woman.

She, too, wore a black coat, but hers was shabby and unkempt, with traces of peanut shells clinging to it as though she might even have joined in the undignified goober grab with the squirrel, the pigeons, and the duck. On her feet were red sneakers with holes in the bunion area through which bits of heavy brown stockings could be seen. Her head and much of her face were swathed in a once-gaudy yellow and red scarf, pulled well down over her forehead. Perhaps she suffered from eyestrain even though or possibly because she was also wearing a pair of cleap blue-tinted sunglasses with preposterously ornate white plastic frames, in a style fashionable a quarter of a century ago. She shuffled across the asphalt path towards Tremont Street, pausing to investigate the trash receptacles along her way, and occasionally to stuff something she found there into the dilapidated paper shopping-bag she carried.

The men paid no more atention to this pathetic wreck of humanity than the younger woman had given to the squirrel, but ambled on to the corner of Boylston and Tremont. There they parted, the younger going into the Little Building and the elder crossing over towards the Masonic Temple and walking back uptown at a far brisker pace. When he got as far as the subway exit, the old woman was there, adding a grubby newspaper to her collection. Again he paid her no tribute of notice, but paused to buy himself a *Wall Street Journal* from the news vendor while she picked up her bag again and slouched along down Winter and up Washington.

Other scavengers were on the streets, some as aimless as this aged female, others rooting through the potential collectibles in a purposeful and efficient manner. Each carried a bag of some sort: a plastic grocery sack, an old army knapsack, anything they could get their acquisitive hands on. The more businesslike, however, had sturdy brown shopping-bags with the initials SCRC stamped on them in green letters six inches high.

The small man nodded approval at one of these as he walked on, glancing at the front page of his *Wall Street Journal*, stopping once or twice to search the inside pages for some story that had attracted his attention. The second time, as he stood reading, the old woman shuffled past him and cast a covetous eye at his newspaper. He heeded not her longing, but folded it under his arm, glanced at his watch, and picked up his pace. No doubt he was on his way to an appointment with his broker.

To maintain a step-by-step account of such meanderings would be tedious. Suffice it to say that, by what the Scottish poet Burns once referred to as 'some devilish cantrip sleight', the misfortunate denizen of the pavements was at no time without the company, though hardly the companionship, of some one of the three who had erst encountered her so chancily on the Common.

When she wandered through Quincy Market, the young matron with the owlish tote bag happened to be browsing at a stall of stuffed animals. She gave serious thought to a scarlet plush moose with beige velveteen antlers, but decided against it at almost the same moment as the old woman with the by now badly disintegrating shopping-bag ambled around to the opposite side of the leaded glass flower shop.

When the ill-shod peregrinator wended her way at last up Cross Street and back to Washington, in the direction of the North Station, the good-looking younger man was behind her. The casual observer, again assuming there was one, might not have recognized him as he had beguiled the interval by growing a luxuriant moustache. He had also swapped his hand-tailored grey worsted suiting for a pair of hairy green tweed slacks and an even hairier jacket in a strange mustardy shade overlaid with large green tattersall checks. His wavy dark hair was mostly hidden by one of those floppy Irish tweed hats in yet a different tweed with a relatively glabrous texture.

This man had further equipped himself with an impressive collection of photographic gear, hung about his person on leather straps of varying widths and lengths. This time, he did acknowledge the presence of the bag lady. In fact, from the shelter of a convenient doorway, he took surreptitious photos of her reaching for a discarded grape drink can. Even as he clicked his shutter, an unmannerly lout in a purple sweat suit and purple running shoes kicked the can away from her outstretched hand, leaving her crouching, bewildered and deprived, in the gutter. The photographer tipped her a quarter before he took himself off in search of more picturesque vistas.

Even more pathetic than this poignant little episode was the metamorphosis of the elderly gentleman. His visit to his broker must have brought heavy tidings. Perhaps he had been speculating in commodities. In any event, he was now woefully reduced in circumstances.

A shrewd student of the human condition might have deduced that the man had impulsively and wrong-headedly decided to recoup his losses by becoming the proprietor of a second-hand furniture shop that was already losing money and could only lose more. He shambled down the broken sidewalk, preoccupied by some inner debate.

He could have been pondering whether the imitation wormholes he'd drilled in the bogus renaissance table-top before he attached it to the relatively undamaged base of the otherwise ruined quasi Sheraton highboy would help him to peddle the *tout ensemble* as a genuine antique something or other, and if so, what? At any rate, he passed the presumably by now footsore waif of the sidewalks with no sign of recognition. She ignored him likewise, and entered the Senior Ctizens' Recycling Center, dragging her sack behind her.

And thus it went, until the day and the bag lady were both far spent. By now, she was in possession of one of the SCRC bags but she was making little effort to fill it. Gradually she was approaching the selfsame convenience station from which she had emerged that morning. One might have thought it was the only home she knew. Then, as if to put the cap on a totally discouraging day, she was bumped into by a roughly dressed man wearing a balaclava helmet, although the weather was hardly inclement enough to warrant such all-encompassing headgear. The man, as it happened, was also carrying an SCRC bag. After a small flurry and a mumbled exchange of apologies, they each took their bags and went on their respective ways.

Sure enough, the old woman entered the convenience station and did not come out. But lo! Exit the stately dame in the plum-coloured turban and the neat black pumps. From her black leather handbag she drew her plum-coloured gloves, and put them on.

Tagged admiringly by the man in the balaclava helmet, the lady walked to the traffic light at the corner of Beacon and Charles. As he paused to inspect a trash can, she went into the grocery store, made some trifling purchase, then made her leisurely way up Beacon to Tulip Street, sought a familiar brownstone front, and rang the bell marked 'Bittersohn'.

'Theonia!' Sarah rushed to open the door.

Max was right behind her with a towel in his hand and traces of soap behind his ears. He didn't appear to be wearing anything but a bathrobe. 'Hi, Theonia. Want a hand up the stairs?'

'No, thank you. I think I can just about make it. Go put your clothes on. What I want is a drink, and a footstool,' the stately dame added once she'd got inside the apartment and been properly hugged. 'Do you realize how far I've walked today?'

'You poor thing. Here, let me take your coat. Max will be out as soon as he's decent. He had an awful time getting that moustache off, and he's got wool rash all over his lower half from those hairy tweed pants. He's been soaking in a hot tub. Bourbon or sherry?'

'Lucky Max.' Theonia sat down in the armchair Sarah offered and put her feet on the hassock. 'A double bourbon, please, and something to eat with it so I shan't go staggering out of here and disgrace myself. Is Brooks coming?'

'He'll be over in a few minutes. He had to sneak into the cellar and get rid of his balaclava helmet.'

'Did you ask him if anything's being done about the boarders' dinner? I've been so engrossed with my histrionics, I never gave it a thought till this minute.'

'And you needn't now.' Sarah brought Theonia her drink, along with a plate of herbed cheese and water biscuits. 'I went over and made a pot of tomato soup and a bœuf bourguignonne. All Mariposa has to do is boil the noodles and fix the salad.'

'And the dessert?'

'Charles is going to do poires flambées at the table. You know how he loves to hurl flaming liqueur around. And there's nothing to them, really. Don't you want to slip your shoes off? I can phone down to Brooks and have him bring some loose ones for you to wear home.'

'What a glorious idea. My feet feel like pumpkins.' Theonia eased off the black pumps and wiggled her toes. 'Please do call him. I'll never get these back on.'

But Brooks was already letting himself in, with a pair of easy-fitting sandals in his hand.

'Here, Theonia, I thought you might be wanting these.'

'My darling, your kindness to the old bag lady is overwhelming. First my clothes, and now my sandals. How can I ever reward you?'

The Kellings are not as a rule given to dramatic public displays of connubial affection. Brooks merely performed a few preliminary steps of the woodcock's courting dance, of course skipping the part where the bird spirals high into the air, then plummets straight to earth. Then he started rubbing Theonia's feet.

'Feel better?'

'If you only knew!'

Theonia leaned back against the soft upholstery, shut her eyes, and sipped at her drink in blissful silence. The other three waited, respecting her need to rest. At last she began the tale they so much wanted to hear.

'I think that man Ashe is a spy.'

'A what?' Sarah exclaimed.

'I don't mean the kind of spy who comes in from the cold. I mean . . .' Theonia ate some cheese, trying to define what she did mean. 'You know what I mean. Those people who get jobs in rival companies to steal the formula for the piccalilli or bribe the chairman of the board so they can buy up all the stock. That sort of thing.'

'You mean Ashe is there to find out something,' Max explained for her.

'Exactly, though don't ask me what, why, or for whom. I can't think why else he'd be going through this charade. He's certainly not the roughneck he's making himself up to be. Aside from the shaving, he simply doesn't smell gamy enough. Believe me, that's something I couldn't miss. I made a point of getting close to him, and there's nothing wrong with my nose. Wherever he spends his nights, I'm sure it's not on a park bench. My guess would be that he has a place somewhere not far off where he goes and cleans himself up for the evening. In the morning he doesn't shave or shower but smears a mixture of olive oil and soot, or some such thing, on his face and hands before he puts on those dirty old clothes. I'm sure this doesn't surprise you, Max.'

'No, but it doesn't make me happy. Would you say he might be an undercover narcotics agent?'

'If he is, he must be from the FBI,' said Brooks. 'Our Boston cops would have sense enough to get genuinely dirty.'

'I doubt whether he's any sort of law officer.' Theonia took some more cheese. 'He doesn't feel like a policeman. Though perhaps my extra-sensory perception in that area has been somewhat dulled of late.'

'At least we know he needs checking out,' said Max. 'Brooks and I will follow up on him. Er—speaking of smells —' Theonia did not only waft but positively gust of Arpège —'you don't suppose anybody—er . . .'

Theonia was amused. 'No fear, my dear. I took the precaution of tying an old gipsy charm in the tail of that head scarf I was wearing. You start with a clove of garlic and a pinch of asafœtida and rather go on from there. That's why I had to douse myself with perfume when I changed back just now. We must allow time for a thorough scrubbing before dinner, Brooks dearest.'

'Certainly, my love. Feel free to call on me for any required assistance. What else did your talented nose sniff out?'

'There's that woman Annie who signed the will.'

'Surely not Annie,' cried Sarah. 'She's one of Mary's props and mainstays.'

'Then Mary had better prop her handbag someplace where Annie can't get her fingers into it. I've met her sort often enough. Do you know anything about Annie's background, Sarah?'

'Only that she used to be a cocktail waitress. She worked at the Broken Zipper for over twenty years, she told me, so she must have given satisfaction.'

'I'm sure she did,' said Theonia drily. One did still have to make allowances for Sarah's sheltered upbringing. 'But I doubt whether they ever let her operate the cash register. I'm not saying Annie's a bad person, merely what one might call temptation-prone. She'd be friendly and efficient serving her customers, but if they got back their right change, it wouldn't be her fault. She's good-natured and generous, only when she gives you the shirt off her back, it turns out she's been wearing somebody else's shirt.'

'Then what about her sidekick, Joan?'

'Joan's all right. My impression was that she's one of those motherly souls who knows Annie's little quirks and worries about her a good deal. You must remember that I'm only going by instinct and what little observation I could manage without making myself conspicuous. As you know, though, I'm a highly experienced sizer-up.'

'And a damned good one,' said Max. 'What did you think of Osmond Loveday?'

'I stayed well clear of Mr Loveday. I don't see how I'm going to avoid meeting him Saturday night at the auction, and I wasn't at all sure my histrionic ability would stand up to those beady little eyes of his. He looks like a sharp one to me. Fortunately he didn't come out himself to check on me, but sent a representative.'

'Who was that? Joan or Annie?'

'Neither. It was Apollonia Kelling.'

CHAPTER 11

Sarah choked on her milk. 'Aunt Appie? Whatever was she doing there?'

'Throwing the place into utter confusion, as far as I could gather,' Theonia replied with uncharacteristic waspishness. 'I felt like the Lady of Shalott when she came bounding towards me. Doom staring me in the face, you know. I just stood there feeling idiotic and fortunately Appie took me at face value and thought I was. She started asking me inane questions in that briskly sympathetic voice she puts on when she's being helpful. I kept croaking "Huh?" as if I were either too deaf or too stupid to understand, and holding out my bag of rubbish. Finally Joan came over and led me into that back room where they take the salvage and pay you. I made a dollar and eighty-five cents. Aren't you proud of me, Brooks dearest?'

'I am indeed, more proud than I can say. You've done a phenomenal job today, but that doesn't mean I'm going to stand for your staging a repeat performance. I don't often play the heavy husband, Theonia—' understandably not, since his wife outweighed him by at least twenty-five pounds —'but you're worth something more than a dollar and eighty-five cents to me. What if whoever killed Chet Arthur happened to be there when you went in? What if Appie had recognized you and spilled the beans, as she surely would have? Sarah, didn't it dawn on you that Appie might take it into her head to do good works? Couldn't you have kept her away?'

'No it didn't, and why me, anyway? Appie's more your relative than mine.'

'I dispute that! Appie is merely the daughter of my father's second cousin Byram.'

'Which makes her your third cousin in the direct line. She was Alexander's third cousin, but Alexander was only my fifth cousin once removed, which puts Byram so far from our particular branch of the family tree that he doesn't even count. The only real connection I have with Aunt Appie is that she married Uncle Samuel who was, I grant you, first cousin to my own grandfather.'

'Makes sense to me,' said Max. 'Brooks, I don't blame you for not wanting Theonia to take such a risk again and I certainly wouldn't ask her myself, but she did handle herself like a pro, and she did get back safe and sound.'

Theonia waggled her abused toes. 'I'm not so sure about the sound, but I knew I was never in any real danger with my stalwart bodyguard around me. I say we were all magnificent. But as far as Appie goes, you know she's such a dear, muzzy-headed soul that she doesn't know whom she's talking to half the time, anyway. The chances of her blowing my cover, as I believe it's called, probably were not great in any case. If she had, I'd simply have said "Huh?" again and faced her down. Now shall I get on with my report, because I really do have to go and bath pretty soon.'

'First, let me just say I did try to call Aunt Appie, not to put her off going to the Center, because that never entered

87

my mind; but to get Tigger's address as I said I would,' Sarah put in. 'However, she wasn't there and the house-keeper couldn't tell me where she'd gone. I'm wondering if Mr Loveday coaxed Tigger into getting her to volunteer, or if he approached her himself. Anyway, I'll track her down this evening, if I can. Do go on, Theonia.'

'Yes, tell us about that little fracas down by the corner of Blackstone Street,' said Max. 'I thought you were in real trouble there for a second.'

'So did I. What happened,' Theonia explained to the others, 'was that I'd spied a soft drink can in the gutter and stooped to pick it up. Just as I was about to put my hand on the can, some young fellow dressed all in purple rushed over and kicked it away, almost kicking me in the process. So naturally I got up and scooted away from him as fast as I could. I didn't know whether he was planning to rough me up, or what. Did he start to come after me, Max?'

'No, he did something I thought was pretty damned strange. He paid no further attention to you, but very carefully kicked the can back to the exact same spot where it had been before. A few seconds later, a woman carrying an SCRC bag and wearing a purple sweater came along, picked up the can, and stuck it in her bag. The guy stood right there watching her, and never moved a muscle. I had to hurry along after you so I couldn't follow up on her, but I'd have liked to. What kind of can was it, Theonia? Did you happen to notice?'

'I did, partly because the can was purple, like the fellow's clothes. It was some kind of grape soda with a name that wasn't familiar to me. Graperoola, something like that. It was a longish name, I know. The lettering went all around the can.'

Brooks, who still took a youthful pleasure in carbonated beverages, shook his head. 'That's a new one on me, as the monkey said when he scratched his back. I must find out who sells it.'

'Purple suit, purple sweater, purple can—wait a second!' Max shot out of this chair, whipped into the tiny spare room he used for an office, and came back with the torn collecting bag that had been Chet Arthur's. 'Take a look at this.'

He spread the remnant out on the floor in front of Theonia's hassock. The bag was no different from the one she'd acquired at the Center, except that it was in far worse condition and had somehow got splashed with purple paint from some graffiti artist's spray can.

'I'll bet if you'd been carrying this bag instead of your own, Theonia, you'd have got to keep the Graperoola can.'

'But it won't even hold anything. Max dear, I don't understand.'

'I think what you and probably Chet Arthur, too, stumbled into was a drug transfer. As we all know, the police are really cracking down on drug dealers these days. They've tightened up everywhere, yet the dealing goes on. It looks to me as if some pusher may be cracking the blockade by using SCRC people as caddies.'

'You said I'd have been allowed to keep that can. Surely you can't think I'd smuggle dope?'

'You wouldn't know. Assuming that by some chance I've guessed right, the mechanics go something like this: first they choose a type of soft drink can that won't attract any particular notice if it's thrown down in the street but is in fact not a common brand in this area. The organizers may even have gone to the bother of designing their own and having a bunch of them made.'

'Wouldn't that be terribly expensive?' Theonia objected.

'Not in proportion to the kind of money involved in narcotics. And it would make the operation more nearly foolproof.'

'Packing heroin in tonic cans and tossing them around the streets?' said Brooks. 'You call that foolproof?'

'They don't just toss them around the streets. They pick their spots, and they watch to make sure the wrong person doesn't get the can, as Theonia found out. The guy in purple was one of the scouts, of course. He'd probably spotted the woman with the purple sweater and the SCRC bag coming along, and had laid his bait especially for her. I expect a good many of the SCRC collectors have more or less regular routes. Those would be the ones who are watched and used.

If he hadn't been able to find somebody wearing the purple code colour, he'd have contrived to mark the bag in purple, as Chet's was marked.'

'So that the peddler making his pick-up will know whom to mug,' said Sarah. 'Max, we must find that woman with the purple sweater before she gets hurt.'

'If you say so, little mother.'

Max stepped over to the telephone, looked up a number in Sarah's book, and dialled. 'Hello, Dolph. Glad I caught you. Look, do you have a heavy-set woman wearing a black skirt and a thick purple sweater in the Center? That's right, the one who got her bag snatched this afternoon. What do you mean, how did I know? My spies are everywhere. Is she okay? Well, of course, naturally she'd be upset. Wouldn't you? No, just give her a pat on the back and another cup of tea. I'll talk to you later. Regards to Mary.'

He hung up and came back to Sarah. 'Want another slug of milk to calm your nerves?'

'Oh, don't be so infuriating! How did you know she'd be at the Center?'

'Simple logic. It stood to reason she wouldn't be allowed to keep the can in her possession for long. There'd be hell to pay if she gave their contact the slip and got back to the Recycling Center with it. I'd guess she got ripped off not more than ten or fifteen minutes after she made the pick-up, and naturally she'd go straight back to the Center with her tale of woe. Where else would she find a sympathetic ear, a free meal, and a new collecting bag so she can go out and play sitting duck again? Damn, I hope we can convince Dolph that his bright idea is getting the Center in big trouble.'

'Try offering him a different lot of free bags,' Brooks suggested. 'Theonia my dear, if you want that bath before the thundering herds descend upon us, we'd better get cracking.'

CHAPTER 12

Sarah was better prepared for dinner tonight. 'Tomato soup and bœuf bourguignonne,' she announced. 'I made enough for us while I was about it.'

'Good thinking, said Max. 'Good soup, too. Not canned, I take it.'

'Perish the thought. These are the last of our own tomatoes from the garden at Ireson's Landing. Well, not the last because Miriam and I put up scads of them for the winter, but the last fresh off the vines. Oh, darn that phone! Go on with your soup, dear. I'll answer it.'

She should have known better. Apollonia Kelling was on the line.

'Sarah dear, I'm so glad I caught you. Now, what we have to do—'

'What I have to do is serve Max his dinner,' Sarah interrupted. 'We were just sitting down.'

'But this will only take a teeny, tiny minute. I have everything organized and written down. Somewhere. Oh dear, I thought—just hold the line a second while I see—'

'I'll call you back.' Sarah broke the connection and went back to her soup, leaving the receiver off the hook.

'What was that?' Max asked her.

'Something dire, I'm sure. Aunt Appie has everything organized and written down.'

'Has what organized?'

'We may never know. She's mislaid the paper. However, that won't stop her from nipping at our heels until we do it. I assume it's something to do with the SCRC. Oh Max, you don't suppose she's calling about Theonia? Maybe she did spot her after all, and thinks she's gone batty and we're all going to have to be very, very kind and take turns reading to her from the works of William Cullen Bryant.'

'Why William Cullen Bryant?'

'Because that's what they read to Great-aunt Perseverance after she started imagining she was Yvette Guilbert.'

Max looked interested. 'Did it help any?'

'I don't suppose so. Bryant wrote *Thanatopsis* when he was only eighteen, as you may remember, and he appears to have spent the rest of his life exploring the ramifications. I remember Great-aunt Perseverance's sister Letitia coming to read Bryant to my mother. That was after Mother got so sick she couldn't get out of bed to hide in the bathroom.'

'Was that your mother's customary practice?'

'Only when Great-aunt Letitia called. She was in her eighties by then. She wore black skirts down to her ankles and so much jet on her bosom that she clattered every time she moved. She managed to get through "No Man Knoweth His Sepulchre" and "Blessed Are They That Mourn". Halfway through "Hymn to Death", though, Mother pulled herself together. "Sarah," she said, "bring me a Manhattan cocktail and fix Aunt Letitia a dose of Epsom Salts. She appears to be suffering a bilious attack."'

Sarah laughed. 'That's one of the fondest memories I have of Mother. She died three days later. Great-aunt Letitia lasted another ten years. She gave a little party for me and Alexander after we got married. I was still in mourning for my father, so we couldn't have had any big splash even if we'd wanted one. But anyway, Great-aunt Letitia recited Bryant's "The Death of the Flowers", which is about a young girl fading away with the violets. I was still only eighteen, you know, and people did wonder.'

'I can see why they might.' Max didn't seem to think it was funny.'

'Cousin Mabel came right out and told me Letitia was giving me a hint to do the same because she'd always wanted Alexander for her own daughter. They were a lot closer in age, I have to admit. Xanthia was about fifty-five by then, and totally devoted to rock-climbing. She fell off a precipice in the Andes in mysterious circumstances not long afterwards. Uncle Jem wanted to read "The Murdered Traveller" at the memorial service, but they wouldn't let him. Here, darling, there's just half a spoonful of beef left.'

They finished their meal, then Sarah bowed to the inevitable and put the telephone receiver back on the hook. She was looking up Apollonia Kelling's number when her aunt beat her to the dial.

'Sarah, I've been trying and trying to get you. Is something wrong with the line?'

'Not now,' said Sarah, 'only I mustn't tie it up because Max is expecting a call from a man in Marseilles. What's on your mind, Aunt Appie?'

'I simply thought if we all put our shoulders to the wheel and pitch right in—one day a week isn't too much, surely?'

'For what?'

'To work at the Center, dear.'

'Why us? Dolph and Mary have it all beautifully organized so that the members take turns, and give them special treats for helping. Outsiders would be dreadfully in the way.'

'Oh no, dear. Osmond Loveday says what they need over there is a refining influence.'

'Well, he couldn't be more wrong. What they need is a chance to retain their self-respect by doing things for themselves and each other, and that's what Dolph and Mary are giving them. If Osmond Loveday wants a bunch of rich do-gooders flapping around him, he'd better find himself a different job. Sooner or later, Dolph's going to realize he's worse than useless at the SCRC, and chuck him out.'

'Sarah, that is hardly a charitable remark. Osmond Loveday is a truly dedicated man.'

'Dedicated to buttering up people with money and nicking them for all he can get,' Sarah retorted. 'Has he started hinting to you about a truly meaningful donation yet?'

'He did touch on the sad fact that so few patrons have come forward,' Appie admitted.

'I'm sure he did. He didn't happen to say that's because Dolph and Mary had never asked for patronage. So far, they haven't needed it. The Center pretty much supports itself through the sale of salvage and the members' volunteer services, and that's the way they want it.'

'Sarah dear, I'm afraid we're straying from the point. Shall I put you down for Thursday or Friday?'

'Neither. I'm already out straight on the auction and Dolph wants me to help on the publicity drive for the new housing facility. Max says that's enough.'

In fact, Max had said no such thing, but Appie had been bullied by Uncle Samuel for forty-three years and took it for granted all wives were willing doormats. 'Oh well, if Max feels—'

'He certainly does. Aunt Appie, I was going to call you myself. What's Tigger's real name?'

'Tigger? What an odd digression, dear. Whatever made you think of Tigger?'

'Wasn't it she who roped you into this nonsense about volunteering at the SCRC?'

'One would hardly say roped in, dear. Tigger did happen to drop by yesterday at tea-time and mention she'd spent the day there in good works. You cannot imagine how happy that made your old auntie. I've tried so hard to steer the poor lamb in constructive directions. I enrolled her in a number of worthwhile courses: Appreciation of Gregorian Chants, Balinese Tie-Dyeing, History of New England Theology with special reference to Cotton Mather—I felt so sure Cotton Mather would catch her interest, but she gave me one of her looks and that was the end of that. I had to take the courses myself in order not to waste the money, and I must say Cotton Mather wasn't quite what I'd— however. So when Tigger came to me last evening and told me she'd volunteered at the Center, it was a vindication of my fondest hopes. You do see why we must all rush to support her in her welldoing. Are you quite sure about Friday?'

'I'm quite sure you ought to find out whether welldoing is what Tigger's really up to before you leap in with both feet,' Sarah retorted. 'You still haven't told me her name, and I have a perfectly sound reason for asking. How she got to the Center yesterday is that she followed me when I went to get the mailing list for the auction. I tried to introduce her to Mr Loveday, then realized I didn't know what to call her. When I said so, she hadn't the grace to tell me. I don't want to be put in that silly position again.'

'Tigger's shy, you know,' Appie apologized.

'She was brassy enough about forcing herself on me when I tried to shake her off. Aunt Appie, please quit dodging the question. What is Tigger's name?'

'Oh dear, I can't seem to—something A. A. Milne-ish, I'm sure. Hence the Tigger, you know.'

'No, I don't know. Is it actually Milne?'

'Not that, but something.'

'Pooh? Eeyore?'

'Dearie, that's hardly kind. I'll think of it. Just let me get the rusty old thinking machine cranked up.'

Appie's cranking brought no spark. 'Never mind,' Sarah said at last. 'I'll call Lionel's place. Surely Vare will know.'

'Oh my dear, you mustn't ask Vare. Lionel has forbidden her ever to mention that name again under his roof. He's growing more like his dear old dad every day. It quite wrings my heart.'

Sarah could see why it might. There were curmudgeons enough in the Kelling family, but Uncle Samuel had been the acknowledged king of snap and snarl. Lionel would never be the grouch his father was, there was too much of the wimp in him, but why shatter Aunt Appie's fond illusions?

In the end, she had to settle for, 'Just be patient, dear. It will come to me,' and a promise to let Appie know if she had to reschedule her hours at the SCRC. She might have known enough to say yes in the first place and then wipe it out of her mind, since Appie would have forgotten, too, in a day or so.

'She really is the most exasperating woman,' Sarah fussed when she at last managed to get off the phone. 'The awful part is that she means so well. Now where did I put that blouse I was going to mend?'

She settled herself under the lamp and searched through her sewing box for the right shade of thread. 'You know, Max,' she remarked as she compared the spools, 'it's odd they chose purple. That's the most deceptive colour there is. Under artificial light, you often can't tell it from brown.'

'Good point, kid. Maybe they had the purple cans, and

figured they had to get the good out of them.'

'A while back you were telling Theonia they had them printed up specially because price is no object with drug smugglers.'

'So I'm willing to consider both sides of the question. Sarah, I have no idea why they picked purple, unless purple is a colour less used for tonic cans than other colours, which it may or may not be, or because purple is less conspicuous than orange, or because somebody just happens to like purple. What's important, as you've pointed out, is that choosing purple for their signal colour has in fact tended to limit the time span during which they can safely make their drops and pick-ups.'

'Maybe they started in June or July, and didn't realize what was going to happen when the evenings began getting shorter,' said Sarah. 'I don't suppose narcotics dealers are much in tune with nature. Oh dear, there's the doorbell. See who it is, would you, darling?'

Max went to the speaking tube. 'Who is it?'

'Your trusted lieutenant,' came the squawky reply.

'Advance and give the password.' Max pushed the release button for the vestibule door. 'It's Brooks, thirsting for adventure.'

'For goodness' sake, hasn't he had enough to last him for one day? Brooks, why aren't you home rubbing Theonia's feet?'

'She's soaking them in bubble bath.' Brooks was frisky as a chipmunk, notwithstanding the hours he'd put in. 'Max, I've been thinking.'

'Congratulations. About the colour purple looking brown under artificial light, right?'

'Ah, you've been thinking, too.'

'Actually Sarah was thinking. We take turns.'

'Then you've also thought of the ramifications?'

'Sarah's in charge of ramifications.'

'Including Chet Arthur's demise?'

'No, demises are my department. It would seem Chet Arthur must have been killed a good while before he was found, otherwise that splash of purple paint on his bag wouldn't have shown up much against the brown paper and whoever killed him wouldn't have known whom to mug. This of course is assuming he was killed for the heroin, but if he wasn't, his death and particularly the shifting of the body makes no sense.'

'I'm quite ready to go along with your assumptions. The autumnal equinox was just this past week, on September 21, so sunset the night he was killed was shortly before six o'clock standard time. Allowing an hour for daylight saving, that means he couldn't have been killed much later than seven, yet it was a quarter to eleven when Dolph got the call that the body had been found. I'd guess close to dusk, myself. It could have been a serious problem, hiding the body for any great length of time.'

'Unless he was killed in a deserted warehouse or a secret cellar,' Max suggested.

'Or a cavern measureless to man,' Sarah put in. She'd ducked into the bedroom and emerged in a warm caftan of a shade between rose and apricot that Theonia had picked up on one of her lingerie raids to Filene's Basement. 'Though I don't suppose there are many caverns around here, unless you count the underground garage at Boston Common. That would be a good place, actually. Whoever did it could stick him in a car, cover him up with something, and just leave him there till it was late enough to take him over to Marlborough Street and dump him.'

'What would Chet have been doing in the underground garage?' asked Brooks.

'Using the men's room?'

'How would the person who was supposed to collect the drugs know he was there?'

'They'd have either followed him or lured him in,' said Max. 'No doubt it's also occurred to you, Brooks, that these drop-and-scoop operations are well orchestrated. Considering how carefully the first part of the transfer was supervised this afternoon, I expect we'll find the rest of it is, too. To begin with, that guy in the purple suit must have known that woman in the purple sweater was on her way to the right spot.'

'More than that, he knew there would in fact be a woman in a purple sweater,' Brooks added.

'He knew there'd be somebody in a purple something, anyway. That means he was working with somebody who'd had the SCRC under close surveillance, who knew where that woman was likely to go and when she'd be likely to get there. They must have been in contact by telephone or walkie-talkie.'

'Or telepathy,' said Brooks. 'You do see, Max, that the dispatcher is most apt to be someone connected with the Center itself.'

'It wouldn't have to be someone who's always there, though, would it?' said Sarah. 'I don't suppose they keep dropping those cans all day.'

'Oh no,' said Max. 'Nothing like it. They couldn't pull this stunt too often without somebody getting wise. Besides, there's so much profit in heroin they wouldn't have to.'

'We can find out easily enough,' said Brooks, 'just by watching to see how many people leave the Center wearing purple.'

'Right,' said Max. 'You might disguise yourself as a hydrant, stand on the sidewalk, and count them as they go by.'

'Unsubtle, my boy. I suppose your idea is to go straight for the rat i' the arras.'

'Annie,' said Sarah, not happily.

'Ah yes,' said Brooks. 'The non-topless ex-waitress from the Broken Zipper with the sticky fingers.'

'That was only Theonia's impression,' Sarah reminded him, even as she herself was recalling how deftly Annie had swiped all the sugar yesterday at the restaurant. 'I shouldn't have mentioned her. The name simply popped into my head.'

'And for good reason, I expect,' her cousin replied. 'She's around the Center a good part of the time, isn't she? Hostessing, or whatever they call it? She must get to know the members pretty well, and no doubt she can tell purple when she sees it.'

'It's her favourite colour.'

'Well, don't say so in that voice of doom. Dash it, Sarah, if we start playing favourites, we'll never get anywhere. Max, do you know anything about that sink of iniquity she worked in?'

'Not really, but I have one of my secret agents casing the joint.'

'Stout fellow. When do you expect a report?'

'Any time now. He said he'd be along.'

'Whom are you talking about, or is that a secret, too?' Sarah asked him.

'He's one of your old boyfriends.'

'I can't remember having had any.'

'I remembered,' said Max. 'I never know when a stray piece of information may come in handy. Such as Annie's liking purple. How did that come out, Sarah?'

'Quite innocuously, or such was my naïve impression. We were talking about what colours to paint the rooms in the new housing facility.'

'Mary didn't take you over to look at the building, did she?'

'No, she didn't. I'm not even sure where it is. Do you know, Brooks?'

'Certainly.' Her elderly cousin whipped a street map of Boston from his picket and spread it out on her lap. 'You see? Right here.'

'But that's right near the harbour. Won't it be terribly chilly for those old people in the wintertime?'

'Name me a place that isn't. And think how pleasant it will be in the hot weather.'

'I can think of a few other things it might be,' said Max. 'Did I hear the doorbell?'

It came again, that merest hint of a tinkle. Max grinned, sidled over to the door, flattened himself against the wall, and eased it open with his foot. Sarah gaped, gasped, then began smiling, too. Brooks looked from one to the other in perplexity. Nor was his puzzlement lessened when a thin, dark wisp of a man in a filthy raincoat, dirty chino pants, and moccasins with no socks despite the raw late fall evening, slunk through the door, hugging the wall.

'Bill Jones!' Sarah came to him with her hand out. 'What a lovely surprise.'

'Yeah-h-h,' he breathed, then added in a confidential murmur, 'Hi, Sarah.'

'And this is my cousin, Brooks Kelling. Brooks, you remember Bill Jones, who was so helpful to us in the Wilkins*affair?'

'Indeed yes, sir, though I don't believe we two actually ever did get to meet. This is a great pleasure.'

Bill Jones allowed his tiny hand to be pumped. He didn't commit himself to the extent of saying it was a pleasure for him, too; but his dark eyes and his excellent teeth flashed a momentary signal to that effect before his not uncomely face settled back into its usual expression of wary watchfulness. Brooks, used to the ways of small creatures in the wild, adjusted to the newcomer without difficulty.

Thus put at his ease, Bill ventured an opinion that this was a nice place they had here. Sarah explained that it was only temporary and told him a little about the house they were building at Ireson's Landing. Bill said, 'Hey-y-y,' and then, the amenities taken care of, they got down to business.

'Who owns the Broken Zipper, Bill?' asked Max.

Bill shrugged, an exercise that involved his entire body, from his dirty bare feet to his curly black hair. 'Who owns all those places?'

'Another blind trust, I suppose.' Max sighed. 'And you have no idea who's behind this one?'

'Bunch of Greeks, I guess. It's called the Thanatopsis Realty Trust.'

'Thanatopsis?' Sarah wrinkled her nose. 'How odd. Max and I were talking about Thanatopsis just a while ago. It's a poem about how to die gracefully, you know. My great-aunt was always quoting it. Thanatos in Greek means death.'

'Yeah-h-h,' said Bill Jones.

'How long have they owned it?' Max wanted to know.

'Only since 1977.'

---

* *The Palace Guard.*

'And who owned it before that?'

Bill became extremely uncomfortable. He wet his lips and looked wistfully at the door as if he had an urgent rendezvous with destiny.

'Come on, Bill.'

'Well, it was somebody who owned a lot of property around the city. Came from one of the old families.'

'All right, Bill,' said Sarah. 'Which of the Kellings was it?'

'Name of Frederick.'

'Great-uncle Frederick? Goodness, I wonder if Dolph knows. At least he got rid of the place before Dolph inherited. How long did he have it, Bill?'

'Just a year.'

'And what was it when he bought it?'

'Same as it is now.'

'Oh. Well, don't look so stricken, Bill. I suppose Great-uncle Frederick meant to start up a redemption centre for barflies or some such thing, found they didn't want to be redeemed, and unloaded the building on to these Thanatopsis people because they reminded him of Great-aunt Letitia.'

'Or because Dolph made him sell,' said Brooks. 'Wasn't it in 1976 that he finally got up his courage to have Uncle Fred declared legally incompetent?'

'I think so,' said Sarah. 'It was after that business of the Boston Common pigeons, I know. But anyway, it's out of the family now so we don't have to worry about that angle. Bill, what can I get you to drink? Coffee, brandy, your usual gin and tonic?'

Bill confided in a barely audible murmur that he could use a gin and tonic. Max brought it, along with tots of brandy for himself and Brooks and a glass of her fizzy grape juice for Sarah.

'So what's doing at the Broken Zipper these days?' Max asked. 'Thanatopsis boys got everything under control?'

Bill shrugged, but only from the waist up. 'Like you'd expect.'

'Any snow on the ground over there?'

Bill took a kittenish lick at his drink. 'I don't go in much for winter sports, pal.'

That meant he knew but didn't want to rat. Max was well aware of the way Bill Jones's mind worked. So was Sarah. She wasn't up on drug-dealers' jargon, but she did know that snow was a name for heroin. Horse was another, though she couldn't imagine why.

'What about horse trading?' she asked, to everyone's surprise including her own. 'Bill, we're not just making conversation.'

'Most places like the Zipper, you get a little buying and selling,' he conceded.

That was a lot from Bill, but not enough for Sarah. 'Bill, we're talking about a great deal more than a little buying and selling. We mean substantial quantities being shifted around right in broad daylight on the streets of Boston. We're pretty sure we know how it's being done and we have reason to suspect there may be some kind of tie-in with the Broken Zipper.'

This was heavy stuff, and heavy stuff made Bill Jones squirm. Since he had nothing on but a thin shirt with his chinos, his squirms were not constricted and a student of modern dance might have found them inspirational to observe. Sarah, Max, and Brooks merely sat and waited till he quieted down and they could get on with the business of the meeting.

CHAPTER 13

'I could maybe—you know—drop in for a drink,' Bill ventured at last.

'Are you known there, Bill?' Max asked him.

The artist made gyrating motions with those incredibly wee hands. 'I've been.'

There were few places around town where Bill hadn't been. Max Bittersohn had found that out long ago. For an almost painfully honest man, which in all truth he was, Bill knew a remarkable lot about what lurked in the dark corners of Boston. He never got into trouble. Everybody knew Bill didn't carry tales. And everybody knew he was the kid brother of Pericles Jonubopoulos, another honest man, and one nobody cared to get on the wrong side of.

'Before we go further, you may wish to familiarize yourself with the appearances of some people we've run across in the course of our explorations,' said Brooks, fishing a small packet from his inside breast pocket. 'I managed to get these developed and printed during odd moments before and after dinner. Here's one you took of that fellow kicking the tonic can away from Theonia, Max.'

'Nice composition,' said Bill with professional interest. 'Theonia? I had an idea she was your wife, Brooks.'

'She is, I'm proud to say. Perhaps you hadn't realized what a talented actress she is. I must say I hadn't, myself. She disguised herself as a bag lady and spent all day yesterday tramping the streets, gathering evidence.'

'Hey-y-y! But where does the tonic can come in?'

'We have reason to believe such cans are the receptacles in which the drugs are distributed, presumably from the supplier to the pushers,' Max told him. 'We have no proof yet, but you'll notice it's a purple can of a brand even Brooks never heard of. The guy kicking it away is dressed in purple from head to foot. And less than a minute later, this same guy stood back and let the can be picked up by a woman wearing a purple sweater.'

'Okay, pal, but why do you say heroin?'

'Because we'd already found a few grains of it in a bag that had purple paint squirted on the side of it. Wait a second, I'll go get it.'

Max fetched the torn bag again. 'The guy who carried this was mugged and killed night before last. He was another SCRC collector—you know, they go around picking up waste and turning it in for salvage. Their bags are marked with the logo, as you see. This one had been ripped open and left beside the body. There were other cans lying around, but none like the one in the photo. I managed to see a photograph the police had taken at the scene.'

'You didn't tell me that,' said Sarah.

'I suppose it didn't seem important at the time. I spun them a yarn about trying to trace his family so the Center wouldn't have to pay for the funeral, but it didn't get me far. They just said forget it, guys like him don't have families interested in paying for their funerals. The photograph wouldn't have helped much, anyway, because he was lying face down.'

'But surely they took other pictures, dear.'

'That was the one they showed me, and I didn't want to make waves. They suggested I wait till the undertaker got him tidied up and take a shot then for identification purposes if I wanted one. That made sense, so I did.'

Max picked out the photograph of Chet Arthur. 'Ever seen him?'

Bill Jones shook his head. 'Not to remember. Who made the identification?'

'Sarah's cousin Dolph. He and his wife run the Center. This man was one of their best workers.'

Bill waited.

'We've managed to fill in a little of his background. His name was Chester Allen Arthur and he used to work over in South Boston, possibly in a boiler factory that went out of business a few years ago.'

'Grotters and Wales,' Bill replied promptly. 'Grotters died, but Wales is still around. Nice old man, looks like Winston Churchill. He plays golf with my brother's father-in-law.'

'Great. Is there any chance you might get your brother's father-in-law to ask Mr Wales if Chester Arthur ever worked for him, what position he held, and roughly how much he got paid? Arthur turned out to have a good deal more money stashed away in the bank than a man who made his beer money collecting other people's bottles might have been expected to, and we'd like to know where it all came from. It may have been on the up-and-up. He was a frugal type, and he hit the lottery for twenty grand a while back. I found the lunchroom where he bought the ticket, pretty much by accident.'

'Su-ure,' said Bill. 'I know your accidents, pal. Anything else you care to tell me? My brother's father-in-law will— you know—' he waved his hands and wriggled a bit— 'wonder.'

'There's the fact that Arthur was killed instead of just having his bag snatched, as happened to the woman who picked up the can today. There's also the fact that his body was found over in the Back Bay. People at the collection centre say he never went there because he was sure it was all going to cave in and he didn't want to get squashed when the Hancock Tower fell over. It appears to have been a genuine phobia with him.'

'So?

'So we think Arthur was killed somewhere else, probably earlier in the day, and hidden away somewhere until it was dark enough to take him over there and dump him. Don't ask me why he had to be moved. Your guess is as good as mine. One thing, though, whoever dumped him either didn't know he was phobic about the Back Bay or didn't think it mattered.'

'Or knew he was faking.'

Max shook his head. 'That's possible, of course, but the people who knew him seem convinced he wasn't. Anyway, if we could get a handle on Chet Arthur's background, we might be able to say for sure, one way or the other. We might also find out whether he was the type to let himself get tied up with a drug ring voluntarily. Right now, I'm going on the assumption that he'd found out he'd been used as a carrier without his knowledge and was murdered to keep him from raising hell about it.'

'What about that woman in the purple sweater this afternoon?' Bill asked.

'This one here?' Brooks tweaked another snapshot out of his collection. 'My wife took this back at the Center, where she returned after having had her collecting bag snatched. That happened not long after she'd picked up the can, as far as we can make out. She put on quite a turn about having been robbed, but didn't appear to be hurt, Theonia said. Not knowing the woman, Theonia couldn't tell whether her agitation was feigned.'

Bill shook his head. 'Phyllis wouldn't know how to feign.'

'You know the woman?'

'Su-ure. Phyllis used to keep a slush shop down in the old neighbourhood. You know, shaved ice in a paper cup with fruit syrup poured over it. Three cents. Phyllis couldn't count higher than three. You never asked for lemon or lime or whatever, you had to say yellow, orange, green or red. Phyllis didn't know flavours, only colours. Nobody ever figured out what flavour the red was supposed to be, but who cared? Phyllis is okay, believe me. Hey, this is a great picture of her. I'm glad she's got something to keep her busy.'

'What happened to the slush shop?' Sarah asked him.

Bill shrugged. 'Urban renewal.'

'Does she have a home? Where does she sleep?'

'Around, I guess. Phyllis has relatives, only she was always pretty independent.'

'Would you say she's the kind who'd go wandering here and there as the mood struck her, or would she map herself out a territory and stick to it, as some of the other SCRC people do?'

Bill inched himself closer to Sarah and gave her the full beam of his big dark eyes. 'Listen, in Phyllis's shop you didn't push up to the counter. You got in line and waited your turn. Before she'd ask you what you wanted, you had to hold up your hand with the three pennies in it. She'd have the four bottles of flavouring sitting in a row on the counter, always in the same order: yellow, orange, green, red. Whichever one you asked for, she'd begin with the yellow and say off the colours till she got to the one you wanted. Then she'd pick up a cup and scoop it full of ice. She'd set the cup on the counter, take the cap off the bottle, and pour out three glugs.'

Bill smiled. 'She'd say it like that, "Glug, glug, glug." We'd all say it with her. Then she'd put the cap back on the bottle, take your three pennies, count them into her box one by one, and give you your slush. Even if the next kid asked for the same colour you got, she'd go through the whole performance again without missing a glug. If you tried to get sassy and hurry her along, she'd come around from behind the counter, pick you up by the back of the neck and the seat of the pants, no matter how big you were, and throw you out in the middle of the street. My guess is, Phyllis has picked herself out a route. If anybody tries to make her change it, she decks 'em.'

'Then if you wanted a messenger who'd be likely to reach a given point at a certain time and proceed from there to her next point by an established route, your feeling is that one could hardly do better than trust to this compulsively one-track Phyllis,' said Brooks.

'You'd have to know what she was like.'

'Surely, Mr Jones. And you'd have to be fleet of foot enough to avoid getting decked. Would you happen to recognize any of these others?'

Brooks fanned out his bundle of photographs for Bill to inspect. 'These are SCRC members who happened to be in the Center when Theonia was there.'

'How did she ever manage to take them?' Sarah marvelled.

'With Brooks's Dick Tracy belt buckle camera.' Max was enjoying this.

With a modified version of it,' Brooks replied modestly. 'You may have noticed today that Theonia was wearing sunglasses with unusually wide and, I may say, unspeakably hideous sidepieces.'

'I wondered where she'd got them,' said Sarah.

'They once belonged to a former landlady of mine, who wore them when she insisted on my taking her boating on Jamaica Pond. Through a regrettable accident, the boat overturned. The incident led to an acrimonious parting.'

'Too bad,' said Max.

'Er—quite. Anyway, after I'd vacated her premises with strict orders never to return, I found the atrocious eyewear in a pocket of the jacket I'd been wearing at the time of the upset. Having been enjoined from any further contact with her and being, moreover, incensed by her having wantonly destroyed some slides of a water ouzel constructing its most ingenious habitation, which I'd managed to take by concealing myself up to the elbows in an oozy marge and having an indignity committed on my head by an American bittern who thought I was a rock, I felt not the slightest compunction at keeping the atrocious objects. I thought they might come in handy for something sometime.'

'So you built the camera into the glasses. Brooks, you're incredible.'

'Actually I only mounted it behind the right temple with the lens pointing out through an interstice in the decoration, if such it can be called. Theonia had only to turn her head slightly away from the person she wanted to photograph and activate the shutter by means of a plunger on the end of a slender black cord that ran down her coatsleeve. Should anyone have spotted the mechanism, which we deemed unlikely, she could have explained it away as a hearing aid. As far as she knows, it went unseen and we feel the results justified the slight risk. There are a few headless forms, as you see, but considering the restrictions under which she filmed, I think she did a commendable job.'

'They're fantastic,' said Max.

Bill Jones was staring through Max's reading glass at a minute but perfectly sharp photo of Ted Ashe with a dough-nut in his hand. 'This is a senior citizen?'

'He claims to be,' said Max. 'We've been wondering about him.'

'Yeah-h-h.'

'He calls himself Ted Ashe. Do you know him?'

'Not as Ted Ashe, pal. How'd he get so dirty?'

'My wife is of the opinion that he greases his face with salad oil every morning, then rubs it in a flowerpot,' Brooks offered. 'You agree, then, that his filthiness is not the result of gradual accumulation?'

'I saw him three nights ago at the Golden Garter. They were having some kind of benefit for the Hangnail Associa-tion. He was MC, wearing a pink dress suit and a purple cummerbund. The week before that, I bumped into him at a cocktail party given by the Wilton-Rugges. That's a rich real estate guy my brother knows. He looked sharp enough then. Country gentleman get-up. Suede jacket, Gucci loafers, LaCoste shirt, the whole bit.'

'The Wilton-Rugges?' said Sarah. 'Their daughter's the girl Eugene Porter-Smith is engaged to. Eugene was saying last night that Ashe claims to have been the bookkeeper in a meat packing plant, but he turned vegetarian and they threw him out.'

'Maybe he was,' Max answered. 'Obviously, the guy gets around.'

'He calls it collecting material,' said Bill Jones.

'For what?' said Max.

'You know that tabloid *Syndicated Slime*?'

'I've seen it around. You mean he writes for that rag?'

'As Wilbraham Winchell and about six other guys. He was calling himself Hetherton Montague at the party. I don't know his real name, but I'll bet it's not Ted Ashe. He was telling Mrs Wilton-Rugge he's been doing a series of exposés of corruption inside allegedly honest charitable organizations.'

'What if he can't find any?'

Bill shrugged. 'That guy would find some.'

'You don't mean he'd create a scandal just to get copy?' cried Sarah.

Bill shrugged again, one of his more wholehearted efforts.

Brooks Kelling sniffed. 'Smear and smirch. No wonder Ashe chose to make himself filthy. It's all based on self-hatred, you know. "I'm so rotten that everybody must despise me, so I'll make you despicable, too, especially if you're one of those goody-goodies who actually try to make things better for others." I can see where Dolph and Mary would be tempting targets for someone who sees life as a can of worms and thinks he can elevate himself by becoming a snake in the grass.'

'Yes, but attacking them would be like using a cannon to shoot a partridge,' Sarah objected. 'The SCRC is only a small local charity, and *Syndicated Slime* is a nationally distributed publication. If Ted Ashe is doing some kind of sting operation with boys in purple kicking cans full of heroin around, it seems to me he's taking a terrible risk for a story that I shouldn't think many people outside Boston would find particularly interesting. Unless he's planning to hang it on Eugene Porter-Smith and blackmail Cousin Percy.'

'Who's Cousin Percy?' Bill Jones asked her.

'He owns an accounting firm in which Eugene's just been made a junior partner. They do handle some awfully big accounts, so Ted Ashe might suppose they wouldn't care for that kind of publicity.'

'Would Cousin Percy pay?'

'Heavens, no. Would you say so, Brooks?'

'A Kelling part with good money to a smut-scribbling rotter? Don't make me laugh. Percy would ring for some clerk to toss Ashe out on his ear, then tell his secretary not to let in any more blackmailers because he's a busy man and can't be bothered listening to fairytales.'

'But Winchell wouldn't know that,' said Bill.

'Then Winchell or Ashe or whoever it is will get a rude awakening, assuming the blackmail hypothesis is a tenable one.'

'Could we lay off the hypotheses for a while?' said Max. 'What we need is to get hold of one of those purple cans and find out what's really in it. If this bird—I think I'll stick to Ashe—is pulling a fake drug-running operation just to get himself a story, he may be filling the cans with baking soda or some damn thing.'

'That wasn't baking soda you found in Chet Arthur's bag,' Sarah reminded him.

'I grant you that, but we have no proof that Chet was carrying a purple can, or that the heroin came out of it if he was. All through looking at those pictures, Bill? Nothing more you can tell us?'

'This guy.' Bill picked up the photo of the neat elderly man whom Sarah had first noticed reading the church magazine.

'Harry Burr,' she said. 'He's some kind of lay preacher, I believe.'

'That's right,' said Max. 'He conducted the service for Chet Arthur.'

'Last time I saw him,' said Bill, 'he was tending bar at the Broken Zipper.'

Sarah's first thought was, 'Oh, poor Mary!' But she didn't say it. 'He could just have been filling in for the regular bartender. Annie Bickens might have recommended him. She still goes over there sometimes to see her old pals.'

'Yeah,' said Bill. 'Well, I'd better be moving.'

He gave Sarah a particularly wistful smile, nodded to the men, and slunk down the stairs into the night.

CHAPTER 14

'What's on your agenda for today, dear?'

Sarah was up, dressed, and ready to go. Max groped for his coffee and turned on Morning Pro Musica, listened until their favourite radio impresario announced that since this was the anniversary of Carl Phillip Emanuel Bach's sister-in-law's cousin Ludmilla's birthday, he was going to play the Sinfonia Concertante in D by Carl Stamitz, who'd no doubt have taken to Ludmilla right away if they'd ever happened to meet. He then addressed his wife's question.

'Today? First I have to call Pepe. Then I thought we might go to look at some real estate.'

'We already have real estate,' Sarah replied, much surprised. 'Do you mean you want us to drive out and see what's happening at Ireson's Landing?'

'I know what's happening. My father's about to have another quiet chat with the architect.'

The elder Mr Bittersohn had his son's house well in hand. As a builder of the old school, he did not always see eye to eye with designers of new houses. Their discussions were never acrimonious, for Isaac Bittersohn was a man of peace. However, they always wound up with the architect humbler and wiser and Isaac going quietly off to straighten out another of those whom he always referred to as his helpers even when they weren't being helpful.

'The real estate I had in mind,' Max explained, 'is that warehouse of Dolph's.'

'Oh good,' said Sarah. 'I'm curious to see it, myself. Can we get in?'

'Probably not. I'll be with you as soon as I run a quick check to see how Pepe's making out.'

Knowing Max's couple of quick checks, Sarah had got the apartment presentable and done a few preliminary things about dinner by the time he announced himself ready to roll. Then they were held up by a visit from Brooks.

'I just spoke with Mary. She says she's been trying all morning to reach you, and the line's been busy. She wonders if either or both of you could possibly go out to Chestnut Hill and help her and Dolph decide what they should put in the auction. They've both taken the day off from the Center to work on it, but Dolph's all confused, time's running out, and Mary sounds as if she's beginning to panic.'

'I don't blame her,' said Sarah. 'I'll go. Can you, Max?'

'Sure. We'll swing by the warehouse on our way over. Care to join the party, Brooks?'

'I should like to very much, but duty in the guise of my beloved wife is whispering low, "Thou must." Charles has an audition today that bodes no good for our domestic economy, Mariposa woke up with a toothache and is off to the dentist, and of course Theonia and I were out of the house all day yesterday, so there's no way we can escape today. She's making the beds and I have the fun of cleaning the bathrooms.'

Now was as good a time as any to bring out the plan she'd been mulling over. 'Brooks,' said Sarah, 'how sick are you and Theonia of running that boarding-house?'

'Do you want an honest answer?'

'Yes, but not necessarily this minute. Let me tell you why. You know Max and I will be giving up this apartment and moving out to Ireson's as soon as the house is ready, but I'm sure we'll find we need a place to stay in Boston sometimes. Since you're getting all that money from Uncle

Lucifer, I was wondering how you'd feel about staying on in the house. I thought perhaps we might turn the place back into a sort of family commune and split the expenses. You and Theonia could always come out to Ireson's and stay in the carriage house when you want a change of scenery. See what Theonia thinks of the idea, and we can discuss the particulars when we have time. Oh, and please let Mary know we'll be there in a while.'

'I didn't know you were thinking of shutting down the boarding-house,' Max remarked as they were walking down to the garage.

'The idea only popped into my head a day or so ago, and since then we've had too much else to think about. But the place has served its purpose, and Brooks and Theonia are getting a bit past it, I think. It seems silly to get rid of the house, when we own it free and clear.'

'You own it.'

'Darling, you don't have negative feelings, do you? I used to, but I don't any more. It's been—depersonalized, I suppose, with so many strangers coming and going.'

'And you do want a town house?'

'I'd like something. There are going to be crises, you know, with all these elderly relatives, and it will be easier to cope from here. And you need a place to stay overnight in Boston, darling. You can't be hopping off a plane from Nairobi in the middle of the night and driving all the way up the North Shore.'

'How often do I hop off a plane from Nairobi?'

'Well, Antwerp or Seattle or wherever. If we didn't have the house, we'd have to rent another apartment or put you up at hotels, either of which would probably average out to more than the upkeep of the house, especially if Brooks is willing to pay something towards it. Besides, our children may want the house some day.'

'Yes, dear.' Max tucked Sarah into the car rather more carefully than if she were a particularly rare piece of early Chinese porcelain, and they were off.

The distance to Dolph's warehouse was not great, but the number of one-way streets and panicked wrong-way drivers from out of state made getting there quite an adventure. Perseverance and dauntless courage brought them to their goal, where they were of course unable to find a parking space and had to content themselves with driving slowly past the building.

The warehouse wasn't much to see, merely a four-storey oblong of red brick with dirty windows and a blacktopped parking lot that must have been sadly inadequate for the needs of the former workers. The two interesting points about the place were that it faced on the harbour and that it was flanked by two other former warehouses that had, by ingenious architectural alterations, been turned into handsome and no doubt expensive condominiums for the upwardly mobile.

'This is fascinating,' said Sarah. 'Aren't you amazed at what they've done, Max? Dolph and Mary won't go in for all those fancy ins and outs, naturally, but at least they can rip out that horrid asphalt and make a pleasant little garden for the lodgers to sit in and look at the harbour, since none of them will have cars. It's not too far from shopping and the subway, and having those condominiums for neighbours will be an advantage, shouldn't you think? Security must be fairly tight, and the senior citizens won't always be getting mugged.'

'Not so many muggings, maybe, but plenty of cold-shoulderings,' said Max. 'Can you picture how the yuppies who've gone in hock for a few hundred thousand to buy these places are going to feel about a procession of Joans and Annies traipsing in and out with their paper bags?'

'Why should they mind? What makes a city interesting is having so many different types of people all mixed in together.'

'Yes, dear.'

For a while Max had to concentrate on getting them away from the waterfront and headed towards Brookline, so the few remarks he made were in reference to other drivers and sometimes discourteous. When they were in the clear, he reverted to the subject that was absorbing them both.

'It's also interesting that Bill Jones ran into Ted Ashe, whose real name may or may not be Wilbraham Winchell, at the rich real estatenik's.'

'Whose name is Wilton-Rugge, which is the name of Eugene Porter-Smith's fiancée whose father is in real estate,' Sarah added. 'Now that we've seen where Dolph's warehouse is, I suppose we ought to be asking ourselves why Eugene took his sudden urge to help at the Center. He's never before shown an iota of interest in any kind of social work that I know of, unless you count tossing quarters to street musicians in front of coffee-houses.'

'I'm wondering if by any chance Wilton-Rugge's the developer in any of those condos,' said Max.

'It shouldn't be hard to find out, should it?'

'Not unless he's hiding behind another blind trust like the Thanatopsis gang. I suppose we could ply the daughter with champagne when she shows up for the auction, and see if we can get any information out of her.'

That got them started on the auction itself, then they got to Dolph's and there was nothing else they could talk about. Dolph and Mary led them through more rooms than Sarah had realized the house possessed. Most of them hadn't been in use for decades. All were crammed with enough stuff to keep the Morgan Memorial going for months.

They found Victoriana, plenty of Art Nouveau and Art Deco, and a vast lot of items that could charitably be called collectibles. Max set aside the best of these for one of the big auction houses. The next best, the not so great, and the mildly amusing were carried down to the ballroom.

Harry Burr had come out on the subway to help the two yard men, Walter and George, with the fetching and carrying. Dressed in clean though shabby overalls and flannel shirt with a nylon windbreaker, he didn't look like either a preacher or a bartender, just an elderly man who'd probably had a fairly tough life and was glad now to have something useful to do.

Before long, they were all at it, even Henrietta the maid and Genevieve the cook. Sarah was delegated to stay down in the vast ballroom that occupied one whole wing of the house, ordering the distribution of the merchandise so they wouldn't have a pigpile to untangle later. Another of her jobs was sorting the more deplorable objects into lots of a few pieces, with one fairly desirable thing stuck in for bait.

She had the inspiration of using SCRC tote bags to pack these lots in, persuading Dolph that they'd be good advertising for the fund drive and congratulating herself that she was getting rid of the dangerous carryalls in a worthy cause. It wasn't likely the sort of people who were coming to the auction would go trailing the bags around Boston afterwards, and even less likely they'd be picking up Graperoola cans. Besides, there weren't anywhere near enough empty boxes in the house, and she was not about to go panhandling around the shops for odd cartons to put the lots in.

By the time they'd knocked off for lunch; Max and Sarah in the breakfast-room with Dolph and Mary, and Harry Burr in the kitchen with Walter, George, Henrietta and Genevieve by his own choice; they already had the makings of a pretty good auction. At tea-time they'd just about filled one end of the ballroom and still had a couple of rooms to sort through.

'What amazes me is that the house looks just as furnished now as it did when we started,' said Mary, 'only better because you're not falling over a beaded footstool every step you take.'

'Don't knock those beaded footstools,' said Max. 'You ought to do fairly well with them. Victorian beadwork's popular these days.'

'Not with me,' growled Dolph, peering into his glass to see if there might be some other saleable article lurking behind the ice cubes, for tea in the Kelling family did not necessarily always mean tea. 'I've loathed the confounded things ever since I can remember. How many did we bring down, for God's sake?'

'Eight beaded so far,' said Sarah, who'd been trying to keep an inventory list of the more describable objects. 'We also have the needlepoint footstools, the turkey work footstools, the tooled leather footstools, the tapestry footstools, the brocaded footstools with the fringe around them, not to mention the stuffed hassocks, of which—'

'Blast it, Sarah, we've already broken our backs lugging the things, we don't have to wear out our eardrums hearing about them. I must say I was surprised, though, to discover that secret compartment in the hassock we took from Uncle Fred's dressing-room.'

'With all those naughty French magazines hidden in it. He really was a sanctimonious old goat, you know, Dolph.' Sarah glanced behind her half fearfully, as if her impiety might bring a spectral voice thundering out of the woodwork, 'Little Sarah Kelling, go stand in the corner!'

All she heard, though, was Mary saying, 'You'll stay to dinner, of course.'

'Oh, we couldn't,' Sarah protested. 'Genevieve must be exhausted.'

'She says she's fine. The staff are always complaining that we don't keep things humming the way Dolph's aunt and uncle used to. It is quiet for them, with us in at the Center so much, I'm sure. Anyway, Genevieve's got a ham and a crock of beans in the oven, and she's baked a couple of her scrumptious deep-dish apple pies, so for goodness' sake stay and eat some of it so her feelings won't be hurt. I don't want my cook mad at me with all that slew of people descending on us Saturday night.'

'Have you any idea how many so far?'

Sarah had put RSVP on her invitations, with little hope that anybody would bother. However, people were calling. They'd got twenty-one acceptances at the Center. Osmond Loveday reported thirty-six irate calls from people demanding to know why the auction had been scheduled at such short notice and insisting it be put off to suit their convenience.

Here at the house, Henrietta had taken down forty-three acceptances, seventeen regrets, and only one complaint. That was from the old crank down the road who wanted the Kellings to know what would happen to any car caught blocking his driveway. Henrietta had assured him there'd be guards posted to supervise the parking. He'd threatened dire consequences to any guard caught trespassing on his property and slammed down the phone. They had every confidence he'd be calling again as soon as he thought of something else to fuss about.

They wouldn't worry about the crank. Sarah was gratified by the figures. Henrietta's responses had been mostly from people in the area, who'd naturally be quickest and most punctilious about answering. They'd come and bring their neighbours, like as not. So far, the crowd was shaping up just about the way she'd hoped.

The ballroom could easily handle two hundred chairs, more in a pinch. Some buyers would leave early, some would come late. They needn't worry about fire hazards with French doors on three sides and plenty of windows. The big triple doors at the end that connected to the main house could be opened and the crowd allowed to spill over into the huge drawing-room and the dining-room beyond, where the champagne would be set out and the actors moving among the patrons with their trays of refreshment. It was a safe bet a good many, notably the husbands, would be more interested in the champagne and the young actresses in their flapper frocks than in the bidding.

Except for the foyer and the downstairs lavatories, the rest of the rooms would be shut off. The house had been laid out for just such grand-scale affairs as this, though none had been held for a long time. It was ironic that Dolph and Mary had finally got around to using the place as it was meant to be used, not for a grand ball or a formal reception but to clear out some of its overflow in preparation for a time when it might never be used again.

They must, Sarah thought, give at least one really dazzling waltz evening here for the benefit of the fund drive. How Theonia would love that! She'd looked positively queenly here the other night, sitting in the dining-room with the candles and flowers on the table in front of her and all Great-aunt Matilda's polished silver gleaming on the sideboard behind her.

Later, back in the library on Tulip Street, Theonia had seemed a different kind of queen. She should have had violins wailing and horses stamping, and a different kind of firelight casting wild gleams and shadows on her crimson gown as she hurled a perfectly good piece of antique Canton ware into the flames and sailed off into the darkness without a word of explanation.

Theonia wasn't crazy, or anything like it. She'd had a mad life, but she'd handled it sanely enough. How many orphans, on their own at thirteen without a cent of money or a whole pair of shoes, in a world whose ways they'd never had a chance to learn, would have managed as well as she? She'd kept herself as respectable as circumstances allowed, educated herself, acquired the social graces and the appearance of the lady she longed to be and in fact always had been, though nobody had ever told her so.

However you looked at her, Theonia was an admirable person and the last in the world to smash a family heirloom on a whim. Then why had she broken that cup?

There were things one didn't ask. If Theonia wanted to, she'd explain sooner or later. Sarah shook her head and went back to bagging up knick-knacks.

Genevieve's dinner was good, but by the time it was over they were all too tired to sit chatting. 'Come on, Sarah,' said Max, 'let's get the kid to bed. Where's Harry Burr, Dolph? I'll be glad to give him a ride back to Boston.'

'I'll go find him,' said Mary, but she came back alone. Harry had eaten his early supper with George and Walter in the kitchen, then said he had to get back because he'd promised to be somewhere. George had run him down to Chestnut Hill Station.

Sarah wondered if Harry was bartending again tonight at the Broken Zipper. Tuesday he'd preached at Chet Arthur's funeral. People really did lead awfully strange lives.

CHAPTER 15

One of the finds Max had set aside for the big auctioneers was a small, quiet landscape Dolph had picked off a wall in one of the never-used bedrooms. Neither Uncle Fred nor Aunt Matilda had ever liked it much, he said. Frederick Kelling's taste had run to battle scenes and enlarged photographs of himself having his hand shaken by persons of note. His wife had preferred huge, dark oil paintings of large, ferocious animals devouring each other.

Max, on the other hand, had liked the landscape well enough to take it home for a better look. While Sarah was getting ready for bed, he gave the surface a gentle preliminary cleaning and went over it inch by inch with a jeweller's loupe. The next morning, even before he started telephoning Marseilles, he showed Sarah what he'd found.

'George Innes? Max, how lovely. Is it authentic, do you think?'

'As far as I can tell, but I'm not an authority on the American school. If you have nothing better to do this morning, I thought you might like to take it over to the Museum and see what they have to say.'

'I'd adore to, but wouldn't you rather go yourself?'

'Somebody's got to mind the store.'

'What's that supposed to mean? That you have bigger fish to fry, I suppose. What are you going to do?'

'Right now I'm going to make some phone calls.'

'As when were you ever not? All right, dear, I'll go. What if they want to keep the painting?'

'If it's for study, get a receipt. If it's for their collection, request a cheque. And look, Sarah, don't go down in the subway. Don't go anywhere by yourself. Take a cab from the house, Wrap the painting in a towel or something and put it in a bag.'

'I know, and guard it with my life.'

'The hell with that.' Max put down the little black notebook in which he kept his jottings long enough to give her a hug, a gentle one in respect for her condition. 'But it could mean a nice chunk of cash for the building fund if Dolph lets us sell the painting for him.'

'I'm sure he will. Dolph doesn't care a rap for art, and Mary's much more interested in doing things for other people than feathering her own nest. I'll put the painting in

120

that tote bag Aunt Appie embroidered for me. It's hideous enough to put anybody off the track.'

'Good thinking. Okay, I'll make an appointment for you.'

Max went to the telephone and Sarah to her closet, wondering what one wore to have an Innes authenticated. When she went into the shower, Max called Brooks.

'Hi, Zorro. Boston Blackie here. Would you care to join me in a brief excursion? Provided the little woman doesn't want you to pick daisies for the table or anything?'

'Daisies are out of season and the household is back to full strength,' his favourite accomplice replied crisply. 'What did you have in mind?'

'I thought we might kidnap somebody.'

'Splendid suggestion. I might point out that your former bedroom is at present unoccupied and that Charles's new role is that of a prison guard.'

'Right on! Yours will be that of a respectable middle-aged member of the Kelling family.'

'Piece of cake. When do you want me?'

'As soon as you see a cab pull away from here with Sarah in it. She has a ten-thirty appointment at the art museum, so I'm calling the taxi for ten, on the flimsy pretext of heavy traffic.'

'I'll be ready.'

Max broke the connection and was talking French to Pepe Ginsberg in a nonchalant and guileless manner when Sarah came out, wearing her green jumper with a cream-coloured silk shirt and Granny Kay's bluebird pin. She had a pretty shrewd idea she was being got rid of and a sound hunch as to why, but there wasn't much she could do about it.

Besides, one didn't get to authenticate an Innes every day. According to Aunt Appie's daughter-in-law Vare, the experience should provide subliminal æsthetic enrichment to her unborn. Vare had dutifully carted her own embryos, one after the other, to places of culture and edification. Jesse, Woodson, James, and Frank were already efficient saboteurs and masters of criminal cunning, but they showed few signs of being attuned to the higher vibrations. Perhaps

Vare had looked at too many Goya prints. Surely the gentle Innes wouldn't hurt a baby.

Sarah had been coming to the Museum of Fine Arts ever since she could remember. Her girlhood dream had been to study painting here. That hadn't worked out, but she had been allowed a private drawing teacher from the time she was ten until she was fifteen. Miss Pefton had been herself a Museum School graduate long ago, and had often brought her here for gallery talks. Sarah tended sometimes to think of the place in terms not of its magnificent collections but of its long galleries, and herself traipsing through them at the heels of a brisk docent, carrying not only her own folding stool but also Miss Pefton's, as her teacher had been well advanced in years. She'd died not long after Sarah married Alexander. Sarah had gone to the funeral by herself because Alexander had been doing something with his mother. It was just as well. She'd cried, and Alexander would have been embarrassed.

Keeping tight hold of her hideous tote bag, she paid off her taxi, explained herself to the receptionist, and was directed to the proper curator's office. Now that she was Mrs Max Bittersohn, she was welcomed there on quite a different basis than when she'd been a Kelling. Sarah found quite a little reception committee on hand to greet her and her tote bag. She was treated to coffee and delightful little pastries. She was given a lengthy technical description of Innes's painting methods, about which she already knew a fair amount thanks to Miss Pefton and her gallery walks. She even got to see the X-rays.

The consensus after much scrutiny was that she did indeed have a perfectly splendid little Innes there, and what did she propose to do with it? She replied that she was only the errand girl and got invited to lunch. While she was eating Brie and French bread and a crunchy Macoun apple, Max and Brooks were kidnapping Annie Bickens.

It wasn't hard, actually. Max had already learned from Mary that Annie wasn't scheduled to help at the Center today. That meant she'd be out collecting salvage, and where she collected mostly was up on Washington Street

122

near the big five-and-ten, because she could usually pan-handle the price of a milkshake at the lunch bar. SCRC members weren't supposed to beg, but Annie had a way of doing it without appearing to. According to Joan, people simply walked up and gave her money. Annie couldn't bear to hurt their feelings by turning down donations, not when she had a milkshake habit to support.

Milkshakes did seem an odd passion for somebody who'd spent most of her life serving cocktails and highballs, but milkshakes were what Annie craved, and milkshakes the conspirators were determined she should have.

Max wasn't wearing a hat, but Brooks had on his grey-green felt with the ruddy turnstone feather in the band. As they approached their quarry, he raised it politely.

'Mrs Bickens? We were hoping to find you here. I'm Dolph Kelling's cousin Brooks and this is my cousin Sarah's husband, Max Bittersohn.'

'We've met,' said Max at his most cosmopolitan. 'At the SCRC on Tuesday morning. I owe you a cup of coffee, come to think of it. Perhaps you'd care to stop in here and have something with us. They make a great milkshake.'

Annie gave him the smile she'd probably saved for big tippers back at the Broken Zipper. 'Yeah, I know.' She was the first one to the lunch counter.

The place wasn't crowded just then, they were able to get three stools together down at the far end, where they could talk in a certain amount of privacy. Annie ordered her milkshake and a huge pastry with green frosting on it. Brooks took root beer and a doughnut, neither of which ever appeared at the boarding-house table. Max said in a somewhat God-help-us voice that he'd just have coffee.

They chatted of this and that. Max and Brooks displayed a lively interest in the daily doings of the Center, with special reference to its members' comings and goings. Max touched on the auction and the work they'd been doing to get ready for it. Harry Burr was being a great help, he told her. The Broken Zipper wasn't mentioned, though, until Max had paid the check and Annie had swiped a few packets of sugar from force of habit.

It was Annie herself who got down to business. 'Okay, boys, what's this all about?'

'That's a most pertinent question and we'll be happy to answer it,' Brooks replied, 'but not here, please. Mrs Kelling is expecting us.'

'Jeez,' Annie whined, 'I just came from the Center a little while ago. Do we have to walk all the way back there again?'

'No, we don't.'

Even though they weren't all that far from Tulip Street as the crow flew, although in fact crows were seldom seen around Tulip Street, Max had decided it would be an excellent idea to get Annie into a small, enclosed space as quickly as possible.

'We'll take a cab,' he assured her. 'We can grab one up by the Parker House.'

They did, but when Max gave the address, Annie yelped. 'Hey, what's the idea? You said Mrs Kelling wanted me.'

'I'm sorry,' Brooks apologized. 'Perhaps I didn't make it clear that I was talking about my wife, Mrs Theonia Kelling. You know, the one who made all those brownies for the funeral. Oh look, they're taking away the swanboats.'

Brooks knew a great deal about the swanboats, those pedal-powered pleasure craft from which generations of Boston children, including Sarah and Brooks and even Dolph Kelling had tossed popcorn to the mallards that came quacking in convoy. He told it all, giving Annie no chance to put a word in edgewise until they'd got her out of the cab and into the house.

Theonia was in truth waiting to greet Annie Bickens. She'd taken no risk of being identified as the crone in the black coat who'd shown up at the Center yesterday. Although it was still morning and she had by no means completed her domestic duties, she'd put on an elegant burgundy wool dress with one of the opulent lace collars she favoured. Her sleek leather pumps and stockings were burgundy, too. There were pearls in her ears and a diamond brooch in the shape of a miniature Samurai sword, part of Uncle Lucifer's legacy, pinned to her lace.

Annie was overawed by so much elegance, but Theonia

gave her no time to freeze up. 'Mrs Bickens, how kind of you to come. Brooks darling, do take Mrs Bickens's bag and jacket. Did these beastly men offer you any refreshment, or did they whisk you directly here?'

'I had a milkshake,' Annie managed to blurt.

'We stopped for a bite uptown,' Brooks amplified. 'What time were you planning lunch?'

'Half past twelve, if that's convenient.'

'But I didn't mean to stay,' Annie protested. 'He said you wanted to talk to me.'

'And so I do, Mrs Bickens. We all do, about something desperately important in which we do so hope you can help us. Why don't we all go into the library, where we can be comfortable?'

'Or downstairs,' Max suggested, 'where we can be private.'

Theonia inclined her majestic head. 'Certainly, if you prefer. Let me take your arm, Mrs Bickens. The stairs can be a trifle confusing if you're not used to them. Would you mind coming out through the back?'

Annie was clearly beginning to mind quite a lot, but there didn't seem to be much she could do about it with a woman twice her size at her elbow, the agile Brooks leading the way, and the gallant but formidable Max Bittersohn right behind. Theonia kept that light but firm grip on her arm all the way down, although the stairway was well lighted and there was a sturdy golden oak banister to hang on to.

She might have felt like a prisoner being shown to her cell, but the room into which they led her was surprisingly attractive with a scrubbed brick floor, white-painted walls, simple furniture in bright colours, and plants growing on the high windowsills. Max smiled.

'This used to be my room, Mrs Bickens.'

'Huh? You live here, too?'

'I did, until I married my landlady. Sarah and I moved next door, and Brooks and Theonia took over here. This is a pretty complicated family. Like the SCRC. I don't know whether you're aware of the fact, but things are getting complicated there, too. That's why we need to talk to you.'

'I didn't do nothing!'

'Nobody's accusing you, we just hope you can help us find out who did.'

'Did what?'

'Murdered Chet Arthur, among other things.'

'That was muggers.'

'You don't think mugging counts?'

'Well, it's not like as if they knew who he was. When you say murder, it sounds more personal, like.'

'We think they did know who he was. Here, Mrs Bickens, you'd better sit down.'

CHAPTER 16

Max steered Annie to a blue-slipcovered armchair that had been brought in from the old Ireson's Landing house for his own use, and drew a red-painted wooden chair up close to it. Brooks and Theonia sat on the bed, which had been perked up with red cushions to look like a studio couch. Annie wet her lips, moving her eyes from one to the other.

'Is it about the will? All I done was sign where Chet told me, honest. Joan signed it, too!'

'Relax, Annie,' said Max. 'You don't mind if I call you Annie? No, it's not about the will. Except that you weren't quite accurate when you said you didn't read it, were you?'

'So what if I wasn't? A person's got a right to know what she's signing, hasn't she? What do you think I am, some kind of a jerk?'

'Not at all. I only wondered what you thought of it.'

'I thought it was weird, if you want to know. I mean, here's this guy out on the streets picking up beer cans for a living, and he's making this will like he's some kind of a millionaire.'

'So you and Joan had a big laugh over it, right?'

'Nah, I didn't tell her. See, Chet said we weren't supposed to read it, just sign. Joan wouldn't have thought it was right. She's always at me about you shouldn't do this and you shouldn't do that. I mean, don't get me wrong. Joanie's my best friend, but she can be kind of a pain sometimes. I just didn't want her getting on my case about something that didn't mean anything, see.'

'But you did tell somebody?'

Annie shrugged, a feeble effort compared to Bill Jones's. 'Well, what the hell? I mean, it was pretty funny, right?'

Max wasn't laughing. 'Whom did you tell, Annie?'

'Nobody special. Just Bulgy.'

'Bulgy who?'

'Like I said, just Bulgy. If he's got another name, I never heard it.'

Theonia cut in. 'I believe what Cousin Max means is, in what connection do you know this Bulgy? Is he a particular friend of yours?'

'I don't know, I guess so. See, I knew him from the Zipper. He was there when I first started. He was just always around, you know what I mean.'

'Where is Bulgy now?'

'Oh, he's still there, him and Dan. They're the only two left that I worked with. Dan's one of the day bartenders. He used to be on nights but he couldn't take it no more so he switched. I don't know the guy who took Dan's place nights. Jeff, his name is.'

'What about Harry Burr?' asked Max.

'Harry tell you he's working at the Zipper?' Annie sounded surprised.

'Did you get him the job?' Max countered.

'Sort of, I guess. See, I'm in there one day an' Dan's bitching because the night guy that's supposed to help Jeff called in sick. So that meant Dan was going to have to work the night shift, too, 'cause they didn't know anybody else they could get at short notice, see. So what the hey, Dan's a friend of mine, so I told him about Harry.'

'Harry used to be a bartender?'

'No, Harry was a minister, only he believes in what he calls hands-on religion. Like when he wanted to preach about the evils of drink, he figured he ought to get some first-hand experience first. He didn't want to start boozing it up himself because he figured the church wouldn't stand for it and neither would his stomach, so he got a part-time job tending bar.'

'Harry told you this himself?'

'Sure, Harry's a friendly guy, only he's always sneaking in little bits of sermons at you. That's why he keeps tending bar, he says it's not much different from being a minister in a way. Everybody's crying on his shoulder and wanting free advice about their problems that you know they're not going to take. But anyway, like I said, I told Dan about Harry and then I went back to the Center and told Harry about Dan and that's how it happened. Harry doesn't like the Zipper much, but they only ask him when they're short-handed and nobody else ever asks him at all, so he goes. The money's not so bad.'

'Does Harry know Bulgy, too?'

'I guess. Bulgy's sort of what you might call the handy-man. Like when they take in a shipment of liquor, Bulgy has to help the men move it down cellar and put it away. Then when the bartender needs anything from down cellar, he yells down the tube for Bulgy to bring it up and take away the empties and like that. I don't know if Harry ever gets to talk to Bulgy because it's always busy at night, and anyway I never go down there after dark any more.'

'When did you tell Bulgy about Chet Arthur's will?'

'Right after we signed it. See, Joanie was on hostess duty that afternoon and I figured what the hey, so I took myself a walk down to the Zipper. Dan wasn't around and the new guys don't like me much, so I went down cellar and hung out with Bulgy for a while. I told him about the will because I thought it was funny.'

'Did Bulgy think it was funny, too?' Max asked her.

'Who knows? Bulgy's none too bright. Anyway, he laughed.'

'Would he have repeated the story, do you think?'

'I guess so,' Annie admitted, 'if he could find anybody to listen. Bulgy'll talk your arm off if you give him half a chance.'

'Does he talk with the customers?

'Not unless there's a fight and somebody yells for Bulgy to come and break it up. Bulgy's pretty strong, see, from lugging all them crates of liquor around. Or like if a customer has a little accident, you know what I mean, and they get Bulgy to mop the floor.' Annie gave Theonia an embarrassed glance. 'Anyway, that's what he does. He doesn't get to mix much.'

'Does he have friends away from his job?' Brooks asked her. 'Anybody he chums around with on his time off?'

Annie looked as if she didn't understand the question, then she shook her head. 'Bulgy doesn't get time off. He's always there. He sleeps in the cellar and eats in the kitchen and takes a bath in the scrub bucket maybe once in a while when the girls get on his case. He doesn't mind, it's what he knows. Like I said, Bulgy's not too bright.'

'I'm sure there are many people worse off than he,' said Brooks, sounding far from convinced. 'Then you—er—still have the run of the place, Mrs Bickens?'

'I don't go into the men's room.' Annie giggled, then gave Theonia another nervous glance.

'I expect what we're interested in would be down in the basement. Take a look at this photograph, please, Mrs Bickens.'

'Hey, that's the woman who was in the Center yesterday.'

'Er—no doubt. What I'd like you to focus on is not the woman but the can she's reaching for. Here, this magnifying-glass will help you.'

'I seen that kid around before. He always wears purple is how I noticed. Purple's my favourite colour.'

'I must show you a picture of the purple gallinule, then. And the purple grackle, I always feel, is a bird that receives less than his just meed of admiration because of the low company he often keeps.'

'In the spring, a livelier iris gleams upon the burnished dove,' Theonia offered.

'The can, Annie,' said Max rather grimly.

'So okay, the can. What about it?'

'You see plenty of cans when you're collecting, right? Have you ever seen another one exactly like that can in the picture. Are you able to read the letters on it?'

'I don't have to, I know what they say. Graperoola. Yeah, I seen some like it.'

'Where?'

'Would you believe in Bulgy's cellar? That's an antique, that can is. See, back during Prohibition, they used to make their own booze at the Zipper. It wasn't the Zipper then, it was something else. But anyway, they'd make the bootleg booze and pour it into these cans so when the Elliot Neff guys came snooping around, all they'd find was cans of tonic. But then it got to be Repeal and they had all those empty cans left over. Bulgy likes having them around. He thinks they're pretty.'

'Did Bulgy tell you all that about the bootlegging?'

'Sure, who else? He don't remember it himself. Bulgy never remembers much unless you keep reminding him. He remembers about the cans because Dan comes down cellar every so often and takes a bunch of them away to sell for antiques. That upsets Bulgy, he hates to see them go.'

'Very interesting,' said Brooks. 'Mrs Bickens, to the best of my recollection, during Prohibition and for some time afterwards, soft drinks were invariably sold in bottles. Steel cans were introduced sometime during the 'forties. These had the crimped metal bottle caps you still had to lift off with an opener. Next came aluminium cans with those lift-off rings which proved to be such an ecological nuisance that the present pop-top cans were developed. If Dan's been around as long as you say, he must know those Graperoola cans are no antiques. And so should you.'

'Well, I'm kind of forgetful myself sometimes,' Annie mumbled. 'You mean the Graperoola cans aren't worth anything?'

'That's not precisely what I said. Why? Do you have some of them yourself?'

'Just one. I took it for a souvenir, like. What the hey, they still got two big cartons left.'

'One full and one open with some of the cans missing, right?' said Max. 'You wouldn't have risked dipping into a fresh carton because somebody would have noticed.'

'That's right. I didn't want Dan on my back. He knows I go down there.'

'Did Bulgy see you take the can?'

'No. Like I said, it upsets him. I had my bag with me, so I just lifted one out and stuck it down in the bottom with a newspaper over it while Bulgy had his back turned, getting me some empty bottles. They always let me take a few empties. Dan doesn't care.'

'Big of him. Do you still have that Graperoola can?'

'Sure, I got it right with me. I always carry it. I thought it was an antique, see?'

'Let's see it,' said Max. 'Is it in your collecting bag?'

'You've got to be kidding. The way our bags have been getting snatched lately?'

'You mean Phyllis and Chet weren't the only SCRC members to have been victimized?'

Annie snorted. 'Name me somebody who hasn't been. It figures out to two or three a week. Funny thing, for a long time nobody bothered anybody, then all of a sudden the past couple of months, it's like somebody's playing a game with us. Joan says it's on account of the bottle bill being passed, but that don't make sense to me.'

'Did the snatching start before or after you took that Graperoola can?'

Annie became wary. 'What do you keep harping on those cans for?'

'Let me tell her,' said Theonia. 'Take another look at that old woman in the photograph, Annie.'

'Okay, so?'

'I'm that woman.'

Annie stared at her. 'You trying to be funny?'

'Not at all. I was heavily disguised, of course.' Theonia touched her diamond brooch ever so fleetingly. 'Anyway, I was about to pick up that can, as you see, when the fellow in the purple suit kicked it away from my hand. Notice how blurred his right foot is in the picture? That shows it was moving.'

'Yeah, I see. So that's you? Jeez, I'd never have believed it.'

'Cousin Max took the photograph. He'll explain what happened next.'

'Theonia got up and beat it out of there,' Max went on, 'which was smart of her. The kid then very carefully kicked the can back to this same spot where you see it in the photograph. Less than a minute later, your friend Phyllis came along, wearing that purple sweater you must have seen her with. She picked up the can and put it in her SCRC bag. As you know, about ten minutes later, Phyllis had her bag snatched.'

'Are you saying somebody's after the Graperoola cans? So they're valuable, after all?'

'The cans themselves aren't valuable, no. But I'll give you a hundred dollars cash right this minute for the one you have with you.'

'Wait a minute. First you say the can's not worth nothing, then you offer me a hundred bucks. What's the deal?'

'The deal is, Annie, that we believe somebody's smuggling something in those Graperoola cans, and using the SCRC members as carriers. How it appears to work is that one of the gang, like this guy in the purple suit, drops the can in a place where he knows an SCRC member will soon come along, see it, and pick it up. Then whoever's supposed to get the stuff is alerted to track down the carrier and snatch the bag.'

'So how do they know who's got the can? There are a lot of us out there.'

'The tip-off seems to be that the carrier will show a purple signal of one sort or another. For instance, Phyllis was wearing a purple sweater. Chet's bag had a splash of purple paint on it. If Theonia had been wearing a purple scarf, say, she might have been allowed to pick up the can. We didn't know all that yesterday, or we wouldn't have to bother you for yours.'

'But mine doesn't have anything in it.'

'That doesn't matter. We're going to put something in it and use it to bait a trap. Our aim is to catch the smugglers and keep any more SCRC members from being mugged or killed. Now do you see why your can's worth that hundred to us?'

'Wow, just like Elliot Neff! Okay, sure, I'm game. Excuse me.'

Annie went through the motion of turning her back, hiked up the baggy old skirt she was wearing, and fished in a pocket she had sewn to the petticoat under it. An old shoplifter's trick. Max wondered what Joan thought of her friend Annie's underwear.

'Here it is.'

And there it was, shiny and purple and ready to roll. The pop top was sticking up, but a neat little transparent cap plugged the opening. Brooks nodded his approval.

'Highly efficient. We're most grateful to you, Mrs Bickens. And now, Theonia, I believe you'll have to excuse Max and me. Enjoy your lunch, ladies.'

'Here's your hundred, Annie.' Max paid it over, in crisp new tens and twenties. 'Now there's one more thing we want you to do, not for us but for yourself. We're going to set a trap, as I explained. We don't know how soon it will work, but when it does, the smugglers are going to know there's an extra Graperoola can gone from Bulgy's cellar, and the likeliest person to have taken it is you. For your own safety, we'd like to keep you right here in this room until we can positively guarantee there's nobody running loose who wants to kill you the way they did Chet Arthur.'

'Hey, are you guys T-Men? Was Chet one, too? Is that how come he made the will?'

'We're not at liberty to say,' Max replied inscrutably. 'While you're in our care, every effort will be made to keep you happy and comfortable. You have your own bathroom, Theonia will show you. She'll provide you with food, magazines, TV, anything you want within reasonable limits. Stay away from the windows,' which in any case were small and had iron grilles over them. 'Keep the curtains drawn as they are now, just in case some passer-by might look in and spot you. You won't have a phone, but we'll get a message to your friend Joan that you're all right and not to worry. Take it easy and enjoy yourself. We'll see you later.'

CHAPTER 17

'There, by gum, I'd say that's a pretty neat job.'

Brooks had been busy in the kitchen. He'd reasoned that the heroin had been put into the cans already measured out into 18-gram lots and wrapped in the usual folded papers. Those grains of heroin they'd found in Chet Arthur's torn collecting bag could have spilled out when Chet got curious and unfolded such a paper, thus making it necessary for the drug dealers to kill him.

A mixture of brown sugar and cornstarch approximated the pale brown colour of cut heroin closely enough. They didn't expect to fool the receiver for long, and surely not long enough for some deluded purchaser to try shooting it into his vein. Folding the papers around the quarter-teaspoonfuls was finicky work, but now that he'd got them all tucked in, the can looked and felt just about the way they thought it ought to look. In Annie's well-used SCRC bag, with a few of Brooks's root beer cans, some empty wine bottles, and a bundle of newspapers on top, it should make a convincing enough decoy.

Half an hour later, the elderly man who'd suffered such a rapid financial downfall yesterday was back on the streets of Boston. His business must have gone completely to pot by now, for he was no longer shabby, but downright ragged. His face was none too clean. His hands might be even dirtier but one couldn't be sure of that. Some clinging shred of respectability had prompted him to hide them inside a pair of grimy old work gloves such as a man in less dire circumstances might wear to do chores around the house when his maid had a toothache and his butler an audition.

This unlucky man might be down, but he wasn't licked. He was lugging an already well-filled SCRC collecting bag, and the diligence with which he looked about him for further salvageables showed that he was throwing himself heart and soul into his latest career.

134

By one of those coincidences Fate loves to contrive, the elderly man was again capturing the interest of a photographer. This was not yesterday's tweedy tourist but a more with-it or possibly somewhat past it type in blue jeans and a bright red windbreaker. The jeans were tight ones, such as might belong to a nephew who sometimes slept over at his uncle's apartment and was careless about leaving stray garments around. The windbreaker had Boston University silk-screened across the back, and conceivably could also have been part of the hypothetical nephew's neglected wardrobe.

In deference, no doubt, to the current fad for wearing older people's cast-offs, the photographer had on a greenish-grey felt hat, circa 1947, with a feather of the ruddy turnstone stuck in the band. He appeared to be quite unjustifiably proud of this adornment, wearing it far back on his head to set off his mirrored sun goggles and his abundant red hair. Like many redheads, he was well endowed with freckles. An artist might have been struck by the tasteful way these were dotted over and around the immense auburn moustache that entirely hid his mouth.

Who could have divined that these two were none other than those past masters of sartorial subterfuge, Brooks Kelling and Max Bittersohn? Sarah would, probably, once she realized Max had swiped her eyebrow pencil to draw his freckles with; but by then, with any luck, their mission would have been accomplished.

They'd talked over the information Annie had given them about SCRC members' work habits. Some were haphazard, some methodical. Most of them worked within a one or two mile radius of the Center, because they were elderly people and full trash bags got heavy to carry. Annie had told them who was reliable, who was wayward, and who was wearing purple today because she'd seen them all at breakfast and purple, as she kept letting them know, was her favourite colour.

There was one man named Joe who'd come in wearing a purple T-shirt, but Joe was on backroom detail today and wouldn't be going out at all. A guy they called Frodo had on a purple baseball cap, but Frodo was such a flake anybody would be crazy to trust him any farther than they could throw him. He'd never been mugged yet, so apparently nobody had trusted him.

That left only Phyllis in her purple sweater. Normally two drops on successive days would be unlikely, judging from the pattern of the bag-snatchings to date, but Max and Brooks were gambling on the fact that something had obviously gone badly wrong with the delivery Chet Arthur had been supposed to make. That must mean the drug dealers were running behind schedule, the week was drawing to a close and after all, why not use Phyllis again?

Whoever was feeding information from the Center must know Phyllis hadn't done anything yesterday except go back to the SCRC and bitch about getting her bag snatched. Mr Loveday had no doubt reported the incident to the police as a matter of form, but they wouldn't have done anything about it either, because there simply wasn't anything they could do. Mr Loveday had suggested Phyllis ought to change her route today and Phyllis had in turn made a few suggestions to him. She'd earned new respect among the members, who hadn't realized Phyllis knew that many words, but she'd be doing exactly the same things today that she'd done yesterday, and nobody would try to stop her.

If Phyllis got her collecting bag snatched again today, in the same place and in the same way, would she learn to think of the incident as a part of her daily round and hand over the bag without a struggle? If she did, they'd have the perfect messenger for so long as nobody except the compulsive Phyllis caught on to what was happening. By then, she'd know her receiver and have to be silenced.

That was why the photographer in the funny hat and tight jeans zeroed in on the corner where Phyllis had picked up her Graperoola can the day before, just as the zealous lady with the purple sweater was heaving into view. Around the bend that Phyllis would take next lurked the ragged man with the SCRC bag just like hers. But where was the dashing fellow in the purple running suit?

Off and running, perhaps. There was only one idler on

the corner, leaning against a lamp-post, wearing hiking boots and a hairy poncho. The photographer raised his camera to his eye, keeping well out of her sight. She didn't appear to notice Phyllis coming, but one hand came out from under the poncho holding a bright purple soft drink can. She raised it to her lips as if to drain the last swallow, tossed it into the gutter, and strolled away. The photographer's shutter kept on clicking.

Phyllis stopped, mouthed some words that might have been, 'Yellow, orange, red, green, purple?', picked up the can, and stowed it among her other finds. The photographer stopped clicking and hurried around the corner.

Right on schedule, Phyllis chugged up the sidewalk, encountered the ragged man with the SCRC collecting bag, and took umbrage. Her method of expressing her displeasure, as Bill Jones had predicted, was to set her own bag down against a hydrant and pick up the little man like a bucket of slush, causing him to drop his own bag. She carried him kicking and sputtering to the corner, gave him a stern lecture on trespass, and left him sitting dumbfounded on the kerbstone. She then went back to the hydrant, picked up her bag, and went on her way.

The photographer handed the remaining bag to the man on the kerb. 'Well, it saved our having to mug her.'

'At least I've got her warmed up for the next chap, God help him.' Brooks was sorting through the rubbish in the bag, as a concerned scavenger would naturally do. 'Yes, it's there and it's not empty. I miscalculated the weight, but not by much. Are you coming with me?'

'No, I'll follow Phyllis and try to get a shot of whoever grabs the bag. You've got a bodyguard, that guy in the grey jersey across the street. His name's Pat Zewitzky. See you in jail.'

Brooks nodded and puttered off in the general direction of the police station. Max waited to make sure Brooks's tail had moved up close enough to protect him if necessary, then lengthened his stride and went after Phyllis.

He knew from Annie what route the woman would take and where she'd been attacked the day before. The muggers had chosen well, a crossroad with twisty alleyways to flee into. That they might decide to mug him if they caught him taking their picture was altogether possible. That Max would let himself be mugged was improbable.

Ah, there she was, looking down at an orange crush can with a connoisseur's eye and perhaps a touch of nostalgia. Phyllis gave the orange can her seal of approval and crammed it in with what she supposed to be the rest of her loot. Luckily there'd been time for Max to switch the top layers of the respective collecting bags before he'd left the dummy by the hydrant and passed hers to Brooks. Phyllis appeared not to have noticed the exchange. Probably she didn't form the same intimate relationship with her daily gleanings that she had with her bottles of slush syrup.

And here came the mugger, a burly white youth with a nasty black eye. And here came another. From the look of that eye, Phyllis had demonstrated once again that she was no pushover. They did it by the book, the first man strolling past Phyllis and jostling her off balance while the second reached from behind and wrenched the SCRC bag out of her grasp. They were off before she could get her mouth open to yell.

But yell she did. Judging from the amount of noise she was making, Max didn't think Phyllis could have sustained any real injury, except to her *amour propre*. He took one last shot of Phyllis yelling, and made himself scarce.

She'd go back to the Center and pour out her tale of woe as she'd done yesterday. As the news of two muggings in a row got around, other members might find themselves less and less eager to go out on the streets and get their bags snatched, too. Damn shame. Those senior citizens were performing a real service, to themselves and to their city.

Max had no time to brood over the broader aspects now. He had to buzz on over to the station and see what was happening to Brooks. It was as well he hurried, that game old bird was getting his feathers ruffled.

'Glad to see you, Max. Perhaps you can convince the captain here that I'm not a drug runner.'

'We haven't accused you of running drugs, Mr Kelling,'

said the captain in what he probably thought was a conciliatory tone. 'You have to realize it's a little bit unusual for an elderly vagrant to drop in on us with a bagful of trash that happens to include a cache of heroin he picked out of the gutter. Who the hell ever heard of Graperoola, anyway?'

'You'll hear plenty about it before we're through,' said Max. 'Brooks Kelling is no vagrant, but a concerned citizen trying to do his civic duty. If you've allowed Mr Kelling to tell his story, you ought to know he knew the heroin was in that bag of trash because he and I both saw it being put there. The Graperoola can was deliberately planted in front of a member of the Senior Citizens' Recycling Center. You know about the organization?'

The captain admitted he did.

'Well, this same woman picked up an identical can in the same place yesterday afternoon, and had her collecting bag snatched shortly afterwards. For your information, I've just come from watching her get her bag snatched again, only we'd switched bags on her, as Mr Kelling may have told you.'

'So?'

'So right now, the two men who pulled the snatch are probably handing over a Graperoola can stuffed with brown sugar and cornstarch to somebody who isn't going to be happy about getting it. Look, I don't know how much of Brooks's story you've heard so far, but would you mind if we started over? It begins with Chester Allen Arthur, a member of the SCRC whose body was found in an alley near the intersection of Marlborough Street and Massachusetts Avenue this past Monday night.'

'That was a mugging.'

'I'm not arguing with you, though I do think there's room for doubt. What apparently wasn't noticed during the investigation was that Arthur's carrying bag, which was returned to Brooks's cousin Dolph, who runs the SCRC, contained grains of heroin.'

'What?'

'My wife noticed them, and I analysed them on my little home chemistry set.'

139

'The hell you did. Go on.'

Max went on. Brooks produced the photographs they'd taken the previous day, along with one of Theonia in her wine-coloured velvet dinner gown to show what she really looked like. That proved to be a mistake, as they had a hard time persuading the captain to quit looking at Theonia and attend to the rest of the evidence.

After he'd finally been allowed to explain the other photographs, Max indicated the camera around his neck. 'I've got a batch more in here. At least I hope I have. I shot everything from the drop to the mugging.'

'Okay, Bittersohn, we'll get them right down to the darkroom.'

'If it's all the same to you,' Brooks objected, 'I'd much rather take the films home and process them myself. Those are my cameras, and I'm fussy about the quality of my prints.'

'So are we,' said the captain implacably.

They compromised at last by sending Brooks to the darkroom with the cameras, so that he could supervise the processing. Max finished their tale, then went to the washroom and removed his red wig, moustache, and freckles. He was stuck with the jacket until he could get home, and Mike's jeans would probably have to be peeled off him with surgical instruments. Walking slightly bowlegged, he went back to the captain's office.

'Well, well,' said the captain genially, 'quite a change. The darkroom just rang up to say they've got a proof sheet on your films. They're anxious for us to go take a look.'

'Brooks is probably driving them nuts with good advice,' said Max. 'Okay, let's see what we've got.'

Thanks either to the darkroom personnel's skill or to Brooks's bullying, the photographs had come out just fine. There was one in particular of Tigger tossing away the Graperoola can that intrigued the captain almost as much as Theonia had done.

'We've got that baby dead to rights, if only we can get some kind of lead on who it is. Or what.'

'Female, possibly human,' said Max. 'Age somewhere in

140

the early thirties, at a guess. Commonly known as Tigger. She's been some kind of protégée of my wife's aunt, Apollonia Kelling, who's trying to remember Tigger's real name for us. Something out of A. A. Milne's the closest Appie's been able to come to it so far.'

'James James Morrison Morrison Weatherby George Dupree?' said the captain, and blushed slightly.

'I shouldn't be surprised. Appie says it will come to her sooner or later. In the meantime, I have to tell you that my wife saw Tigger quarrelling over near Park Square with that guy Ted Ashe, whom I pointed out to you upstairs; the one who's been identified as Wilbraham Winchell, a reporter for *Syndicated Slime*, a muckraking tabloid.'

'What were they fighting about?'

'My wife doesn't know. Tigger claims Ashe tried to rape her but my wife says that's baloney. Anyway, she used the incident to tag on to my wife and gatecrash the SCRC, where she's since done some volunteer work, don't ask me what. She's also roped Appie Kelling into working there, which in itself is a form of sabotage. Captain, why don't you let Brooks and me follow up on the Tigger angle while you track down those two muggers we fingered today and the guy in the purple running suit? It might also be helpful to run a check on who's behind the Thanatopsis Trust.'

'You telling me how to run my department, Bittersohn?'

'I wouldn't dream of it, Captain.'

'In that case, why don't you and Mr Kelling check out this Tigger while we handle the rest of it? Let me know the minute you come up with a result. You're not the Lone Ranger and Tonto, you know.'

'Right, Kemo Sabe. Are we dismissed?'

'What's your hurry?'

'These goddamn jeans are threatening to destroy my marriage.'

'Next time wear a mini skirt. Dismissed.'

The captain flipped a switch on his intercom. 'Have an unmarked car waiting downstairs to drive two gentlemen, one of them slightly disabled, to the address they'll give you. The driver should be prepared to take a statement from a witness who's being held in protective custody. Need a wheelchair, Bittersohn?'

'Levity is unbecoming in an officer of your rank,' Max told him coldly. 'After you, Brooks.'

CHAPTER 18

Back at Tulip Street, they found their witness bearing her confinement with fortitude. Since Theonia and her aides-de-camp couldn't be riding herd on Annie every moment of the day, Mariposa had put in an emergency call to her Uncle Pedro, a widower of suitable age and friendly disposition. She'd equipped Annie with a portable TV, Charles's walkaround stereo, a deck of playing cards, and several good things to eat. Pedro had brought along a jug of sangria and his maracas. Theonia had gone downstairs to see whether they might like a nice historical novel to read aloud together, but hadn't been able to make herself heard over the cries of 'Cha cha cha.'

Annie was pleased to meet Sergeant Cooley, but she didn't want to make a statement. She wanted to form a conga line. After less unsober heads had prevailed, however, and Mariposa had made her a lovely milkshake, Annie talked a blue streak. By now, she'd decided she'd committed an act of heroism by stealing that Graperoola can from the Broken Zipper, though she hoped she hadn't got Bulgy in trouble.

At last Sergeant Cooley closed his notebook, regretfully declined a glass of sangria and a turn with the maracas, and went away to file his report. Max went home to be excavated from Mike's jeans, soak his chafed limbs in a hot bath, and receive Sarah's welcome news about the Innes.

'Good work, little mother. Have you told Dolph and Mary?'

'I tried to. Mary said wasn't that nice and did I think she'd better tell the rental company to bring another hundred chairs, just in case? They've had a hundred and thirty-seven acceptances so far and Mr Loveday's in a tizzy because I didn't put "black tie" on the invitation.'

'To an auction? Is he out of his mind?'

'He thinks it would have elevated the tone and encouraged the patrons to bid higher. I wish he'd keep his bright ideas to himself. Mary'd be fine if he'd only leave her alone and quit harping on how to treat the right people. He's getting her down.'

'Loveday ought to be locked up in the basement with Annie,' said Max. 'She'd straighten him out fast enough.'

'What's happening over there, anyway? Theonia told me Annie has a boyfriend. I hope she doesn't lift his watch and spoil what could be the start of something beautiful.'

'I don't think it's his watch she's after.' Max decided his legs were back in working order, and got out of the tub. 'Hand me a towel, please, *angela mia*. I think I'll slip into something comfortable. Bed, for instance.'

'Surely you can't be that badly off. What have you been doing?'

Max told her.

'And it was actually Tigger who threw that Graperoola can with the drugs in it? Max, that's appalling. She couldn't possibly have been recruited in so short a time, could she? It appears she and Ashe must have been working together all along. You know, I shouldn't be surprised if Tigger was a *Slime* reporter, herself. That could be why she always hung around at Aunt Appie's parties never saying a word but taking everything in. Writers are always rather crazy, aren't they?'

'Not always, but I suppose it helps. Oh, I forgot to tell you Bill Jones checked out Chet Arthur with that boiler-maker friend of his brother's. Arthur did work for Grotters and Wales. He was foreman of the mop-and-broom depart-ment, at least he had a couple of guys to help him sweep the floors. But he earned a steady salary, never spent a cent he didn't have to, and did have pension money coming to him when the factory shut down, so there's no reason to suppose Mary's inheritance isn't perfectly safe.'

'That's one piece of good news. At least I hope it is. I'd

better call Aunt Appie and see if she's remembered Tigger's name yet.'

'Try her on James James Morrison Morrison Weatherby George Dupree,' Max suggested.

'Where did you ever pick that up?'

'I have my methods.'

'Well, let's hope Aunt Appie has her wits about her for a change, and has dropped that asinine schedule business. Oh dear, why couldn't I have been born into some other family? Darling, I'm terribly afraid we'll have to give our son Kelling for a middle name. Unless you're willing to stand for Jeremy Frederick Adolphus Beddoes? Aunt Emma would be shattered if we left out Uncle Bed. I thought if we simply use Kelling, we can say it's for all of them.'

'I don't know,' said Max. 'There's a certain ring to Jeremy Frederick Adolphus Beddoes. Speaking of rings, isn't she answering?'

'Too soon. She's still hunting for the phone. She has it on one of those extra-long cords, you know, because Uncle Samuel would never pay for an extension, and she never knows where she put it last time, so she has to get hold of the cord and track it down hand over—Aunt Appie? It's Sarah. No, not Sarah Gamp, your niece Sarah. The one who's married to that amusing man whose name you can never remember. Speaking of names, I was wondering if you've remembered Tigger's?'

Appie began to talk. Sarah closed her eyes and prayed for patience. Max brought her a chair and, after a while, a glass of milk.

'Getting back to Tigger,' she managed to put in at last, 'what's her proper name? You said it was out of *Winnie the Pooh*.'

'She said it was out of A. A. Milne,' Max hissed, but his whisper was drowned by a happy shriek from the receiver.

'That's it! You clever, clever child. It's Perdita. Perdita Follow. Because Perdita means lost, you see, and Pooh got *lost* in the woods. And when he saw more and more tracks going around the tree, he thought some other animal was *following* him. You see how obvious it is? Silly old me, I've been wearing holes in my thinking cap and here it was, right in front of me. All I'd have needed to do would have been to look at dear old Sam's teddy bear. I keep Winnie—short for Winston, you know—sitting in Sam's favourite chair for company now that my darling's not with me any more. Vare thinks it's silly. I expect you do, too.'

'Not a bit,' Sarah replied. 'It makes perfect sense to me, Uncle Sam was the beariest man I've ever known. Give Winnie a pat for me. And you're marvellous to remember, Aunt Appie. Perdita Follow. Max, you'd better write that down before we forget again.'

'Max,' crowed Appie from the far end of her telephone cord. 'Wasn't he that boarder of yours who had the affair with Alice Beaxitt ages ago.'

'No, you must be thinking of James James Morrison Morrison Weatherby George Dupree. I have to say goodbye now, but don't hang up. Max wants to talk with you.'

Max had not in fact wanted to talk to Apollonia Kelling. He'd wanted Sarah to ask Appie how she'd become acquainted with Perdita Follow, and where Perdita Follow was living now that Vare had severed connections with her. He gave it his best shot. When at last he extricated himself from a maze of *non sequiturs* and hung up no wiser than when he'd started, Sarah had the grace to apologize.

'I'm sorry, darling, but I simply couldn't have taken any more. Aunt Appie's rather like sunburn, you know. If you expose yourself too long, the suffering becomes unbearable. Did you manage to get any sense out of her about Tigger?'

'In a word, no. But at least we got the name. I'll call it in to the police right now. Are we eating in, or do you want to go someplace?'

As Max was still wearing only his bathrobe and slippers, his offer struck Sarah as being somewhat less than wholehearted. 'They treated me to lunch at the museum. Why don't you light the gas log and we'll have trays in front of the fire instead? Did you get lunch yourself, by the way?

'I grabbed a hunk of cheese and an apple next door while Brooks was inventing the heroin.'

'Then you must be famished. Just a minute.'

The microwave oven had been Max's idea, not Sarah's, but she had to admit it came in handy at times like this. Though she hadn't yet stooped to commercially frozen dinners, she'd learned how to package her own, freezing single-plate servings so she'd have emergency meals ready to accommodate her husband's often unpredictable comings and goings. By the time he'd finished the one modest scotch and water that was his usual pre-dinner drink, she had Yankee potroast with mashed potatoes and gravy, Wayside Inn style, steaming in front of him, and another tray with salad and hot corn muffins at his elbow.

'This looks great,' he told her. 'Aren't you having any?'

'Of course.'

She fetched her own tray and sat down in the other armchair, which he'd drawn up to the fire beside his own. For a while they didn't talk much. When Max had emptied his plate, he reached over and took her hand.

'Very good, dear. What's on your agenda for tomorrow?'

'I thought I might ask you to run me out to Chestnut Hill right after breakfast. Theonia was going to help, but she won't be able to now that she has Annie to look after, and Mary's going to need all the help she can get. Or I could take the subway and have Dolph pick me up at the station.'

'Nothing doing. You stay out of the subway.'

'But I shan't be carrying an Innes this time.'

'You're carrying a Bittersohn. The start of one, anyway. What if somebody shoves you down the stairs?'

'Nobody ever has before. Max dear, are you getting paranoid about this baby?'

'Why the hell shouldn't I? He's mine, isn't he?'

'Of that you may rest assured, my darling. But as you so rightly remarked, I'm the one who's carrying him, so I think you ought to tell me straight out if you think I may possibly be in any personal danger over this Graperoola business.'

'Sarah, think about it. We can be fairly sure there's been hell to pay somewhere not far from here over that trick Brooks and I played this afternoon, or soon will be. Whoever Perdita Follow's working for can't know we're the ones who got on to their delivery system, unless they've got somebody planted in the police department or unless Annie's a double agent with a walkie-talkie pinned to her garter belt. However, Perdita Follow knows you're Dolph's cousin, she knows you have a connection with the SCRC because she trailed you there, and she knows you're married to a detective. She was at Ireson's Landing with Vare that* time, remember?'

'Yes, of course, and since Tigger was the one who dropped the heroin, she'll be the first person suspected of stealing it and substituting the dummy. Therefore, she's going to need a scapegoat in a hurry and I'll do as well as anybody. Is that what you're thinking?'

'I just hope it's not what she's thinking. I'm going to give the police another call.'

Sarah shrugged and began filling the dishwasher. The idea was too weird to be frightening, but then Tigger was weird, too. She was more relieved than she'd have cared to admit when Max came back to her smiling.

'You'd never believe it. The captain had to go over to the State House on business. He was going around to park the car and there she was, strolling along right in front of the Swedenborgian Church. So he hopped out and made the collar in person. She's not talking, even to call a lawyer, so they've got her in the cooler to think it over.'

'I always said she was crazy,' said Sarah. 'Now whoever she's working for will be sure she's run off with the heroin. That's a break for our side, isn't it?'

'Looks that way, kid. You do understand why we had to plant that dummy?'

'Max darling, what else could you do? You had no case for the police until you had the heroin to show them, and how else could you have got hold of it, short of mugging Phyllis yourself? Now, with all those photographs and everything, you've handed the responsibility over to them without putting Dolph and Mary on a limb. It was an absolutely brilliant manœuvre, and you know it. Want some dessert?'

'Sure. Come here.'

* The Bilbao Looking Glass

CHAPTER 19

Sarah left Max talking Fractured French to Pepe Ginsberg, called a Boston cab, and was in her working clothes by half past nine. Since Theonia hadn't been able to line up costumes for the young actors and actresses, her first stop had to be the attic. It was going to be a longer one than she'd intended, because Mary had not a glimmering of where anything was in that vast expanse of trunks and boxes.

'I should have done something about this place by now,' Mary fretted, 'but I get cold feet just looking at it. I'd be tempted to call in the junkman, myself, but you know Dolph.'

'I don't mind a bit. It'll be fun rummaging around,' Sarah lied bravely. 'Why don't you go out in the garden and pick as many flowers as George will let you have? The frost will be getting most of them soon anyway, so we might as well get the good out of them. Aunt Emma says there's nothing like lots of big, splashy floral arrangements to create a party atmosphere and loosen people up.'

'Just so it loosens up their pocketbooks. When you say many, do you mean a bucketful?'

'I mean all the buckets you can fill. You can't imagine how many flowers a big arrangement uses up until you've done one.'

Filling the pails kept Mary busy most of the morning, and did her good. By the time she came in from the garden, rosy, relaxed, and complaining about her back, Sarah had unearthed a cache of wonderful flapper dresses that must have belonged to Dolph's mother, who was considered flighty and had once done the Charleston at a debutante cotillion. She'd also found straw boaters, derbies, blazers and crew sweaters with preposterously high necks that would do for the boys.

They had a bite of lunch, with the inevitable glass of milk

for Sarah, then they got to work on the flowers. Gradually, the atmosphere of the great, still rooms lightened.

Mary had sent Dolph off early to the SCRC, knowing he'd drive them crazy with helpful suggestions if he stuck around. He was back by half past four, though, bringing Harry Burr, Jeremy Kelling, and Jem's faithful squire, Egbert. A while later, Max arrived with a carload of half-fledged thespians, dumped them at the door, and went back to collect a few more.

Sarah was dying to ask him whether there'd been any further developments during the day, but there were the actors' costumes to be fitted, their duties to be assigned, and Uncle Jem to be kept at bay. Max and Dolph might have realized what a bevy of bright young things in Roaring Twenties garb with rolled stockings and rouged kneecaps would do to Jem's ageing hormones.

And of course everyone had to be fed. There was no way Genevieve could have fixed enough canapés for the expected crowd, baked two thousand cheese straws, and managed to serve a sit-down dinner. At Sarah's suggestion, she'd set out platters of ham and chicken sandwiches and filled Great-aunt Matilda's second biggest tureen with hot clear soup that could be drunk from a mug. People simply went and helped themselves when they felt hungry, which in the actors' case appeared to be most of the time.

No liquor was served. Mary had asked Sarah about that and got a firm thumbs down. 'Don't do it, Mary. These are just kids who mightn't know when to stop. The last thing you want is a bunch of half-stewed waiters slopping champagne all over the guests. Give them each a bottle to take home afterwards, if there's any left.'

This was not to say that Jeremy Kelling didn't get his customary pitcher of martinis, or that he wouldn't have shared them with the cutest and giggliest of the actresses if Sarah hadn't offered to wring his neck the moment he tried.

'God, you're getting to be a worse prude than Aunt Matilda ever dared to be,' he sputtered. 'Since when can't a man perform the purely altruistic gesture of offering a lady a little refreshment?'

'You're here to raise money, not whoopee,' was Sarah's unfeeling retort. 'Give Dolph some if you're feeling altruistic. He looks as if he could use a mild anæsthetic about now. Good heavens, is that Aunt Emma's bus already?'

It was, and the already wasn't so early, either. Time had flown, as time has a way of doing when one could best use an extra half-hour to catch one's breath. Emma floated in at the head of her brigade, bestowing smiles and kisses right and left, exclaiming over the massed flowers in the majolica jardiniéres, the servers in their amusing costumes, the luscious canapés on their silver platters, the silver buckets full of cooling champagne.

'Absolutely perfect! I couldn't have planned it better myself.'

This, from Emma, was the ultimate accolade. 'No, really, Mary dear, we're none of us a bit hungry at the moment. We picnicked on the bus. Just let's get these dear people out of their wraps and set up the chairs for the musicians. Perhaps if some of these muscular young men could roll the piano just a wee bit closer to the archway . . .'

The muscular young men were as eager to be of service to Emma Kelling as young men everywhere always were. The piano was moved, the strings and the woodwinds comfortably settled.

'We didn't bring the brasses or the tympani, we didn't want to drown out the auctioneer. It'll be just nice, soft hearts and flowers music, to mellow them up. There, don't you think that will do?'

'Need you ask?' Sarah gave her favourite aunt another kiss and hoped to goodness Mary had remembered to get the piano tuned.

Emma sat down to give the musicians an A. Right on pitch. Everything was going to be just fine.

'For God's sake, didn't you bring anything else to put on?' Max murmured. Sarah gasped. Everything was ready but herself.

She fled upstairs, remembering to close off rooms as she went. By the time she got back, clean and combed and wearing a rose-coloured velveteen float dress with a string

150

of pea-sized pearls Max had rushed out and bought in Zürich six minutes after she'd phoned him with the news of her pregnancy, the prospective buyers were flocking in and the champagne was beginning to flow.

As she came back down the front stairway, Sarah was amused to see Osmond Loveday standing just inside the door. He'd shown up in black tie, sure enough, and was greeting all comers as if he owned the place. Well, why not? Those he recognized would no doubt be pleased that he remembered their names and the rest would think he was the butler. Dolph and Mary must be relieved that Loveday had taken on a chore neither of them wanted.

They'd agreed to start the bidding at eight o'clock sharp whether anybody was there or not, but they needn't have worried. By the time Jeremy Kelling put down his cocktail glass and picked up his gavel, almost every chair in the ballroom was occupied. At his opening knock, clearly audible in the front hall, Osmond Loveday abandoned his post.

'Where are you going?' Sarah asked him.

'To say a brief word of welcome and explain the purpose of the auction.'

'Don't you dare.' This was no time to mince words. 'Dolph will be livid if you interrupt the bidding. You'd better stay by the door, people are still coming and someone will have to let them in. Unless you'd rather let one of the actors do it and go serve champagne,' she added, knowing he'd rather die.

Luckily Apollonia Kelling and her entourage arrived just then, all of them in a tizzy. 'I was sure I could flap my way straight here like a good old grey-haired pigeon,' Appie was panting, 'but somehow or other, I got a teentsy-weentsy bit confused.'

'We've been up and down every back road from here to West Roxbury,' snapped one of her companions, a woman about Appie's age, dressed from cap to socks in strange garments all knitted from the same batch of mulberry-coloured wool. Her face was mulberry-coloured, too. Sarah recognized her as Mrs Plinth. Clever Mrs Plinth, Appie always called her. Nobody knew why, but it was clear that any friend of Mrs Apollonia Kelling could be as clever as Appie wanted her to be, as far as Osmond Loveday was concerned.

He bore the new arrivals off to shed their outer wrappings and refresh themselves at the champagne table before they sat down and opened their pocketbooks. Or didn't, as was more apt to be the case. Sarah had no great hopes of Appie's crowd, but they weren't going to matter. When she peeked into the ballroom, she could see that the auction was taking off in grand style.

Jeremy Kelling was everyone's dream of an auctioneer: fast-talking, funny, rattling off information about the merchandise that Max was feeding him, interspersed with nuggets of family history, mostly invented and often slightly wicked, to get the crowd bidding madly on even the least exciting of Dolph's alleged family heirlooms. She'd have loved to stay and watch the fun, but since Osmond Loveday was showing every sign of being enraptured by the clever Mrs Plinth, she thought she'd better get back to the door.

'God, the world lost a magnificent snake-oil salesman when Jem opted to spend his life chasing chorus girls,' Dolph remarked when he wandered out into the foyer a little while later. 'What are you doing here?'

'Nothing, at the moment,' Sarah answered quite truthfully. 'How's Mary bearing up?'

'Having the time of her life. She looks wonderful, don't you think?'

Mary was wearing the blue dress she'd had on the day Dolph asked her for their first date. At the time, it had been the only decent thing she owned. How like her to put it back on for her debut as lady of the manor, Sarah thought.

'She's marvellous, Dolph,' she said, and meant it. 'Let's make our next fund-raiser a waltz evening so you can show her off properly.'

'Don't know how Mary would like that,' he grunted. 'Loveday would, though. Damn fool, coming here in black tie like the headwaiter at a goddamn nightclub. Where's he got to now? I thought he was tending door.'

152

'Aunt Appie came in with a gaggle of her friends and he's gone to get them settled. How many people do we have by now, Dolph?'

'Upward of three hundred and fifty, Porter-Smith says. I hope to God we don't get many more.'

'Some are sure to leave early.' Sarah hoped she knew what she was talking about. 'How's the champagne holding out?'

'Fine. Nobody's drinking much so far. Jem's got 'em all mesmerized. Who'd have thought the old coot had it in him? Oh damn, here comes another gang.'

'Only three. No, there's another one coming behind them. I wonder if these could be Eugene's fiancée and her family. That girl looks awfully bridal, somehow.' It might have been because she was wearing a shiny new diamond, with her left hand slightly extended and the fingers arranged in a gentle droop that showed off the ring to its fullest advantage.

The older woman came forward a step and introduced her party. 'Good evening. We're Diane and Henry Wilton-Rugge and our daughter Jennifer.' How nice Jennifer had her own hyphen, Sarah thought. 'And this is our friend—'

'Ted Ashe,' Dolph finished for her. 'Great Scott, Ted, you needn't have got yourself all togged out like a hog going to war. All I wanted you to do was help Harry Burr park the cars.'

The Wilton-Rugges stared blankly at Dolph. The fourth member of their group only smiled.

'They say everyone has a double. This Ted Ashe must be mine. Actually I'm Hetherton Montague, Mr—ah, Kelling, I believe?'

'Hetherton Montague, my eyeball! Now look here, Ted, a joke's a joke, but if you've been bamboozling Mary and me for the past two months, I want to know why.'

Sarah thought she'd better intervene. 'Mrs Wilton-Rugge, why don't we go along in? Eugene's clerking, but I know he's impatient to see you and your husband. And Jennifer, too, needless to say.'

'Yes, let's go.' Mrs Wilton-Rugge fell into step with Sarah.

Her husband and daughter followed, though somewhat reluctantly.

'What an odd mistake for Mr Kelling to have made,' said Mr Wilton-Rugge.

'It wasn't a mistake,' Sarah told him. 'I recognized Mr Ashe, too. He's not quite the master of disguise he seems to think he is. Since he's a friend of yours, though, I expect you realize what he's up to.'

'Hetherton's not what you'd call a friend.' The man knew when to backtrack, obviously. 'Hardly more than an acquaintance. Someone brought him to a cocktail party a couple of weeks ago, and since then I've bumped into him a few times. He happened to mention that he was coming to your auction tonight. I said we were, too, so he said why not let him take us to dinner somewhere and then all come together. What did you mean about what he's up to?'

Sarah shrugged. 'I assumed you must know what he does for a living.'

Before he could press the issue, she hailed one of the young actresses. 'Magda, do give the Wilton-Rugges some champagne and take them into the auction room. I believe Eugene Porter-Smith is saving them seats down front. Excuse me, I'd better go back and see what's happening.'

What was happening was about what Sarah had expected. Dolph was fast coming up to the boil, and Adolphus Kelling in a rage was not a quiet man. Once he let go, he'd have no trouble outshouting Emma's chamber music group, the chatter around the champagne table, and even Jeremy Kelling on the auction block. They'd have all three hundred and fifty people racing out here to see the fight.

Ashe-Winchell-Montague, to give him his fair share of hyphens, wasn't fighting, exactly. He was merely sneering and making remarks about phony philanthropists who only care to involve themselves with those of the downtrodden who allow themselves to stay trodden down. Sarah's first thought was to run back and get Max. By the time she reached the auction room, though, Max was on the auction block, giving Jem a martini break. He was holding up a beaded footstool by one leg, had the bidding up to a hundred and twenty dollars, and appeared confident of getting a good deal more. She'd be crazy to interrupt him now.

Sarah scurried back to the foyer. She could raise her own voice in a pinch, and she did

'Dolph, shut up. You'll scare off the bidders. Mr Winchell, why don't you save your views for your readers, if you have any?'

They were both surprised enough to obey. The snappily dressed outsider with the strangely clean face was first to recover his aplomb.

'What is this? First he calls me Ashe, then you call me Winchell. Are you both nuts?'

'No, but you are if you think you can fool anybody just by getting your face dirty,' Sarah retorted. 'It's awfully unconvincing when you forget to let your whiskers grow, too. But then the unshaven look would hardly go well with your pink and purple tuxedo, would it?'

'Pink and purple tuxedo?' Dolph had found his voice again. 'Good God, what is he? Some kind of pervert?'

'You might call him that. He writes smear stories on organized charities for *Syndicated Slime*, and signs them Wilbraham Winchell. He uses a number of different names. Don't ask me why he took the risk of coming here tonight calling himself Hetherton Montague. I suppose he either expected to get some more material for a trumped-up exposé of the SCRC or hoped to plant some.'

'That's actionable,' cried the man of many names.

'Then sue me. Now, Mr whoever you are, let me remind you that this is a private auction. I sent out the invitations myself, and I'm sure none went to either Hetherton Montague or Wilbraham Winchell. That means you must be here at Dolph's original request as Ted Ashe. Therefore, we may as well call you that and I'm going to let him decide what to do with you. Only please take him outside, Dolph, before you start to bellow.'

'Sarah.' Osmond Loveday had come up behind her. He sounded rather frantic. 'Did I hear you say Ted Ashe is really some kind of reporter?'

'You make it sound like a dirty word, Ozzie,' Ashe gibed.

'Apparently you do, too,' said Sarah. 'That's right, Mr Loveday. As you may have heard me say, he writes for *Syndicated Slime*.'

'And he's planning to do a story about the SCRC?'

'I can't think why else he's been haunting the place. Can you?'

'This is terrible!' Loveday was actually wringing his hands.

'Damn right it's terrible,' barked Dolph. 'Biting the hands that fed him. Outside, Ashe. We'll settle this—I was going to say man to man, but I'm dashed if you qualify as one.'

'I'll come with you,' cried Loveday. 'Wait till I get my coat.'

'Who the hell needs you?'

Dolph slammed out of the house, herding Ashe in front of him like an angry gander. Sarah debated calling for reinforcements, but she didn't think they'd be necessary. Harry Burr was out there, and George and Walter the gardeners. She wasn't about to go herself, Max would have a fit if she did. Besides, she had a more urgent errand.

'Mr Loveday, I'm going upstairs. Go find one of the actors to watch the door. You'd better see what's happening in the drawing-room. If anybody's curious to know what the commotion was all about, tell them a reporter was trying to gatecrash and that you and Mr Kelling threw him out, which is perfectly true.'

It wasn't, but Osmond Loveday would surely not be averse to sharing the hero's role. He nodded and bustled off. She went on upstairs to one of the bathrooms that had been declared out of bounds to visitors. There she dawdled, attending to her creature comforts, dabbing at her face and hair, sitting down on the padded stool and putting her feet up against the side of the tub to rest them a little.

She hadn't realized how tired she was. Perhaps she ought to stretch out on one of the guest-room beds, just for a moment.

CHAPTER 20

Sarah was dimly conscious of voices downstairs, of cars in the drive. Then Max was bending over her, smoothing her hair. She smiled up at him through what was left of her sleep.

'Hello, darling. How's the auction going?

'It's gone. Don't you realize what time it is?'

'Oh no! Don't tell me I've slept through the whole thing. How maddening! Did we make lots of money?'

'Would you believe twenty-seven thousand, nine hundred and forty-six dollars and thirty-two cents? The thirty-two cents was your aunt's friend, Mrs Plinth. And Appie bought all the seaweed mottoes.'

'That I can believe. But how wonderful. By the time we sell the Innes landscape and those other things, they'll have enough to do the whole renovation.'

'Well, maybe. But we'd never have done it tonight without Jem. He was fantastic.'

'You did your share, darling. I saw you up there waving that beaded footstool around. That was why I didn't call you to help Dolph throw Ted Ashe out.'

'What? When was this?'

'Somewhere around half past nine, I think. He came with Eugene's fiancée and her parents, the Wilton-Rugges, all dressed up in a lovely suede jacket and calling himself Hetherton Montague.'

'I'll be damned. So what did you do?'

'Nothing much, actually. Dolph recognized him right away as Ted Ashe and asked why he'd put on those clothes to park cars. Ashe insisted Dolph was mistaken and that he was this other man, and I said no, Dolph wasn't mistaken and he was Wilbraham Winchell. Things began to get sticky, so I shooed the Wilton-Rugges into the auction room and was going to get hold of you, but you were asking for a hundred and thirty dollars and it looked as if you were going to get it, so I decided that was no time to interrupt. Did you, by the way?'

'Sarah!'

'Oh, all right. I went back and told Dolph to quiet down, which he did for the moment. Ashe started going on about mistaken identity again, so I told him flat out that we knew who he was and what he was up to. I assumed you or Brooks would already have told Dolph, but either you hadn't or else it didn't sink in. Dolph's isn't the swiftest brain, you know.'

'I did try to tell him,' said Max, 'but he wasn't listening. I don't think Dolph's any dummy, he's just good at shutting out anything he doesn't want to hear.'

'If you'd known Great-aunt Matilda, you'd understand why,' Sarah agreed. 'I'm not sure he was listening to me, either. He was mostly annoyed because Ashe had turned out to be someone else. Dolph likes things plain and simple, which goodness knows they never were when his aunt and uncle were alive. It was Mr Loveday who was really shaken about Ashe's being a reporter.'

'Loveday was there?'

'Yes. That is, he'd gone off to get Aunt Appie and her crowd settled, but he came back while I was straightening Ashe out. I thought he was going to faint when he found out Ashe was a reporter for *Syndicated Slime*. He was all set to help Dolph throw Ashe off the place,' Sarah giggled, 'only Mr Loveday wanted to get his overcoat first, and Dolph wouldn't wait.'

Max laughed, too. 'Hell of a job trying to be a hero these days. So Dolph did it alone?'

'Dolph scooted Ashe outside, anyway. I knew George and Walter and Harry Burr were around, so I wasn't worried. Anyway, Dolph's bigger than Ashe. I sent Mr Loveday to quell any curiosity in the other rooms by explaining if he had to that a reporter had gatecrashed and that he and Dolph had thrown the man out. That was a diplomatic touch, don't you think?'

'Machiavellian. Did you wait to see what happened?'

'No dear, I ran madly to the bathroom. Then I thought

I'd rest a minute, and here I am. What's happening downstairs?'

'The kids are getting their glad rags off and finishing up the food. Mary's picking up the pieces. Jem's having a martini. Loveday's making a pest of himself. You know.'

'What about Aunt Emma?'

'She and her troupe pulled out over an hour ago.'

'And I never even said goodbye. What must she think of me?'

'She thought you were most likely upstairs taking a nap, so she came and looked and you were. She said to kiss you for her and I kissed her for you, so it's all taken care of.'

'You're so efficient, dear. I must get up.'

'Mary says you're welcome to stay the night if you want. Jem and Egbert are staying. I have to take Dolph's station wagon and ferry that gang into town, but I could come back.'

'You're not going without me. What if Jem delegates you to kiss those actresses good night for him? Help us up.'

'Are you sure you feel all right?'

'I expect I feel better than you do. You must be exhausted. I wonder if there's any of that soup left.'

'Let's go see. I could use some, myself.'

That was how Max and Sarah happened to be in the kitchen when George came looking for Dolph.

'Oh God, Mr Bittersohn, am I glad to see you! Is the boss around?'

'What's the matter?' Max pulled out a chair. 'Here, sit down. Did you hurt yourself? You look like hell.

'I'm all right, but there's a dead man in the tool house.'

'Are you sure he's dead?'

'He's cold, he ain't breathing, and he's got a pickaxe stuck in his chest. That dead enough for you?'

'Plenty. Sarah, I think we'd better call the police. Do you know who the man was, George?'

'No, but that don't mean anything. There must have been at least three hundred people here tonight I never set eyes on before.'

Sarah found Genevieve's cooking brandy and poured out

a stiff shot for the jittering gardener. 'Here, George, you'd better drink this. How did you happen to find him?'

'We'd put out ropes on stanchions to keep the cars out of the flowerbeds, the way we used to when old Mrs Kelling gave her lawn parties. I'd been going around coiling up the ropes and putting the stanchions together in little piles, the way we always did. Then I thought I'd open the tool house so Walter and Harry could get out one of the big garden carts and pick them up to put away. Used to be you could leave things till morning and nobody'd bother them, but not any more. So anyway, I just opened the door and there he was.'

'Did you turn on a light?'

'Sure. The switch is just inside the door. I reached in and flipped it on and—Christ! Where's the boss?'

'In the ballroom, I think. My wife will find him,' said Max. 'Come on, George, we'd better get back there.'

'I don't want to go back.' Nevertheless, George gulped the last of his brandy and hoisted himself out of the chair.

Sarah found the card Genevieve had posted over the telephone, with numbers on it for the fire department, the doctor, the police, and, though this last was hardly the sort of thing to inspire one's confidence in a cook, the hotline to the poison clinic. Sarah dialled the police and gave her message to a cool, matter-of-fact voice at the other end of the line. Somebody, she was assured, would be right over. Then she went to look for Dolph.

In the meantime, Max was hurrying George back to the tool house. This was no paltry garden shed, but a sturdy little one-storey building of grey granite blocks trimmed in red brick. A concrete ramp for the carts and mowers led up to a pair of extra-wide wooden doors like the ones that used to be put on garages back in the days of the Hupmobile and the Pierce Arrow. A new-looking brass lock held them together.

'Just a second.' George took out a bunch of keys and went to work on the complicated lock. 'Got to keep everything locked up nowadays,' he grunted. 'Guys come around with trucks and clean you out if you give 'em half a chance.'

'But you didn't keep the doors locked this evening?'

'I sure as hell did. So many cars coming and going, all you'd need would be one closed van and whammo! I don't know whether you realize it, Mr Bittersohn, but garden equipment's expensive these days. One riding mower alone could set you back a few thousand bucks depending on what you get. The boss always wants the best, he says it saves money in the long run. So like I said, I keep everything locked up. So maybe you can tell me how that guy got inside without me knowing?'

'Is this the only way in and out?'

'That's right.'

'Aren't there any windows?'

'Two at the back and one on each side, but they've got heavy iron grilles bolted over them, right into the bricks.' George gave his key one last turn, pushed open the right-hand door, and flipped the light switch without going in, to show Max how he'd done it before. 'You look. I don't want to.'

Max looked, and said, 'Christ!'

'Do you know who he is, Mr Bittersohn?'

'Have you ever had a man out here from the SCRC who called himself Ted Ashe?'

'According to Harry Burr, Ted was supposed to come tonight, but he never showed up. But this is nobody from the SCRC. Look at his clothes.'

'Is Burr still around?'

'Far as I know.'

'Get him, will you?'

Harry Burr couldn't have been far away. When he came, Max was still standing in the same spot, looking down at the grotesque unreality of a pickaxe with a heavy oak handle, one tine pointing up at the roof, the other buried in a well-cut, neatly buttoned, expensive light brown suede sports jacket. There wasn't any blood showing, just that deadly sweep of tempered steel.

Max couldn't see whether the pickaxe was pinning the body to the floor, but it was standing so stiff and firm that he thought it must be. Ashe was lying quite peacefully on his back. His legs weren't contorted, his arms were not raised to ward off the blow. His dead face showed no look of horror, but dead faces seldom look anything but dead.

'Go on in, Harry,' he heard George say. 'He wants you.'

'I want you, too, George,' Max called out. 'And Walter, if he's around. Stay outside if you want, but don't go away.'

'We're all here.' Somewhat shamefaced, George followed Harry Burr into the tool house. A third man in denim pants and jacket came after them.

'The police should be along soon,' said Max. 'No doubt you'll have to answer a lot of questions again for them, but humour me, will you? Harry, can you recognize this man? Forget the clothes, just concentrate on the face.'

Harry concentrated, then nodded. 'I know him, it's just that I'd never seen him cleaned up before. He's a recent member of the SCRC who's been calling himself Ted Ashe.'

'You never thought that was his actual name?'

'I suspected from the start that Ted was playing a role.'

'Had you any idea why?'

'Not really. At first I hoped he might be a plainclothes policeman trying to get a line on all those bag-snatchings our people have been subjected to lately. Somebody seems to be taking too fundamentalistic a view of the text, "From him that hath not shall be taken away even that which he hath." Perhaps Dolph Kelling has mentioned the muggings to you? You're a relative of his, I understand?'

'My wife is. Yes, I've heard about the trouble you've been having. But why do you say at first?'

'Because the snatchings have continued right up through yesterday and Ted hadn't seemed particularly interested, even when one of our most loyal workers was killed by a mugger. That happened this very week, so you see the situation is steadily worsening. We buried him on Tuesday, and Ted didn't even attend the funeral service. That wasn't what made me change my mind, though; it was more what you'd call the final disillusionment. Once I'd got to know him, Ted simply didn't *feel* like a policeman. That sounds absurd to you, I expect, but then you can't have been arrested as many times as I have. And am about to be again, I suppose.'

'Why? Did you kill Ted Ashe?'

'No, but I don't expect the police will believe me. They seldom have in the past. But what a hideous way for anyone to die. Would you mind if I said a little prayer?'

'Go right ahead.'

Max felt ashamed that he hadn't been thinking of Ashe as a human being with a life to lose, but only as a sleazebag who'd most likely set himself up for what he'd got. Nobody deserved to die like this. Nobody had the right to appoint himself another's executioner. He tried to pay respectful attention to Harry Burr's prayer, but couldn't help hoping it wouldn't be a long one. He was damned uneasy about who might have been on the business end of that pickaxe, and there were some things he wanted to find out before the police got here.

'Who besides yourself has a key to this place,' he asked George as soon as he decently could. 'Walter, have you?'

'Not me,' said the other gardener. 'The boss has one, of course. I guess old Mr Kelling did when he was alive, though I can't remember him ever using it.'

'Me neither,' George put in. 'Mr Kelling never did anything around the place but march along the paths taking a swat with his cane at any plant that wasn't growing the way he wanted it to. Us guys had to trail along like we was the privates and he was the general, listening to him tell us all the things we were doing wrong.'

'The boss now,' said Walter, 'he's different. Something goes wrong, he'd just as soon roll up his sleeves and help you fix it. Remember the year of the big blizzard, George, when the ice started to melt and the drains were backing up into the cellar and we couldn't get 'em unclogged? The boss grabbed that pickaxe and—'

Walter became aware of what he was saying, and shut up fast.

'Getting back to the keys,' said Max, 'aren't there any more of them around anywhere? What happened to old Mr Kelling's key after he died? And shouldn't there be a master

163

key up at the house? Suppose you're not around for some reason, George, and Walter has to get into the tool house? What does he do?'

'Damned little, from the look of the place when I get back. Aw, I'm only kidding. Walt's okay. That's right, Mr Bittersohn, he'd go up to the house and ask Genevieve to let him take the key off the big board. It's hanging right beside the kitchen door.'

'Convenient.'

'Yeah. Mr Kelling liked to keep everything where it could be got hold of in a hurry in case we got invaded by the Martians or whoever. The boss is so used to having the board there, I don't suppose he ever noticed it's not the smartest place in the world to keep the keys. Anyway, I don't suppose he goes into the kitchen much.'

'Besides, I think he still feels funny about changing things around from where his aunt and uncle put them,' Walter added. 'I guess I would, too, if I'd been brainwashed all those years like he was. God, it was pitiful. Here's this great big grown man, old enough to be somebody's grandfather and the only one of 'em that knew which end he was standing on, and they still bossed him around like he was a little kid. He'd come out to the tennis court and whack balls around to let off steam. The boss had one hell of a forehand. Sometimes you'd think the ball was going right through the backboard.'

'Mr Bittersohn doesn't want to hear all this stuff, Walt,' George interrupted. 'Getting back to those keys, Mr Bittersohn, I don't suppose it would be too hard for somebody to get hold of one if he had access to the house and knew where the master was kept.'

'Nobody could have swiped yours and put it back without your knowing?'

'No way.' George hauled out his bunch of keys again, and showed Max how the ring was attached to his trouser loop by a slim chain. 'They'd have had to take my pants, too, and I'd sure as hell have noticed that. The key must have come from the house. You better go talk to Genevieve.'

CHAPTER 21

Genevieve would have to wait, the police were already here: Lieutenant Codfin in a smart blue suit and Sergeant Blue in a trim blue uniform. Osmond Lovejoy brought them around from the front entrance. He'd managed to get his outer garments on this time: a sedate black homburg, a black cashmere topcoat, and the *de rigueur* white silk scarf. Dolph came lumbering up from the ballroom wing at full bellow and met them just as they entered the tool house.

'What the hell's going on here?' he roared. 'Sarah tells me somebody's been—oh, him.'

'You know this man?' asked Lieutenant Codfin.

'I damned well ought to. He's been cadging meals off me under false pretences for the past two months. What's he doing here? I told him to get out and stay out.'

'When was this?'

'Who are you, since you're so damned free with your questions?'

'Oh, sorry. Lieutenant Codfin, and this is Sergeant Blue. And you're Mr Adolphus Kelling, the owner of this property, if I'm not mistaken?'

'You're not. This is my cousin, Max Bittersohn.'

'Max Bittersohn is your cousin?'

'Married my cousin. Same thing, isn't it? Where the hell was I? Oh, Harry Burr, who came to help out; and these two are my gardeners, George Hanover and Walter Presman. Both of them, I may say, are thoroughly reliable men who've been with us for—how long, George? Twenty years?'

'Twenty-three years this past June, boss. I'm the one who found him, in case they want to know.'

'My God! Must have given you an awful turn. Better go ask Genevieve for a slug of whiskey.'

'I'm okay, boss. Mrs Bittersohn gave me some brandy.'

'Mr Hanover,' said Lieutenant Codfin with considerable determination, 'how did you happen to find him?'

'How could I miss him? I opened the door and there he was, just like he is now.'

'You didn't touch him at all?'

'I started to try for a pulse, but as soon as I laid a finger on his wrist, I knew it was no good. So I locked the door again and ran up to the house yelling for the boss. But Mr and Mrs Bittersohn were in the kitchen when I got there. He said he'd come with me and she'd find the boss. I figured him being a detective, he'd know what to do, so I came back with him.'

'And exactly what did you do, Mr Bittersohn?'

'Asked my wife to telephone the police, came out here and took a look, got George to round up the other two men who'd been working in the grounds, and waited for you.'

'Quite right and proper,' said the lieutenant, making it plain by his tone that he knew perfectly well Max was leaving out all the more interesting parts. 'Now, Mr Hanover, you said you locked the door again before you went to the house. Does that mean you'd had to unlock it in order to discover the body?'

'I didn't open it to discover the body. I opened it to put away some ropes and stanchions we'd been using to mark off the parking areas.'

'That's right, you held some sort of charity function here this evening, Mr Kelling. I hope it went well. Was the dead man one of your guests?'

'He was supposed to be one of our workers.'

'Perhaps I can explain,' Osmond Loveday interrupted.

'Why the hell should you?' Dolph retorted sourly. 'I've got a mouth on me, haven't I?'

'Excuse me,' said the lieutenant, 'I still don't have this gentleman's name.'

'Osmond Francis Loveday, formerly confidential assistant to Mr Frederick Kelling, now serving Mr Adolphus Kelling in a somewhat similar capacity,' Loveday replied smartly. 'That was why I thought I should endeavour to make myself useful. If I'm not needed here, I may as well go back to the house.'

'Go ahead,' said Dolph.

'Stick around,' said the lieutenant. 'Sergeant, you'd better go back to the cruiser and contact the station. Ask for the homicide team and tell them to put a rush on it. Mr Loveday, your employer has stated he told the deceased to get out and stay out. Were you present when he did so?'

'I certainly was, and I may add that Frederick Kelling himself could not have handled the incident more forcefully.'

Walter snickered. 'Are you kidding? Mr Kelling used to pick 'em up by the scruff of the neck and the seat of the pants and pitch 'em into the geranium beds. I've replanted more geraniums than you can shake a stick at. He chucked a policeman half way down the front drive once, just for trying to sell him a ticket to the Policemen's Ball.'

'I recall the incident as if it were yesterday,' Osmond Loveday replied with what must have struck Lieutenant Codfin as decidedly misplaced pride. 'Mr Kelling was a man of firm principles. He believed policemen ought to be out guarding the public welfare, not prancing around a dance floor.'

'Blast it, Osmond, will you leave Uncle Fred out of this?' Dolph shouted. 'You're getting as soft in the head as he was. I do not go hurling people around. I never laid a hand on Ted Ashe. Ask Sarah, she was there.'

Loveday cleared his throat. 'In point of fact, Sarah went upstairs right after you—er—ushered Ashe out and closed the door behind you.'

'You're saying that both Mr Kelling and Mr Ashe were then on the outside, while you and this woman you refer to as Sarah were left on the inside?' demanded the lieutenant.

'That is correct. I'd offered to help, but Dolph said my assistance was not required.'

'So what did you do then? Did you look out the window to see what was happening?'

'No, I didn't. Sarah—formerly Sarah Kelling and now Mrs Bittersohn—had suggested I circulate among the guests in the adjoining rooms to find out if they'd noticed the disturbance.'

'And had they?'

'Apparently not. Mrs Emma Kelling's musical ensemble

was playing, people were chatting, and of course the auction was going on. Most of their attention seemed to be on the bidding.'

'I see. Just out of curiosity, Mr Loveday, what would you have said if you'd been asked for an explanation?'

'Mrs Bittersohn had told me to say a reporter had tried to gatecrash and had been ejected, which was true as far as it went.'

'Then you knew Mr Ashe was a newspaperman?'

Loveday glanced at Dolph. Dolph turned to Max. 'You tell it.'

'According to my information, Lieutenant, the man we'd known as Ted Ashe wrote feature articles for a publication called *Syndicated Slime*, using the name Wilbraham Winchell. I've been told he also had other *noms de plume*, but I don't know what they were. Anyway, as Winchell, he'd been doing a series about graft and corruption in charitable agencies, and was reputed to have been in the habit of manufacturing evidence himself if he couldn't find any in the course of his so-called investigations. He'd recently attached himself to the Senior Citizens' Recycling Center, which was established by Dolph Kelling and his wife Mary, and which tonight's auction was designed to benefit. We assume Ashe had selected the SCRC as his next target. We also assume Ashe was another of his aliases, but we'd only just discovered the Wilbraham Winchell identity and hadn't had time to pursue the matter.'

'How was the imposture discovered, Mr Bittersohn?'

This was a tricky bit. 'Serendipitously, as you might say. I was showing some photographs of the SCRC people to a friend of mine a couple of nights ago, and he happened to spot Ashe, whom he'd met as Winchell in a nightclub recently and also at a cocktail party.'

'Would you mind giving us this friend's name, just for the record?'

'Not at all. It was Bill Jones. Know him?'

'Oh, Bill Jones? Sure, I know Bill. Doesn't everybody?' Lieutenant Codfin's affability became a degree less professional. 'Then it was Bill who told you Ashe falsified his information when he was writing as Winchell?'

'Well, you know Bill.' Max shrugged and waved his hands, and Lieutenant Codfin actually laughed.

'One gets the message. Mr Kelling, when Ashe was at the Center, did he wear some kind of disguise?'

'He dressed like a bum and got himself so filthy nobody cared to get close enough for a good look,' Dolph sputtered. 'Showed up tonight dressed to the nines, calling himself Hetherton Montague and thinking I wouldn't recognize him because he'd washed his face.'

'What a strange thing to do,' said Lieutenant Codfin politely. 'When you escorted him out of your house, Mr Kelling, was either of your gardeners around, or Mr Burr? I take it you're a friend of the Kellings, Mr Burr?'

'It would be more accurate to say the Kellings have been good friends to me,' Harry replied. 'I'm a bona fide member of the SCRC. I'm sorry, but I was not near the door at the time. One of the neighbours had taken exception to having cars parked near his property, so Mrs Kelling asked me to stay down by the end of the drive and make sure they parked up here instead of on the street.'

'Precisely where up here?'

'Back by the tennis courts,' said George. 'I can show you if you want, but there's nothing much left to see. Walter and I were back there most of the evening. We got a lot more cars than we'd figured on, and we had to keep opening up more places to put them. Then people who'd come early started wanting to leave, so we'd be helping them find their cars and steering them out the right way. We kept pretty busy.'

'I see, thank you. Mr Kelling, after you'd gone out and shut the door as Mr Loveday testifies, you didn't bring Mr Ashe out here to the tool house?'

'What kind of damn fool question is that? No, I did not. I merely walked out with him as far as the front terrace, told him I'd punch his face in if I ever laid eyes on him again either here or at the Center, and pointed out the way to Chestnut Hill Station.'

'Why did you do that? Didn't Mr Ashe have a car?'

'I never thought to ask. I assumed he didn't because he'd come with some other people.'

'Were these people friends of yours?'

'No, but they're all right. Their daughter's engaged to Eugene Porter-Smith. Young fellow who boards with my Cousin Brooks and works for my Cousin Percy. Gene clerked at the auction.'

'Can you add anything to that, Mr Bittersohn?'

'Only that my wife chatted with them for a few minutes as she was showing them into the auction room, and got the impression that Ashe had been simply making use of the Wilton-Rugges. That's their name, don't ask me why. When Dolph confronted Ashe at the door, Sarah thought she'd better get the Wilton-Rugges away and also find out how well they knew Ashe. Assuming what they told her is true, he'd shown up with somebody or other at their cocktail party, where Bill Jones met him, calling himself Hetherton Montague. He bumped into the husband a couple of times after that, and it was his suggestion that they meet for dinner and go on to the auction together tonight.'

'Why do you think he picked on the Wilton-Rugges?'

'Presumably because he knew their daughter's engaged to Eugene Porter-Smith. Gene's done some volunteer work for the SCRC and, as Dolph mentioned, he was also working here tonight. The auction hadn't been announced at the time of the cocktail party, but I suppose Ashe went on speculation, so to speak. Scavengers like him are always looking around for an angle, you know.'

'Thank you, Mr Bittersohn. Mr Kelling, the station is a fair distance from here. Did you actually expect this man you call Ashe to walk that far?'

'Walked it myself often enough, why shouldn't he? Exercise would have done him good.

'It would have done him more good than staying here, obviously. What did you do after you'd shown him the way?'

'I went back into the house. The place was crawling with people and I had my duties as a host.'

'And Mr Ashe went off quietly?'

'Of course not. He's still here, isn't he? I assumed he

would because I'd told him to. I now assume the crafty swine sneaked back here to see if he could cadge a ride from somebody. He couldn't find anybody leaving, saw the tool house door open—'

'Sorry, boss, but he couldn't have,' said George. 'My orders are to keep it locked, and I do.'

'Then he picked the lock. Had a lock-picker taped to his leg, I suppose. That's how they do, I've seen 'em in the movies. Anyway, he came in here to hide out till somebody came, tripped over the pickaxe, and stabbed himself. Hell of a way to go, but there it is. Plain as the nose on my face. Get him out of here, can't you? I said I didn't want him around, and I still don't. I'm going back to the house.'

'Just a moment, please, Mr Kelling,' Lieutenant Codfin protested. 'This man is lying on his back. The pickaxe has penetrated his ribcage and pinned him to the floor. It's not reasonable to assume he got into such a position by accident.'

'Seems reasonable enough to me. Well, you figure it out. My wife will be wondering where I've got to. Come along, Osmond. No sense in your standing around cluttering up the place. If you have any notion of keeping George and Walter up all night, Lieutenant, kindly bear in mind that they're getting time and a half for overtime and it's my pocket the money's coming out of.'

'Yes, Mr Kelling. Neither you nor Mr Loveday were planning to leave this house tonight, I hope?' Codfin glanced over at the tremendous agglomeration of misguided architecture whose lights still showed through the trees. 'I expect you could find room to put Mr Loveday up?'

'A suite is always kept ready for me,' Loveday informed him with a deprecating little laugh. 'At least I assume it still is. I haven't had occasion to use it lately.'

'Nobody's swiped your pink pyjamas that I know of,' Dolph growled. 'No, Lieutenant, I'm not going anywhere tonight except to bed. Max, you and Sarah had better stay, too. She should have been asleep hours ago, in her condition.'

'As a matter of fact, she was. Don't forget I still have to deliver those kids back to Boston.'

'The hell with that. We'll send 'em home in taxis.'

'What kids are you talking about, Mr Bittersohn?' asked Codfin.

'A group of young actors and actresses who donated their services this evening. I doubt if any of them left the house at any time. They were all in costume, mingling with the guests, passing food and champagne and so forth. I expect you'd like their names as a matter of routine, but they may not be able to help you much.'

'These young people are in no way connected with the Senior Citizens' Recycling Center?'

'Not at all. They were recruited solely for this occasion by a part-time actor named Charles C. Charles who also works for my wife's cousin Brooks Kelling and lives at 30 Tulip Street in Boston.'

'I see. Thank you. Sergeant Blue, why don't you go back to the house with Mr Kelling and Mr Loveday, and see what you can get out of the actors? Now, Mr Burr, I haven't meant to neglect you, but you know how it is.'

'Oh yes, I know how it is. My name is Harold Eustis Burr. My address is the Come-All-Ye Community Church, 27 Amber Street, Boston.'

'You're the minister there?'

'No, but they let me sleep in the basement as a professional courtesy.'

'I thought I recognized the name. I once had the honour of arresting you myself, Mr Burr, back in the 'sixties when I was still on patrol duty. You were sitting at the intersection of Boylston and Hammond Streets, holding up a sign that said "Give Peace a Chance".'

'I expect I was,' said Burr. 'I don't recall the precise incident, but those were busy times.'

'I should have said Reverend Burr, shouldn't I?'

'No, you shouldn't. Reverend is merely an adjective. You could say the Reverend Dr Burr if you wanted to, but it's been so long since I held a pulpit that the title sounds ridiculously pretentious. In jail they generally called me plain Harry and I've grown to prefer it.'

The lieutenant wasn't quite ready for Harry. He cleared his throat. 'I'm required to ask whether you've had any convictions other than for civil disobedience.'

'Yes, one for assault on a police officer who was roughing up a young girl for what I considered to be no valid reason. I took away his truncheon and did unto him that which he'd been doing unto her, in order to give him a clearer understanding of the Golden Rule. The judge was only lukewarm to my argument that I'd acted solely for the purpose of religious instruction and gave me sixty days.'

Harry shrugged. 'But I mustn't bore you with personal reminiscences. You want to know when I last saw Ted Ashe alive, I expect. It was yesterday at lunch-time, in the Center. He'd made a point, as he often did, of standing next to me in the chow line and engaging me in conversation.'

'What about?'

'Usually small details concerning the members.'

'Did he ever ask you about their collecting methods?' Max broke in. 'Which of them worked hit-or-miss, and which had regular routes, that sort of thing?'

'I believe he did, now that you mention it. Many of us are quite serious about our collecting, you know, and some incline to be rather territorial. Ted might have been asking merely because he didn't want to encroach on someone else's hunting ground, though I admit it was this habit of his that made me think at first he might be an undercover agent. But you say he was a newspaperman named Wilbraham Winchell? I don't suppose there could be two?'

'It doesn't seem likely,' said Max. 'Why? Do you know him?'

'He was younger then, of course, and he had a beard, but I think it must be the same man. He interviewed me once in jail.'

'Really?'

'Yes, we had a long talk. He seemed like such a pleasant fellow. Then he sent me a copy of the published article. I don't know why he did that. It was a chastisement I didn't think I needed just then, but maybe the Lord knew better.'

'What do you mean, a chastisement?' Max asked him.

'What Winchell had done was to twist and distort every single thing I'd said so that it came out sounding like hypocrisy and self-aggrandisement. Having turned me into a fascist, he then accused me of being a Communist. At that time, I'd been getting a fair amount of press coverage because of my intransigence on certain issues, so naturally some of the other publications picked up his article and did their worst with it. When I got out of jail, I found Wilbraham Winchell had effectively rendered me a zero. Affiliating with a minister who's been tagged as a Commie, however unjustly, doesn't do much for the credibility of an association, a church, or even a private person.'

'So you had good reason to hate Wilbraham Winchell,' said Lieutenant Codfin.

'My dear sir, nobody, and least of all a practising Christian, has good reason to hate anybody else. We may not care for what some of our fellows stand for, but that doesn't give us a right to destroy them. No, Lieutenant, I did not drive a pickaxe through this poor man. Frankly, I doubt whether I could if I wanted to. I'm an old man and the life I've led has not been particularly conducive to physical well-being. I have endurance, but no great muscular strength.'

'You wouldn't need a great deal,' said Codfin. 'A tool that heavy would do much of the work for you.'

'Not that much,' George argued. 'You'd have to know how to swing it. It's not just the arms, you know, you've got to be able to get your back and legs into it. Harry gets a crick in his back every time he bends over.'

The gardener wasn't afraid of the corpse any more. He was staring at that expensive suede jacket. 'What gets me is there's no blood showing. I mean, cripes, a blow like that, you'd think—'

'I expect the medical examiner will have an explanation,' said Codfin.

'I'll bet I know what his explanation will be,' said Max.

'If you don't mind, Mr Bittersohn, we'll wait for the

official report. By the way, I don't believe I have your statement of where you were when the incident between Mr Kelling and Mr Ashe, as we may go on calling him, took place.'

'According to my wife, I was auctioning off a beaded footstool. She came looking for me after the fracas broke out.'

'She didn't approach you in the auction room?'

'No, the bidding was going well and she didn't want to interrupt, so she just went back and told them to put a lid on it. In case you have any ideas about my wife, I may add that she's small, delicately built, and eight months pregnant. Physical violence isn't her bag. She copes pretty well without it,' Max added with a grin. 'As Loveday testified, she went upstairs right after that. She fell asleep in one of the bedrooms and didn't even wake up when her aunt went to kiss her goodbye. I finally woke her myself, after the auction was over. I suppose you'll want her personal statement, but that's the gist.'

'Thank you. Have you anything further to add?'

'Yes. So you won't have to waste your time thinking Ashe's death is an isolated incident, you should know that it may quite possibly be the latest chapter in a long story that Brooks Kelling and I presented to the Narcotics Division of the Boston Police yesterday afternoon, along with photographs and other corroborative evidence. You'd be well advised to get in touch with them as soon as possible.'

'Narcotics?' Lieutenant Codfin blinked. 'I shall certainly do so. Er—you said you had an idea of how Ashe was killed.'

'Let's say that if I were in charge here, I'd check those garden carts, especially that big one over there, for fresh dirt on the wheels, possible bloodstains in the box, and a noticeable lack of fingerprints on the handles before anybody's had a chance to clean them up. I don't suppose you'll find the bullet, but it wouldn't hurt to look.'

'What bullet, Mr Bittersohn?'

'The small-calibre one Ashe was most likely shot with

shortly after Dolph Kelling kicked him out and before he was brought here to the tool house. That would explain the lack of blood George so rightly remarked on, and also the position of the body. Surely you don't think anybody would meekly lie down on the floor and wait for somebody to drive a pickaxe through him, unless he was already either dead or damned close to it.'

CHAPTER 22

'But people would have heard the shot,' Mary protested.

There'd been a long, long night of waiting around and answering Lieutenant Codfin's questions before any of them had to go to bed. The enigma of keys to the tool house had been gone into with little result. Nobody could remember whether Great-uncle Frederick had one or not, much less what might have happened to it. Dolph had his, but it turned out he'd changed his clothes for the auction and left his key ring lying on his dresser since he wouldn't be needing to unlock anything that night. As far as he could tell, the keys were where he'd left them, but who could be expected to notice a detail like that?

As for the keyboard in the kitchen, Genevieve confessed that she'd been worried about leaving it where it was with a bunch of young strangers running in and out all evening, so she'd quietly and gently taken the board off the wall and set it in the pantry behind the cookie sheets. None of them had gone into the pantry because they'd had no call to, and they wouldn't have seen it if they did. That appeared to narrow down the list of possible suspects, most of whom wished Genevieve had left the board alone.

The way matters stood now, Max, Jem, Egbert, and Eugene Porter-Smith were all in the clear. None of them had left the auction room for more than a few minutes from the time they went in until the last bang of the gavel. Every one of the young actors had enthusiastically alibied Mary, but nobody could be a hundred per cent sure about how long Dolph had been away from the party after he'd ejected Ted Ashe.

Genevieve and Henrietta hadn't had time for any shenanigans. Sarah was technically a suspect since she'd admitted to having been alone upstairs for hours, and could easily have borrowed Dolph's key for herself or a confederate. Osmond Loveday was still iffy. He'd been popping in and out of the various rooms so often that neither Mary, Henrietta, nor any of the servers could pinpoint his movements.

Then of course there were an indefinite number of other possibles, since nobody could say how many of the patrons had been milling around outside during the crucial period, or even how long the crucial period had been. By the time Lieutenant Codfin left them to get what little sleep they could, though, he'd made it fairly clear that his primary suspects were Dolph Kelling and Harry Burr. Harry had gone back to the gardener's cottage with George. Dolph was here at the table, eating a great deal and saying little.

'Surely people would have heard the shot,' Mary repeated.

'Maybe some did, but not as a shot,' Max replied, helping himself to another biscuit. The household had been so late pulling itself back together that breakfast had turned into brunch. 'A small-calibre pistol doesn't bang. It pops.'

'And champagne corks had been popping all evening,' Sarah finished for him so that he could get on with his biscuit.

'Why do you say a small pistol?' said Osmond Loveday. 'It seems to me that if I were to embark on so picaresque an enterprise, I'd want the biggest pistol I could get.'

'You'd be borrowing trouble if you did,' Max told him. 'Large calibre handguns are awkward, heavy, and conspicuous to carry. They make a lot of noise and a messy wound, and they're harder to get rid of afterwards.'

'If you're right about the small-calibre pistol, they ought to find the bullet still in the body, shouldn't they?' Sarah asked. 'I wonder if the murderer really meant it to be thought that Ashe was killed by the pickaxe, or if he was

177

just buying time to confuse the issue and give him a chance to get rid of the gun? Or if he hated Ashe so much that he went a little bit crazy? Ugh.'

'Well, it's my guess,' said Mary, 'that sticking him in the tool house and using the pickaxe was a deliberate attempt to pin the killing on Dolph. And I'm pretty mad about it, I can tell you. Sarah, you finish your milk and don't be dwelling on guns and pickaxes. You shouldn't be thinking of such things, in your condition.'

'Yes'm,' said Sarah. She was used to being bossed around by elderly relatives. 'All the same—'

'Excuse me, Mrs Kelling.' That was Henrietta. 'Lieutenant Codfin's here again, wanting to speak to Mr Kelling.'

'Oh he is, is he?' said Mary. 'Well, you show him right into the breakfast-room. Anything he's got to say to my husband he can say in front of me, and you tell him I said so.'

'Shall the rest of us leave?' Sarah asked.

'Hell, no,' said Dolph. 'Stick around and watch the fur fly. Mary's pretty spectacular when she gets her Irish up. Don't be too hard on the poor fellow, dear. He's only doing his job.'

'Well, he'd better do it right or he'll wish he had.'

Mary wiped her lips, laid down her napkin, and stood up to greet Codfin. She came about to his elbow. 'Good morning, Lieutenant. Would you like some coffee?'

'No, thank you.' Lieutenant Codfin was as spruce and straight as he'd been the previous evening, notwithstanding the fact that he probably hadn't had a wink of sleep. His expression, however, was that of a man nonplussed.

'I'd really prefer to speak to Mr Kelling alone.'

Mary planted her fists on her hips, cocked back her head and gave him the full force of her bright blue eyes. 'And would you, now? Come on, spit it out and get it over.'

'If you insist.' Codfin drew a long breath. 'Adolphus Kelling, I have a warrant for your arrest on a charge of—'

'Don't you dare say it! If you think my Dolph's the kind of man to go shooting people and clobbering them with pickaxes to cover up what he did—'

'The charge is not murder, Mrs Kelling. If you'd please let me finish what I have to say—'

'Whatever it is, you're wasting your time because he didn't do it. Go ahead and get it out of your system if you have to, but don't expect any of us to believe a word you say.'

Osmond Loveday pushed back his chair. 'I'd better go telephone Mr Redfern.'

'Not yet, Osmond,' Dolph objected. 'Hadn't you better wait and see what I'm getting pinched for first? Somebody ought to get Jem out of bed. He'd hate to miss this.'

'You'd all better pipe down and let Lieutenant Codfin read his warrant before he runs the pack of us in for obstructing an officer in the performance of his duty,' Max suggested mildly.

'All right, Max, if you say so. What the hell, it's rather interesting. I've never been in the toils of the law before. Go ahead, Codfin. Hang me the rap.'

'Hang you the what?' Jem was among them, disgustingly pink-cheeked and full of beans after a far longer sleep than anybody else had got. Egbert had put him to bed nicely oiled just a little while before George brought the direful news from the tool shed. 'Egbert says I missed a murder. Why didn't somebody come and tell me?'

'Because you were out like a light, you old souse,' snarled Dolph. 'Shut up and pay attention, I'm getting arrested. And for God's sake, everybody quit interrupting. This a solemn occasion, damn it.'

He straightened up in his chair like an elder statesman about to get his portrait painted, and glared at the by now pretty well demoralized representative of the law. 'Well, get on with it, can't you? What do you think we're paying you for?'

Codfin cleared his throat and took another stab at the warrant. 'Adolphus Kelling, I arrest you on a charge of trafficking in narcotics.'

'What?' roared Dolph, Max, Jem, and Egbert in unison.

'You're crazy,' shrieked Mary.

'You certainly are,' Sarah confirmed. 'Wherever did you pick up that absurd notion?'

Codfin gave her a glance that could have been called smug. 'Acting on information received from licensed private detective Max Bittersohn and his assistant Brooks Kelling, the Boston Police Narcotics Squad last night conducted a raid on a downtown nightclub known as the Broken Zipper. A large quantity of heroin and two cartons of empty cans purporting to have been intended for a fictitious soft drink and in fact used to make drops of the drug were seized. Five persons, including one Daniel Purffle, a bartender and apparent leader of the operation, were taken into custody. All five insisted they were working under the direct orders of the club's owner.'

'That's interesting,' said Max. 'According to my information, the Broken Zipper is owned by an outfit calling itself the Thanatopsis Trust.'

'It is,' said Codfin. 'That trust is controlled solely by Adolphus Kelling.'

'That is a vicious fabrication,' shouted Dolph. 'Now look here, Lieutenant, I shouldn't mind so much getting arrested on half-way reasonable grounds, but accusing me of owning some goddamned sink of vice and depravity under the cover of some goddamned trust I never heard of is downright asinine and I'm not going to stand for it. Osmond, call Redfern.'

'We'd better line up your accountant, too,' said Max. 'Who is it?'

'Cousin Percy, of course.'

'The one Eugene Porter-Smith works for.'

'What's that got to do with the Thanatopsis Trust?'

'Nothing, if we're lucky. Where are you taking him, Lieutenant?'

'Boston. They're sending out a car.' Lieutenant Codfin did not add the pious ejaculation he was so obviously feeling.

'All right,' said Max. 'He'll go quietly. Won't he, Mary?'

'If you say so, Max, but you'd better know what you're doing. Shall I pack your overnight bag, dear?'

'No, don't bother. I don't suppose they'd let me keep it. Afraid I'd strangle myself with my spare socks, no doubt.

Which I damned well wouldn't. Where's Harry Burr? He's the expert on getting arrested.'

'Harry took off.' Genevieve was standing in the doorway, making no effort to hide her tears. 'To think I should live to see the day! I could bake you a cake with a file in it, boss.'

'Great idea. How about coconut frosting? Come on, Codfin. Let's get out of here before I forget I'm cooperating.'

'We'll see you in a while, Dolph,' Max assured him. 'Come on, Loveday, we'd better do some telephoning. The rest of you get your things together and prepare to move out.'

'I'm coming, too,' said Mary. 'Genevieve, you and Henrietta will have to keep the home fires burning. Don't you worry, I'll bring the boss back alive. It's a blessing we don't keep the Center open on Sundays, at least we don't have that to worry about. Where do you suppose Harry Burr went? Back to Boston on the subway, I suppose. They have a coffee bar at the church today. I was going to send them the leftover food by Harry, but those youngsters polished off every bite.'

She was chattering to keep from crying. Sarah gave her a hug.

'Don't fret, Mary. This is all some crazy mistake, and Max will fix it. Go put on that pretty green suit Dolph likes so much.'

'I must say I should be glad of a chance to change my own suit,' sighed Osmond Loveday.

'I should think you might,' Sarah agreed tactlessly. He did look silly in evening dress at this hour of the day. 'Your landlady will think you've been making a night of it.'

'Fortunately, I don't have one.'

Of course he didn't. He'd have a prissy bijou apartment up on Bowdoin Street or somewhere, with a signed photograph of Great-uncle Frederick in a silver frame on the mantelpiece. Sarah realized how little she knew about Mr Loveday's personal life, and how little she cared. She went upstairs and got the extra things she'd brought with her yesterday, and walked out to meet the car Max had gone to bring around to the front door.

They filled the car, with Jem, Egbert, and Loveday in the back seat and Mary and Sarah in front with Max. 'Good thing the gendarmes took Dolph with them,' Jem remarked.

'That's a matter of opinion,' Mary snapped back. 'How soon can I see him, Max?'

'I honestly can't say, Mary. I thought I'd drop you and Sarah at Tulip Street until we find out what the score is. You might give Theonia a hand with Annie.'

'Oh my gosh, I'd completely forgotten about Annie. I'd better see if I can get hold of Joan somewhere and tell her not to worry.'

'I'm not so sure she shouldn't.' Sarah began describing to Mary some of the ways Annie was beguiling the time during her protective detention. That got Jem reminiscing, naturally. They all laughed harder at his yarns than they normally would have. It was better than stewing over what might be happening to Dolph.

'I'm going to the station with Max,' Jem insisted when they got into town.

'No you're not,' Sarah vetoed. 'You'd wind up poking some sergeant in the nose and we'd have two of you to bail out. You're going home and gargle your throat so you'll be in shape to sing bawdy songs at Dolph's coming-out party.'

So Osmond Loveday, the only one who didn't want to, wound up going alone with Max. He'd pleaded to stop off at the apartment and shed his absurd tuxedo, but Max said sorry, there wasn't time.

In truth they were none too soon. Redfern was already in the room with Dolph, the captain, and an assortment of minions. The prisoner and his lawyer were poring dazedly over a number of documents that had been laid out on the table.

'Don't try to tell me you're unfamiliar with Adolphus Kelling's signature, Mr Redfern,' the captain was insisting. 'You must have seen it thousands of times.'

'Never in the context of this transaction,' Redfern insisted right back, 'if indeed any such business ever took place, which I find impossible to believe. I cannot understand it.'

'Why not? It's simple enough. Frederick Kelling bought the Broken Zipper in 1976 and deeded it over to his nephew a year later, which would have been two years before he died, according to our information. No doubt this was done to avoid his nephew's having to pay inheritance taxes. This is Frederick Kelling's signature, and you needn't try to deny it. We've got plenty of samples to compare it with. The guy must have spent all his time writing letters.'

'Nevertheless—'

The captain cut Redfern short. 'Okay, so as soon as Adolphus Kelling obtained possession of the property, he put it into a blind trust in which he himself retained the sole financial interest. Maybe Mr Kelling didn't want his high class friends to know he owned a crummy dive in the Combat Zone. Anyway, this is Adolphus Kelling's signature, whether you say so or not. Furthermore, the taxes have been duly filed and paid each year through a bank account in the name of the Thanatopsis Trust, with cheques signed by the treasurer, one William C. Bryant. Who's William C. Bryant, Mr Kelling?'

'I've already told you I don't know any William C. Bryant. Nor do I know this James R. Lowell who's down as secretary. And who the hell's Oliver W. Holmes?'

'Come on, Mr Kelling, quit trying to kid us. This is your handwriting and you know it.'

'I'm not denying that's my handwriting, I'm merely telling you I did not sign those confounded papers. I've never seen them before in my life.'

'You refuse to admit your uncle deeded the Broken Zipper over to you?'

'I don't refuse to admit the possibility that he might have done so. How can I? By 1976, Uncle Fred was loopy enough to have done anything. What I'm saying is that if he did, I never knew it. Redfern never knew. Cousin Percy never knew. Osmond, did you know?'

Loveday swelled up like an angry penguin. 'How should I? You know perfectly well I didn't handle your uncle's personal affairs, I only worked on the organizational accounts.'

'And a fine mess you made of them,' Dolph grunted.

'But you must have been familiar with both Frederick Kelling's and his nephew's signatures, Mr Loveday,' the captain pressed.

'Oh yes, thoroughly familiar. I couldn't have helped being, considering how many letters I bullied them into signing over the past thirty-seven years. I'm sorry, Dolph old boy, but I'm afraid I'd have to testify that to the best of my knowledge, both your and Mr Kelling's signatures are absolutely authentic in every instance.'

'And all of them are absolutely identical,' said Max. 'Dolph, how long ago was it that Loveday got rubber stamps made of your and your uncle's signatures so that you two wouldn't have to sign all those thousands of letters in person?'

'God, Max, so he did. Must have been upwards of thirty years ago. Not long afterwards, Uncle Fred bought one of those automatic letter-writing machines that sign your name in a different colour, so we never used them much. I'd completely forgotten. But you hadn't, you bastard!'

'Rubber stamps?' The captain took the pocket magnifier Max held out to him, studied the signatures, and shook his head. 'I'll be damned.'

'I'm the one who's being damned without cause,' cried Loveday. 'Anybody could get a rubber stamp made.'

'Who but you would think of it?' snarled Dolph. 'And who else is expert enough with them to get a perfect impression every time? You've been rubber-stamping all your life.'

'Wait a minute,' said Max. 'Let's call in another witness. Is Perdita Follow still in custody, Captain?'

'The one with the poncho? Sure.'

'Has she talked yet?'

'Not a yip.'

'Can we get her up here?'

'No problem.'

'This is absurd,' Osmond Loveday sputtered.

184

'Think so?' said the captain. 'You're entitled to phone your lawyer if you'd like.'

'Thank you, I shall certainly do so.'

In this, Loveday was fortunate. His attorney was at home, he lived just over near the river end of Berkeley Street, and could be there in ten minutes. Fetching Tigger from the lock-up where she'd spent the night took longer, but not much. She clomped in wearing her poncho and boots, glaring out from behind her hair, her lips clamped tight together. When she caught sight of Osmond Loveday, though, the lips parted.

'Lover-boy!'

'Lover-boy?' cried Dolph in understandable amazement. 'Can she mean you, Osmond?'

'I have no idea whom she means,' Loveday replied, his own lips not working too well.

'So!' wailed Tigger. 'I was but the plaything of an idle hour, a mere bauble to reflect the rays of your coruscant passion and then be cast aside. Ozzie-babe, how could you?'

'Christ Almighty!' Dolph's eyes were bulging as they'd never bulged before. 'You been sullyin' the fair name of maidenhood with *her*?'

'I—I couldn't help myself,' Loveday stammered. 'For thirty-seven years it was just one mink coat after another tossed over the foot of my bed, then one day those feral little eyes gleamed out at me above that ratty old poncho and—'

The lawyer from Berkeley Street cleared his throat. 'Er—Osmond, don't you think it would be wiser not to give out any information?'

'What have I said? Merely that I admit to a brief amorous dalliance with Miss Follow.'

'Miss Follow?' Tigger burst into cataclysmic sobs. 'He told me I was deliciously uncouth!'

A middle-aged man's passion for a younger woman is a dangerous thing. Osmond Loveday could contain himself no longer. 'Oh, you are! You are! Please, Tiggywinkle, don't cry.'

'Tiggywinkle?' Dolph Kelling's jaw dropped half way to

his tie-clasp. 'Great balls of fire, if Uncle Fred were only alive to see this day!'

CHAPTER 23

'Osmond Loveday and his little rubber stamps.' Mary Kelling shook her neat grey head. 'Whoever would have thought it?'

'Actually Loveday had stuck out like a sort thumb from the beginning,' said Max, 'only I couldn't figure out how to hang it on him until he murdered Ted Ashe.'

'And started Tiggywinkle spilling the beans,' snickered Dolph. 'I suppose I shouldn't laugh. As it turns out, Ted was really her elder brother, Wilbert Follow.'

'So that's why they were cussing each other out in the alley,' said Sarah.

'No doubt,' Max agreed. 'Tigger was furious with Wilt, as she called him, for muscling in on the SCRC and threatening to put a crimp in Lover-boy's drug running operation. Wilt refused to give up the chance of a sensational exposé, even for his sister, and she was scared stiff Loveday would find out who he was and blame her. She'd been half tempted to bump off Wilt herself, we gathered, but she couldn't take it when she found out Ozzie had done the job for her last night. That was when she really started running off at the mouth. I'll bet she hasn't shut up yet.'

'Did Tigger say Osmond killed Chet Arthur?' Mary asked.

'In graphic detail. By the way, Sarah, you were right about the garage, only it wasn't the Under-Common one. What happened was that Hoopie made a drop—Hoopie being that bird in the purple sweatsuit, who's now in custody and chirping for all he's worth—and Chet picked up the can. Only Chet, being no dummy, realized there was something strange about it. He investigated, found the little folded papers, and opened one of them.'

'That must be how the heroin got spilled inside his SCRC bag,' said Brooks.

'Undoubtedly,' Max agreed. 'Chet realized what he'd got hold of, didn't feel competent to face the police with it by himself, and hightailed it back to the Center to tell Dolph. As luck would have it, he got there just as Loveday was leaving, at five o'clock. Naturally, when Loveday saw Chet still had his bag, he knew something had gone wrong with the drop. He stopped Chet, got the story out of him, and told him the Kellings had left for the night but he'd be glad to run Chet out to their house in his own car.'

'I didn't know he had one,' said Mary.

'There must have been an awful lot about Loveday you didn't know. According to Tigger, he gave Chet a pretty hard time about what the drug dealers would do to him if they caught him. By the time they got to the car, Chet was only too happy to lie down on the floor in the back and let Loveday cover him up.'

'With what?' Brooks asked.

'A couple of big black trash bags from the kitchen. Loveday'd run back and got them as soon as he saw Chet coming down the sidewalk with his bag. No question of unpremeditated murder there. So once he'd got Chet conveniently stowed away, Loveday conked him with a tyre iron—the same one that was found at the scene, no doubt —and went home to Tiggywinkle.'

'God!' said Dolph.

'Oh, Osmond's quite a guy. According to Tigger, they spent an interesting evening. When intermission time rolled around, Loveday sauntered back to the garage, drove Chet out to that place where he was found, and dumped him, ripping the bag and scattering the cans to make it look like the routine mugging the police took it to be.'

'And outsmarted himself by not having been interested enough in the members to know Chet had a phobia about the Back Bay,' said Mary. 'I don't see where he was so darn clever.'

'God, when I think how Uncle Fred used to hold Osmond up to me as a model of all the virtues,' Dolph snorted. 'And there he was, embezzling Uncle Fred's money to buy that dive in Uncle Fred's name. No wonder he kept the accounts in such a mess. Did it so he could siphon off a little at a time and nobody would notice, I suppose.'

'What intrigues me is his setting up that Thanatopsis Trust with William Cullen Bryant, James Russell Lowell, and Oliver Wendell Holmes as officers,' said Brooks. 'He must have the gall of an ox.'

'You don't know the half of it,' said Max. 'Tigger says he was planning to use some of his drug-running earnings to buy Dolph's warehouse in the Thanatopsis name, so that he could build some more condominiums instead of a senior citizens' housing project.'

'With a penthouse for him and Tiggywinkle,' Dolph added, 'and make me look like the world's greatest hypocrite if the truth ever came out. Even Harry Burr's going to have a hard time finding a good word for Osmond when he hears that.'

'I expect Harry will manage one way or another,' said Sarah. 'What a life that man's had, all because he's honestly tried to practise what he preaches. Isn't it amazing how few people can tolerate someone who's thoroughly good?'

'It's much easier to follow someone who puts on a good show and caters to one's personal prejudices,' Brooks agreed. 'Speaking of shows, Dolph, I hope you're prepared to perform. I'm sure the media people are waiting for you out at Chestnut Hill already.'

'I know they are,' said Mary. 'That's why I wanted to stay here for a while and give Dolph a chance to catch his breath. As soon as I found out things were going to be all right, I phoned the house on that old private line of Uncle Fred's. Henrietta says the other phone's been ringing off the hook, and there are a slew of people out front with cameras and microphones. I told her to shut off the phone and keep the doors locked till we get back. The police were already out in the tool shed looking for bloodstains in the wheelbarrows when the trucks began to roll up, so they're doing emergency crowd control, bless their hearts, and Genevieve's sneaking coffee and doughnuts out to them through the old coal chute. But, Max, didn't you say it's already established that Osmond killed Ted Ashe?'

'No doubt about it, Mary. I didn't give Loveday a chance to go home and change his clothes because I was hoping he'd kept the weapon on him. And damned if the arrogant twerp didn't have this cute little pearl-handled popgun stuck down between his sock and his garter when the cops made him take off his pants.'

'Just the way Dolph said they did in the movies. You're so brainy, dear.'

Mary gave her husband a look of complete and utter worship. Dolph bridled and stuck out his lip, but refrained from saying he wasn't. Jeremy Kelling, who until now had been saving his voice for 'On Her Horsehair Sofa in Her Bombazine', emitted a strange noise somewhere between a snort and a chortle.

'By gad, a couple more episodes like this one and you'll almost have me believing you, Mary macushla. Only how did Loveday manage to shoot Ashe in the midst of that mob?'

'In the first place,' said Sarah, 'they weren't in the mob. Dolph put Ashe out, remember, and left him there alone. In the meantime, I'd told Mr Loveday to see to the guests and gone upstairs. I'm sure as soon as my back was turned, he slipped into one of the shut-off rooms and slipped out of whatever door or window came handiest. He knows the house inside and out, you know, having stayed there so often when Dolph's aunt and uncle were alive. I suppose he ran after Ashe, offered him a ride, led him to some convenient spot, and shot him. It's rather awful to think that if I'd stayed downstairs a few minutes longer, the murder wouldn't have happened.'

'Don't feel that way, dear,' said Max. 'It had to happen. Once Loveday found out he'd been letting a smirch artist like Wilbraham Winchell infest the SCRC, he'd never have dared leave Ted Ashe alive. Ashe's cover was blown, he'd been chucked out on his ear, he was a vindictive bastard and a damned effective mudslinger. It stood to reason he'd go straight to his typewriter and start ripping the SCRC to shreds. Even if he hadn't yet caught on to the drug running, and Loveday had no way of being sure about that, Ashe could have thrown enough dirt to focus official attention on the Center. He'd have played up Chet Arthur's death and perhaps told something pretty close to the truth even if he hadn't meant to. At the very least Ashe could have made it impossible for Loveday to continue his highly lucrative delivery service and maybe got him in trouble with his own suppliers.'

'But Loveday's such a pipsqueak,' Jem argued. 'We're supposed to believe he shot Ashe with that popgun he had on him, lugged him to the tool house, picked the lock, got the body inside, and whammed a pickaxe clean through it. How could he?'

'He did,' said Max. 'A 22-calibre bullet matching Loveday's gun was found in Ashe's body, as I'd hoped it might be. A good deal of leafmould was adhering to the back of that suede jacket Ashe was wearing. George keeps that tool house floor clean as a kitten's whiskers, so the leafmould had to come from the ground. Loveday probably used one of the garden carts to get him inside.'

'Why didn't he just lure Ashe into the tool house and shoot him there?'

'Probably because Ashe would have smelled a rat and not gone. As for picking the lock, I'm sure Loveday didn't have to. Most likely Frederick Kelling did have a key at one time, and Loveday got hold of it.'

'Wouldn't surprise me,' said Dolph. 'Osmond stole Uncle Fred's name and his money, why should he stop short at pinching a key? Kept it because he thought it might come in handy some day, I suppose. Like the rubber stamps, eh?'

'I expect so,' said Max. 'The key hasn't been found on him, so we have to assume he tossed it into the shrubbery or somewhere after he'd taken care of Ashe. He wouldn't be needing it again.'

'But how could he have known he was going to need it this time?' Jem insisted.

Brooks shrugged. 'Precognition, maybe. What do you think, Theonia?'

His wife settled her lace and smiled her Gioconda smile. 'I should be inclined to believe Mr Loveday carried the key simply because it tickled his vanity to know he could move more freely around the estate than its present owner thought he could. He must have resented the fact that Dolph and not he was Frederick Kelling's heir.'

'I think Theonia's absolutely right,' said Sarah. 'Remember how he swanked around in that silly dinner jacket last night, greeting people at the door as if he owned the house? He even wanted to make a speech of welcome before the auction started. I practically had to trip him up and sit on him.'

'Good thing you headed him off,' Jeremy Kelling grunted. 'I'd have picked him up and chucked him off the auction block single-handed.'

'In a pig's eye you would,' said Dolph, force of habit proving too much for his new-found bonhomie. 'Osmond's in a damn sight better shape than you ever were. Walks, lifts weights, eats wheat germ. I've seen him.'

'God, the follies people will commit! No wonder Loveday took to a life of crime. Everybody knows wheat germ warps the mind. Egbert, I believe we're out of martinis.'

'In this house, Egbert's a welcome guest like the rest of you,' Brooks said firmly. 'Sit down, Egbert. I'll fix the drinks.'

'What happened to your retinue of servants?' Max wanted to know.

'Charles has a rehearsal and Mariposa's gone to visit some of her relatives,' Theonia told him. 'I believe they're holding an engagement party for Annie and Uncle Pedro. And I'm afraid you'll have to excuse me. We do a Sunday-night buffet for our boarders, you know, and it's time I did something about the food.'

'I'll help you,' said Sarah. 'Max will take Mary and Dolph back to face the onslaught, and I'd suggest Uncle Jem go with them. The SCRC will have to be defended to the media, and after last night I'm convinced Uncle Jem could talk anybody into anything.'

'Damn right,' said Dolph. 'Come on, you old barfly. Make

yourself useful, since you're long past being ornamental.'

'If you wish,' Jeremy Kelling replied with immense dignity. 'As the Prince of Wales said to Lillie Langtry, *Ich dien*. All I ask is a chance to collect a pair of my own pyjamas. I slept in some of Dolph's last night and dreamed I'd been swallowed by an elephant. Devilish disconcerting experience, I don't mind telling you. Have you any idea how complicated elephants are inside those ill-fitting grey skins?'

'No, and for goodness' sake don't tell us,' said Mary. 'You're right, Sarah, we really should get started. I hate to think what Genevieve and Henrietta are going through out there without us.'

'I'll phone and tell them you're on your way,' Brooks promised. 'I'd go with you myself, if we weren't short-handed here.'

'You and Theonia have already done more than your share, Brooks. Goodness knows how we'd ever have managed without you.'

'Before you get on the phone, Brooks, I'd like to make a quick call, if you don't mind,' said Max. 'Mind if I use the one upstairs, Theonia?'

'Not at all.' Why should she, considering that the house was by now more his than hers?

The quick call stretched out a good five minutes. Mary began to fidget. 'Dolph, do you think we should call a taxi?'

'I'll go see what's keeping Max,' said Sarah.

She got there just in time to hear him say, 'Oh Jesus! *Eh bien, Pepe, tant pis.* Keep your moustache on, we'll work it out somehow.'

'What's the matter?' she asked when he'd hung up. 'Couldn't Pepe get back the two Paul Klees and the Winslow Homer?'

'Oh yeah, he got them. Also a Utrillo and a Vuillard.'

'But our client didn't lose a Utrillo and a Vuillard.'

'*Précisément, ma chérie.* That's why I have to buzz over to Marseilles before the Sûreté catches up with Pepe.'

'Mary's awfully anxious to get home.'

'Come on, then. First things first.'

They got downstairs in time for a little more hugging and

back-slapping. Then Max and his passengers were on their way and Sarah was alone with Theonia. It was while they were setting out the china for the buffet that she saw her opening.

'Theonia, would you forgive me if I asked you something rude?'

'My dear Sarah, there would be nothing to forgive. Ask what you like.'

'It's about that first night, when we'd come back from Dolph's and you threw the teacup into the fireplace.'

'Oh, that.' Theonia hesitated, turning a perfectly clean cup in her shapely hands as if searching for words on the delicate porcelain. 'I suppose you might call it forensic fortunetelling. I believe I told you once, my dear, that when I used to do readings, I'd sometimes get what I called a flash.'

'When you knew something for a positive fact, I remember.'

'Yes. Well, there's another kind of flash, when you become aware of something but can't put it into words. That was the kind of flash I had then, a feeling of great evil and terrible danger directed towards our circle. My gipsy grandmother would have said somebody was practising black magic against us. I may as well tell you that my immediate concern was for Max, but that was my mind working, not my spirit. I couldn't tell where the curse was coming from or whom it was meant to harm. So all I could do was turn it around.'

'Turn it around?'

'Ill-wishing will always return to the ill-wisher if the person against whom it's directed simply refuses to accept the curse. I knew I wasn't going to hurt anybody except the person or persons from whom the evil was emanating, so I just let go and did what felt right to me. I grant you I was hard on your lovely old china, like the old tyrants killing the messengers who brought them bad news. But you see, the same principle applied. The bearer of the tidings was assumed to have become impregnated with their aura.'

'Like mailmen who read all the postcards?' Sarah suggested.

'You're laughing at me,' said Theonia, 'and I don't wonder.'

'I am not. How could I? It worked, didn't it? One ill-wisher is dead and the other's a good deal worse off than he, in my opinion. And they did both bring it on themselves, when you come to think of it. Ted Ashe set himself up to be killed by crashing the auction as Hetherton Montague, for no good reason that I can see. If he'd been content to come as Ted Ashe and park cars the way Dolph expected him to, he could have done whatever he came for and got away with it, most likely.'

'Yes, that's true. Nobody would have challenged him, so Osmond Loveday wouldn't have panicked and shot him,' Theonia agreed.

'Then Mr Loveday made his own punishment inevitable by keeping the gun,' Sarah went on. 'That was a really crazy thing to do, you know, especially for someone so pernickety as he. It's as if the pair of them were both blinded by their own cockiness. And now it's over and Dolph and Mary are in a better position than ever to get on with their good work. Surely that's worth a teacup.'

'Thank you, my dear. Now let's talk about something pleasant. I still haven't heard any details about the auction. Was it fun?'

'I'm afraid I can't say. I slept through most of it. All I know is that Aunt Appie bought all those seaweed mottoes.'

'Oh my!' An odd expression flitted across Theonia Kelling's superbly moulded countenance.

'What's the matter?' Sarah teased. 'Another flash?'

'I'm afraid so, dear. I have a hideous feeling Appie's planning to give us each one of them for a Christmas present. Would you mind terribly if I smashed another teacup?'

———

Born on November 21, to Mr and Mrs Max Bittersohn of Beacon Hill and Ireson's Landing, a son, David Josiah Kelling.

Letter from Mrs Beddoes Kelling to Mrs Max Bittersohn

Darling Sarah,

Max called just after midnight with the joyful tidings . . .
I am too, too delighted! Wanted to jump right into the
car and have Heatherstone drive me straight to Phillips
House, but there's this bothersome kick-off luncheon for
the Children's Fund Drive and then the Garden Club's
Beautification Benefit . . . for the parks, dear, not the
members, though I'm sure some of us could use a bit of
titivating . . . but anyway, I'll come as soon as I can. I'm
simply bursting to see if Little Kell's as handsome as his
daddy and as adorable as his mummy . . . you were such
a precious tyke, sweetie! Do remember that your old
babysitting service is ready and eager to be reactivated
at a moment's notice. Mrs Heatherstone is thrilled to
pieces at the mere notion of filling your bunny mug again,
and so am I. Take care of yourself, dear. Oceans of love
to you all,

Aunt Emma

Letter from Mrs Isaac Bittersohn to Mrs George Gordon

Dear Leah,

Just to let you know my daughter-in-law Sarah had her
baby last night at half past eleven. Max is all excited. I
hope it doesn't wear off when he starts getting waked up
in the night. It's a boy. They're calling him David Josiah
after his two grandfathers and Kelling for her side of the
family, which isn't so bad. I'd have liked a granddaughter
but at least he's healthy, though only six and a half
pounds. It would have been nice if she'd gone to a closer
hospital, but what can you do? Miriam and Ira are taking
us in to see Davy Joe as soon as Ira can get away from
the garage. You know how Isaac hates driving in Boston.
By the way, we're having the *briss* here next Thursday
afternoon, so maybe you and George might like to come
if you have nothing else to do.

Your sister,
Bayla

Letter from Miss Mabel Kelling to Mrs Apollonia Kelling

Dear Appie,

There was no need for you to squander a long-distance telephone call just to inform me that Sarah's second husband has acquired a new income tax deduction. At least I assume that was the message my maid took down. Zeriah is tolerably efficient in some ways, but stenography is not what I pay her for.

Where on earth did Sarah get such an absurd name for the child? There hasn't been a David nor a Josiah in the family during its entire history, to my knowledge. At least she had sense enough to insert a Kelling in the proper place so that the child can drop the Bittersohn as he will surely wish to. I hope she remembered to change her will before she went into labour, just in case, but anything so sensible probably never entered her head. We must be thankful she pulled through all right, it would have been unthinkable for those in-laws of hers to get their hands on Walter Kelling's money.

Your aff. cousin,
Mabel

Letter from Jacob Bittersohn, Esq. to Max Bittersohn, PhD

Dear Nephew,

Mazel Tov! Would you believe your father tracked me all the way to my hotel in Chicago at one o'clock in the morning your time? He said he had to phone himself because your mother was too excited to talk. That I believe! I swear to God, Max, he was crying. So was I. A grandson to carry on the family name, Isaac and I were both afraid we'd never live to see. Giving him the grandfathers' names was another mitzvah we didn't expect, and you needn't tell me who thought of it. That Sarah of yours is a jewel above rubies. She openeth her mouth with wisdom and in her tongue is the law of kindness.

Now, Max, don't get me wrong. I know you're a fine husband and a good provider. But would it be an insult for an old uncle to do for David what I did for your sister's boy Mike? And would have done for you if I'd had a nickel to spare at the time, you know that. So anyway, I'm starting a little trust fund for his education and I hope you and Sarah, God bless her, will take it the way it's intended.

If the judge stays awake long enough, we should wind up this case in another couple of days. I'll head back to Boston as soon as the jury brings in its verdict. The right one, *kain ayin harah*. Kiss Sarah for me. Kiss the baby if the nurse will let you. What the hell, kiss the nurse, too. Or maybe I should handle that myself.

See you soon,
Uncle Jake

Bestselling Crime

☐ Moonspender	Jonathan Gash	£2.50
☐ Shake Hands For Ever	Ruth Rendell	£2.50
☐ A Guilty Thing Surprised	Ruth Rendell	£2.50
☐ The Tree of Hands	Ruth Rendell	£2.50
☐ Wexford: An Omnibus	Ruth Rendell	£5.95
☐ Evidence to Destroy	Margaret Yorke	£2.50
☐ No One Rides For Free	Larry Beinhart	£2.95
☐ In La La Land We Trust	Robert Campbell	£2.50
☐ Suspects	William J. Caunitz	£2.95
☐ Blood on the Moon	James Ellroy	£2.50
☐ Roses Are Dead	Loren D. Estleman	£2.50
☐ The Body in the Billiard Room	H.R.F. Keating	£2.50
☐ Rough Cider	Peter Lovesey	£2.50

Prices and other details are liable to change

ARROW BOOKS, BOOKSERVICE BY POST. PO BOX 29. DOUGLAS. ISLE OF MAN, BRITISH ISLES

NAME..

ADDRESS...

....

....

Please enclose a cheque or postal order made out to Arrow Books Ltd. for the amount due and allow the following for postage and packing.

U.K. CUSTOMERS: Please allow 22p per book to a maximum of £3.00.

B.F.P.O. & EIRE: Please allow 22p per book to a maximum of £3.00

OVERSEAS CUSTOMERS: Please allow 22p per book.

Whilst every effort is made to keep prices low it is sometimes necessary to increase cover prices at short notice. Arrow Books reserve the right to show new retail prices on covers which may differ from those previously advertised in the text or elsewhere.

Bestselling Thriller/Suspense

☐ Hell is Always Today	Jack Higgins	£2.50
☐ Brought in Dead	Harry Patterson	£1.99
☐ Russian Spring	Dennis Jones	£2.50
☐ Fletch	Gregory Mcdonald	£1.95
☐ Black Ice	Colin Dunne	£2.50
☐ Blind Run	Brian Freemantle	£2.50
☐ The Proteus Operation	James P. Hogan	£3.50
☐ Miami One Way	Mike Winters	£2.50
☐ Skydancer	Geoffrey Archer	£2.50
☐ Hour of the Lily	John Kruse	£3.50
☐ The Tunnel	Stanley Johnson	£2.50
☐ The Albatross Run	Douglas Scott	£2.50
☐ Dragonfire	Andrew Kaplan	£2.99

Prices and other details are liable to change

ARROW BOOKS, BOOKSERVICE BY POST, PO BOX 29, DOUGLAS, ISLE OF MAN, BRITISH ISLES

NAME...

ADDRESS..

....

....

Please enclose a cheque or postal order made out to Arrow Books Ltd. for the amount due and allow the following for postage and packing.

U.K. CUSTOMERS: Please allow 22p per book to a maximum of £3.00.

B.F.P.O. & EIRE: Please allow 22p per book to a maximum of £3.00

OVERSEAS CUSTOMERS: Please allow 22p per book.

Whilst every effort is made to keep prices low it is sometimes necessary to increase cover prices at short notice. Arrow Books reserve the right to show new retail prices on covers which may differ from those previously advertised in the text or elsewhere.

Bestselling Fiction

☐ Hiroshmia Joe	Martin Booth	£2.95
☐ The Pianoplayers	Anthony Burgess	£2.50
☐ Queen's Play	Dorothy Dunnett	£3.95
☐ Colours Aloft	Alexander Kent	£2.95
☐ Contact	Carl Sagan	£3.50
☐ Talking to Strange Men	Ruth Rendell	£5.95
☐ Heartstones	Ruth Rendell	£2.50
☐ The Ladies of Missalonghi	Colleen McCullough	£2.50
☐ No Enemy But Time	Evelyn Anthony	£2.95
☐ The Heart of the Country	Fay Weldon	£2.50
☐ The Stationmaster's Daughter	Pamela Oldfield	£2.95
☐ Erin's Child	Sheelagh Kelly	£3.99
☐ The Lilac Bus	Maeve Binchy	£2.50

Prices and other details are liable to change

ARROW BOOKS, BOOKSERVICE BY POST, PO BOX 29, DOUGLAS, ISLE OF MAN, BRITISH ISLES

NAME...

ADDRESS..

.............................:...

....

Please enclose a cheque or postal order made out to Arrow Books Ltd. for the amount due and allow the following for postage and packing.

U.K. CUSTOMERS: Please allow 22p per book to a maximum of £3.00.

B.F.P.O. & EIRE: Please allow 22p per book to a maximum of £3.00

OVERSEAS CUSTOMERS: Please allow 22p per book.

Whilst every effort is made to keep prices low it is sometimes necessary to increase cover prices at short notice. Arrow Books reserve the right to show new retail prices on covers which may differ from those previously advertised in the text or elsewhere.

Bestselling SF/Horror

☐ The Labyrinth	Robert Faulcon	£2.50
☐ Night Train	Thomas F. Monteleone	£2.50
☐ Malleus Maleficarum	Montague Summers	£4.50
☐ The Devil Rides Out	Dennis Wheatley	£2.50
☐ The Shadow of the Torturer	Gene Wolfe	£2.95
☐ Contact	Carl Sagan	£3.50
☐ Cobra Strike (Venture SF 17)	Timothy Zahn	£2.95
☐ Night Visions	Campbell, Barker, Tuttle	£2.95
☐ Bones of the Moon	Jonathan Carroll	£2.50
☐ The Island	Guy N. Smith	£2.50
☐ The Hungry Moon	Ramsey Campbell	£2.95
☐ Pin	Andrew Neiderman	£1.50

Prices and other details are liable to change

ARROW BOOKS, BOOKSERVICE BY POST, PO BOX 29, DOUGLAS, ISLE OF MAN, BRITISH ISLES

NAME..

ADDRESS...

....

....

Please enclose a cheque or postal order made out to Arrow Books Ltd. for the amount due and allow the following for postage and packing.

U.K. CUSTOMERS: Please allow 22p per book to a maximum of £3.00.

B.F.P.O. & EIRE: Please allow 22p per book to a maximum of £3.00

OVERSEAS CUSTOMERS: Please allow 22p per book.

Whilst every effort is made to keep prices low it is sometimes necessary to increase cover prices at short notice. Arrow Books reserve the right to show new retail prices on covers which may differ from those previously advertised in the text or elsewhere.

A Selection of Arrow Bestsellers

☐ The Lilac Bus	Maeve Binchy	£2.50
☐ 500 Mile Walkies	Mark Wallington	£2.50
☐ Staying Off the Beaten Track	Elizabeth Gundrey	£5.95
☐ A Better World Than This	Marie Joseph	£2.95
☐ No Enemy But Time	Evelyn Anthony	£2.95
☐ Rates of Exchange	Malcolm Bradbury	£3.50
☐ Colours Aloft	Alexander Kent	£2.95
☐ Speaker for the Dead	Orson Scott Card	£2.95
☐ Eon	Greg Bear	£4.95
☐ Talking to Strange Men	Ruth Rendell	£5.95
☐ Heartstones	Ruth Rendell	£2.50
☐ Rosemary Conley's Hip and Thigh Diet	Rosemary Conley	£2.50
☐ Communion	Whitley Strieber	£3.50
☐ The Ladies of Missalonghi	Colleen McCullough	£2.50
☐ Erin's Child	Sheelagh Kelly	£3.99
☐ Sarum	Edward Rutherfurd	£4.50

Prices and other details are liable to change

ARROW BOOKS, BOOKSERVICE BY POST, PO BOX 29, DOUGLAS, ISLE OF MAN, BRITISH ISLES

NAME..

ADDRESS..

....

....

Please enclose a cheque or postal order made out to Arrow Books Ltd. for the amount due and allow the following for postage and packing.

U.K. CUSTOMERS: Please allow 22p per book to a maximum of £3.00.

B.F.P.O. & EIRE: Please allow 22p per book to a maximum of £3.00

OVERSEAS CUSTOMERS: Please allow 22p per book.

Whilst every effort is made to keep prices low it is sometimes necessary to increase cover prices at short notice. Arrow Books reserve the right to show new retail prices on covers which may differ from those previously advertised in the text or elsewhere.